Claude Tillier, Benjamin Ricketson Tucker, Ludwig Pfau

My Uncle Benjamin

A Humorous Novel

Claude Tillier, Benjamin Ricketson Tucker, Ludwig Pfau

My Uncle Benjamin
A Humorous Novel

ISBN/EAN: 9783743435544

Printed in Europe, USA, Canada, Australia, Japan

Cover: Foto ©Andreas Hilbeck / pixelio.de

More available books at **www.hansebooks.com**

MY UNCLE

Benjamin

A HUMOROUS, SATIRICAL, AND PHILOSOPHICAL
NOVEL

BY

CLAUDE TILLIER

Translated from the French by

BENJ. R. TUCKER

———

With a Sketch of the Author's Life and Works by

LUDWIG PFAU

———

BOSTON, MASS.
BENJ. R. TUCKER, PUBLISHER
1890

CONTENTS.

TRANSLATOR'S PREFACE.

I RESURRECT a buried treasure; a novel unlike any
other, by an author unlike any other; a novel, as
Charles Monselet says, that "has no equivalent in the
literature of this century"; a novel which, despite the
pessimism with which it opens and the pathos with
which it closes,—yes, even in these,—must take rank
among the wittiest and most humorous ever written;
a novel of philosophy, of progress, of reality, of humanity; a novel of the heart and of the head; a novel
that is less a work of art than a work of genius,—the
work of an obscure genius, a child of the French Revolution, who lived and died early in the nineteenth
century and will be famous early in the twentieth.

BENJ. R. TUCKER.

MY UNCLE BENJAMIN.

CHAPTER I.

WHO MY UNCLE WAS.

I REALLY do not know why man so clings to life. What does he find that is so agreeable in this insipid succession of nights and days, of winter and spring? Always the same sky, the same sun; always the same green pastures and the same yellow fields; always the same speeches of the crown, the same knaves and the same dupes. If this is the best that God could do, he is a sorry workman, and the scene-shifter at the Grand Opera is cleverer than he.

More personalities, you say; there you are now, indulging in personalities against God. What do you expect? To be sure, God is a functionary and a high functionary too, although his functions are not a sinecure. But I am not afraid that he will sue me in the courts for damages, wherewith to build a church, as a compensation for the injury that I may have done to his honor.

I know very well that the court officials are more sensitive in regard to his reputation than he is himself; but it is precisely that of which I complain. By virtue of what title do these men in black arrogate to themselves the right to avenge injuries which are wholly personal to him? Have they a power of attorney signed by Jehovah that authorizes them?

Do you believe that he is highly pleased when the police magistrates take in hand his thunderbolts and launch them brutally upon the unfortunate for an offence of a few syllables? Besides, what proof have these gentlemen that God has been offended? He is there in the court-room, fastened to his cross, while they sit in their arm-chairs: let them question him; if he answers in the affirmative, I will admit my error. Do you know why he tumbled from the throne the Capet dynasty, that old and august salad of kings so saturated with holy oil? I know, and I am going to tell you. It is because it enacted the law against sacrilege.

But this is not to the point.

What is it to live? To rise, to go to bed, to breakfast, to dine, and begin again to-morrow. When one has performed this task for forty years, it finally becomes very insipid.

Men resemble the spectators, some sitting on velvet. others on bare boards, but the greater number standing, who witness the same drama every evening, and yawn every one of them till they nearly split their jaws. All agree that it is mortally tiresome, that they would be much better off in their beds, and yet no one is willing to give up his place.

To live, is that worth the trouble of opening one's eyes? All our enterprises have but a beginning; the house that we build is for our heirs; the morning wrapper that we wad with love to envelop our old age, will be made into swaddling-clothes for our grandchildren. We say to ourselves: "There, the day is ended!" We light our lamp, we stir our fire; we get ready to pass a quiet and peaceful evening at the corner of our hearth; tic, tac, some one knocks at the door. Who is there? It is death; we must start. When we have all the appetites of youth, when our blood is full of iron and alcohol, we are without a cent; when our teeth and stomach are gone, we are millionaires. We have scarcely time to say to a woman: "I love you!" at our second kiss, she is old and decrepit. Empires are no sooner consolidated than they begin to crumble: they resemble those ant-hills which the poor insects build with such great efforts; when it needs but a grain to finish them, an ox crushes them under his broad foot, or a cart under its wheel. What you call the vegetable stratum of this globe consists of thousands and thousands of shrouds laid one upon another by successive generations. The great names that resound upon the lips of men, names of capitals, monarchs, generals, are the clattering *débris* of old empires. You do not take a step that you do not raise about you the dust of a thousand things destroyed before they were finished.

I am forty years old, I have already passed through four professions: I have been a monitor, a soldier, a school-teacher, and now I am a journalist. I have been on land and on sea, under tents and at the corner of the fireside, behind prison bars and in the midst of the broad expanses of the world; I have obeyed and I have commanded; I have had moments of wealth and years of poverty. I have been loved and I have been hated; I have been applauded and I have been ridiculed. I have been a son and a father, a lover and a husband; I have passed through the season of flowers and through

the season of fruits, as the poets say; and under none
of these circumstances have I found any reason to congratulate myself on being confined in the skin of a
man rather than in that of a wolf or a fox, rather than in
the shell of an oyster, in the bark of a tree, or in the
jacket of a potato. Perhaps if I were a man of property, a man with an income of fifty thousand francs, I
should think differently.

In the meantime, my opinion is that man is a machine
made expressly for sorrow; he has only five senses with
which to receive pleasure, and suffering comes to him
through the whole surface of his body: in whatever
spot he is pricked, he bleeds; in whatever spot he is
burned, he blisters. The lungs, the liver, the bowels
can give him no enjoyment: nevertheless the lungs
inflame and make him cough; the liver becomes ob-
structed and throws him into a fever; the bowels gripe
and give him the colic. You have not a nerve, a
muscle, a sinew under your skin that cannot make you
howl with pain.

Your organization unjoints at every moment, like a
bad pendulum. You raise your eyes to heaven to in-
voke it, and a swallow's dung falls into them and dries
them up; if you go to a ball, you sprain your ankle and
have to be carried home on a mattress; to-day you are
a great writer, a great philosopher, a great poet: a
fibre of your brain breaks, and in vain will they bleed
you or put ice on your head, to-morrow you will be
only a poor madman.

Sorrow hides behind all your pleasures; you are
gluttonous rats which it attracts with a bit of savory
bacon. You are in the shadow of your garden, and

you shout: "Oh! what a beautiful rose!" and the rose pricks you; "Oh! what a beautiful fruit!" there is a wasp on it, and the fruit bites you.

You say: God has made us to serve him and to love him. It is not true. He has made you to suffer. The man who does not suffer is an ill-made machine, an imperfect creature, a moral cripple, one of nature's abortions. Death is not only the end of life, it is its remedy. One is nowhere so well off as in the grave. If you believe me, you will order, instead of a new overcoat, a coffin. It is the only garment that does not pinch.

What I have just said to you you may take for a philosophical idea or for a paradox, it certainly is all one to me. But I pray you at least to accept it as a preface, for I cannot make you a better one, or one more suitable to the sad and lamentable story which I am going to have the honor of relating to you.

You will permit me to trace my story back to the second generation, like that of a prince, or of a hero, when his funeral oration is delivered. Perhaps you will not lose thereby. The customs of that time were well worth those of ours: the people carried swords, but they danced with them, and made them rattle like castanets.

For, note this, gayety always keeps company with servitude. It is a blessing that God, the great maker of compensations, has created especially for those who become dependent upon a master, or fall under the hard and heavy hand of poverty. This blessing he has given them to console them for their miseries, just as he has made certain grasses to grow between the

pavements that we tread under our feet, certain birds
to sing on the old towers, and the beautiful verdure of
the ivy to smile upon grimacing ruins.

Gayety flies, like the swallow, above the splendid
roofs of the great. It stops in the school yards, at the
gates of barracks, on the mouldy flaggings of prisons.
It rests like a beautiful butterfly on the pen of the
school-boy scrawling in his copy-book. It hob-nobs
at the canteen with the old grenadiers; and never
does it sing so loud — provided they let it sing — as
between the dark walls that confine the unfortunate.

For the rest, the gayety of the poor is a sort of
pride. I have been poor among the poorest. Well,
I found pleasure in saying to fortune: I will not bend
under your hand; I will eat my hard crust as proudly
as the dictator Fabricius ate his radishes; I will
wear my poverty as kings wear their diadem; strike as
hard as you like, and strike again: I will answer your
scourgings with sarcasms; I will be like the tree that
blooms while they are cutting at its roots; like the
column whose metal eagle shines in the sun while the
pick is working at its base.

Dear readers, be content with these explanations, I
can furnish you none more reasonable.

What a difference between that age and ours! The
man of the constitutional *régime* is not a merry-maker,
quite the contrary.

He is hypocritical, avaricious, and profoundly selfish;
whatever question strikes against his brow, his brow
rings like a drawer full of big pennies.

He is pretentious and swollen with vanity; the grocer
calls the confectioner, his neighbor, his honorable friend,

and the confectioner begs the grocer to accept the assurance of the distinguished consideration with which he has the honor to be, etc., etc.

The man of the constitutional *régime* has a mania for wishing to distinguish himself from the people. The father wears a blue cotton blouse and the son an Elbeuf cloak. To the man of the constitutional *régime* no sacrifice is too costly to satisfy his mania for making a show. He lives on bread and water, he dispenses with fire in winter and beer in summer, in order to wear a coat made of fine cloth, a cashmere waistcoat, and yellow gloves. When others regard him as respectable, he regards himself as great.

He is prim and stiff; he does not shout, he does not laugh aloud, he knows not where to spit, he never makes one gesture more violent than another. He says very properly: "How do you do, Sir"; "how do you do, Madam." That is good behavior; now, what is good behavior? A lying varnish spread upon a bit of wood to make it pass for a cane. We so behave before the ladies. Very well; but, before God, how must we behave?

He is pedantic, he makes up for the wit that he has not by the purism of his language, as a good housewife makes up for the furniture which she lacks by order and cleanliness.

He is always observant of the proprieties. If he attends a banquet, he is silent and preoccupied, he swallows a cork for a piece of bread, and uses the cream for the melted butter. He waits till a toast is proposed before he drinks. He always has a newspaper in his pockets, he talks only of commercial treaties and railway lines, and laughs only in the Chamber of Deputies.

But, at the period to which I take you back, the customs of the little towns were not yet glossed with elegance; they were full of charming negligence and most agreeable simplicity. The characteristic of that happy age was unconcern. All these men, ships or walnut-shells, abandoned themselves with closed eyes to the current of life, without troubling themselves as to where it would land them.

The *bourgeois* were not office-seekers; they were not miserly; they lived at home in joyous abundance, and spent their incomes to the last louis. The merchants, few in number then, grew rich slowly, without devoting themselves exclusively to business, and solely by the force of things; the laborers worked, not to amass savings, but to make both ends meet. They had not at their heels that terrible competition which presses us, and cries to us incessantly: "On! On!" Consequently they took their ease; they had supported their fathers, and, when they were old, their children in turn would support them.

Such was the abandonment of this society to merry-making that all the lawyers and even the judges went to the wine-shop, and there publicly took part in orgies. Far from fearing lest this might be known, they would willingly have hung their wigs upon the branches of the tavern bush. All these people, great and small alike, seemed to have no other business than to amuse themselves; they exercised their ingenuity only in playing some joke or in concocting some good story. Those who then had wit, instead of expending it in intrigues, expended it in merriment.

The idlers, and there were many of them, gathered in the public square; to them, market-days were days of fun. The peasants who came to bring their provisions to the town were their martyrs; they practised on them the most waggish and witty cruelties; all the neighbors hurried to get their share of the show. The police magistrates of to-day would prosecute such things; but the court officials of that time enjoyed these burlesque scenes as well as anybody, and often took part in them.

My grandfather was a summons-server; my grandmother was a little woman whom they reproached with not being able to see, when she went to church, whether the holy-water basin was full. She has remained in my memory like a little girl of sixty. When she had been married six years, she had five children, some boys and some girls; they all lived upon my grandfather's miserable fees, and got along marvellously well. The seven of them dined off three herrings, but they had plenty of bread and wine, for my grandfather had a vineyard which was an inexhaustible source of white wine. All these children were utilized by my grandmother, according to their age and strength. The eldest, who was my father, was named Gaspard; he washed the dishes and went to the butcher's shop, there was no poodle in the town better tamed than he; the second swept the room; the third held the fourth in his arms, and the fifth rocked in its cradle. Meantime my grandmother was at church or talking with her neighbors. All went well, however; they succeeded in reaching the end of the year without getting into debt. The boys were strong, the girls were not ill, and the father and mother were happy.

My uncle Benjamin lived at his sister's ; he was five feet ten inches in height, carried a big sword at his side, and wore a coat of scarlet ratteen, breeches of the same color and material, pearl-gray silk stockings, and shoes with silver buckles ; over his coat bobbed a large black cue almost as long as his sword, which, incessantly going and coming, had covered him with powder, so that my uncle's coat, with its shades of red and white, looked like a peeling brick. My uncle was a doctor ; that was why he had a sword. I do not know whether the sick had much confidence in him ; but he, Benjamin, had very little confidence in medicine : he often said that a doctor did very well if he did not kill his patient. Whenever my uncle Benjamin came into possession of a franc or two, he went to buy a big fish and gave it to his sister to make a matelote, upon which the entire family feasted. My uncle Benjamin, according to all who knew him, was the gayest, drollest, wittiest man in all the country round, and he would have been the most — how shall I say it not to fail in respect to my great uncle's memory? — he would have been the least sober, if the town drummer, named Cicero, had not shared his glory.

Nevertheless my uncle Benjamin was not what you lightly term a drunkard, make no mistake about that. He was an epicurean who pushed philosophy to the point of intoxication,— that was all. He had a very elevated and distinguished stomach. He loved wine, not for itself, but for that short-lived madness which it brings, a madness which engenders in the man of wit an unreasonableness so naïve, piquant, and original that one almost prefers it to reason. If he could have intoxicated himself by reading the mass, he would have read the mass every day. My uncle Benjamin had principles: he maintained that a fasting man was a man still asleep; that intoxication would have been one of the greatest blessings of the Creator, if it had not injured the head, and that the only thing that made man superior to the brute was the faculty of getting drunk.

Reason, said my uncle, amounts to nothing; it is simply the power of feeling present evils and remembering them. The privilege of abdicating one's reason is the only thing of value. You say that the man who drowns his reason in wine brutalizes himself: it is the pride of caste that makes you hold to that opinion. Do you really think, then, that the condition of the brute is worse than your own? When you are tormented by hunger, you would like very much to be the ox that feeds in grass up to his belly; when you are in prison, you would like very much to be the bird that cleaves the azure of the skies with a free wing; when you are on the point of being turned out of house and home, you would like very much to be the ugly snail whose shell there is none to dispute.

The equality of which you dream, the brute possesses. In the forests there are neither kings, nor nobles, nor a third estate. The problem of common life studied in vain by your philosophers was solved thousands of centuries ago by the poor insects, the ants, and the bees. The animals have no doctors; they are neither blind, nor hump-backed, nor lame, nor bow-legged, and they have no fear of hell.

My uncle Benjamin was twenty-eight years old. He

had been practising medicine for three years; but medicine had not made him a man of income, far from it: he owed his tailor for three scarlet coats and his barber for three years of hair-dressing, and in each of the most famous taverns of the town he had a pretty little account running, with nothing on the credit side but a few drugs.

My grandmother was three years older than Benjamin; she had cradled him on her knees and carried him in her arms, and she looked upon herself as his mentor. She bought his cravats and pocket-handkerchiefs, mended his shirts, and gave him good advice, to which he listened very attentively,— so much justice at least must be done him,— but of which he did not make the slightest use.

Every evening regularly, after supper, she urged him to seek a wife.

"Bah!" said Benjamin; "to have six children like Machecourt,"— that was the name he gave my grandfather,— "and dine off the fins of a herring?"

"But, poor fellow, you would at least have bread."

"Yes, bread that will have risen too much to-day, not enough to-morrow, and the day after will have the measles! Bread! what does that amount to? It is good to keep one from dying, but it is not good to make one live. I shall be far advanced indeed when I shall have a wife to tell me that I put too much sugar in my vials and too much powder on my cue, to come to the tavern in search of me, to rummage in my pockets when I am asleep, and to buy three cloaks for herself to one coat for me."

"But your creditors, Benjamin, how do you expect to pay them?"

"In the first place, when one has credit, it is the same as if he were rich, and when your creditors are good-natured and patient, it is the same as if you had none. Besides, what do I need to enable me to square my accounts? Only a first-class epidemic. God is good, my dear sister, and will not abandon in his embarrassment him whose business it is to repair his finest work."

"Yes," said my grandfather, "and render it so unserviceable that it has to be buried in the ground."

"Well," responded my uncle, "that is the usefulness of doctors; but for them there would be too many people in the world. Of what use would it be for God to take the trouble to send us diseases if men could be found to cure them?"

"In that case you are a dishonest man; you rob those who send for you."

"No, I do not rob them, because I reassure them, I give them hope, and I always find a way to make them laugh. That is worth a good deal."

My grandmother, seeing that the conversation had changed its current, decided that she had better go to sleep.

CHAPTER II.

NEVERTHELESS a terrible catastrophe, which I shall have the honor to relate to you directly, shook Benjamin's resolutions.

One day my cousin Page, a lawyer in the bailiwick of Clamecy, came to invite him together with Machecourt to celebrate Saint Yves. The dinner was to take place at a well-known tea-garden situated within two gun-shots of the faubourg; the guests, moreover, were a select party. Benjamin would not have given that evening for an entire week of his ordinary life. So after vespers my grandfather, adorned in his wedding coat, and my uncle, with his sword at his side, were at the rendezvous.

Almost all the guests were there. Saint Yves was magnificently represented in this assembly. In the first place there was Page, the lawyer, who never pleaded a case except between two glasses of wine; the clerk of the court, who was in the habit of writing while asleep; the government attorney, Rapin, who, having received as a present from a litigant a cask of tart wine, had him cited before the court that he might get a better one from him; Arthus, the notary, who had been known to eat a whole salmon for his dessert; Millot-Rataut, poet and tailor, author of "Grand Noël"; an old architect that had not been sober for twenty years; M. Minxit, a doctor of the neighbor-

hood, who consulted urines; two or three notable merchants,— notable, that is, for their gayety and appetite; and some huntsmen, who had provided the table
with an abundance of game. At sight of Benjamin all
the guests uttered a shout of welcome, and declared that
it was time to sit down to table. During the two first
courses all went well. My uncle was charming with
his wit and his sallies; but at dessert heads began to
grow hot; all commenced shouting at once. Soon the
conversation was nothing but a confusion of epigrams,
oaths, and sallies, bursting out together and trying to
stifle each other, the whole making a noise like that of
a dozen glasses clashing against each other simulta-
neously.

"Gentlemen," cried Page, the lawyer, "I must entertain you with my last speech in court. The case
was this. Two asses had got into a quarrel in a
meadow. The owner of one, good-for-nothing scamp
that he is, runs and beats the other ass. But this
quadruped, not being disposed to endure it, bites our
man on the little finger. The owner of the ass who
inflicted the bite is cited before the bailiff as responsible
for the doings of his beast. I was counsel for the
defendant. 'Before coming to the question of fact,'
said I to the bailiff, 'I must enlighten you as to the
morals of the ass that I defend and that of the plaintiff.
Our ass is an entirely inoffensive quadruped; he enjoys
the esteem of all who know him, and the town constable holds him in high regard. Now, I defy the man
who is our adversary to say as much of his. Our
ass is the bearer of a certificate from the mayor of his
commune,—and this certificate really existed,— which

testifies to his morality and good conduct. If the
plaintiff can produce a like certificate, we consent to
pay him three thousand francs damages.'"

"May Saint Yves bless you!" said my uncle; "now
the poet, Millot-Rataut, must sing us his 'Grand
Noël':

'A genoux, chrétiens, à genoux!'

"That is eminently lyrical. It must have been the
Holy Spirit that inspired that beautiful line."

"I should like to see you do as much," cried the
tailor, who was very irascible under the influence of
Burgundy.

"I am not so stupid," answered my uncle.

"Silence!" interrupted Page, the lawyer, striking
with all his might on the table; "I declare to the court
that I wish to finish my plea."

"Directly," said my uncle; "you are not yet drunk
enough to plead."

"And I tell you that I will plead now. Who are
you, old five-foot-ten, to prevent a lawyer from talking?"

"Have a care, Page," exclaimed Arthus, the notary,
"you are only a man of the pen, and you are dealing
with a man of the sword."

"It well becomes you, a man of the fork, and a
devourer of salmon, to talk of men of the sword;
before you could frighten anybody, he would have to
be cooked."

"Benjamin is indeed terrible," said the architect.
"He is like the lion; at one stroke of his cue he can
knock a man down."

"Gentlemen," said my grandfather, rising, "I will answer for my brother-in-law; he has never shed blood except with his lancet."

"Do you really dare to maintain that, Machecourt?"

"And you, Benjamin, do you really dare to maintain the contrary?"

"Then you shall give me satisfaction on the instant for this insult; and, as we have here but one sword, which is mine, I will keep the scabbard, and you shall take the blade."

My grandfather, who was very fond of his brother-in-law, accepted the proposition, to avoid vexing him. As the two adversaries rose, Page, the lawyer, said:

"One moment, gentlemen. We must fix the conditions of the combat. I propose that each of the two adversaries shall hold on to the arm of his second, in order that he may not fall before it is time."

"Adopted!" cried all the guests.

Benjamin and Machecourt stood promptly face to face.

"Are you there, Benjamin?"

"And you, Machecourt?"

With the first stroke of his sword my grandfather cut Benjamin's scabbard in two as if it had been an oyster plant, and made a gash upon his wrist sufficient to force him to drink with his left hand for at least a week.

"The clumsy fellow!" cried Benjamin; "he has cut me."

"What!" answered my grandfather, with charming simplicity, "does your sword really cut?"

"All the same, I still want my revenge; and the

remaining half of this scabbard is enough with which
to make you beg my pardon."

"No, Benjamin," rejoined my grandfather, "it is
your turn to take the sword. If you stick me, we shall
be even, and we will play no more."

The guests, sobered by this accident, wanted to return to town.

"No, gentlemen," cried Benjamin, with his stentorian voice, "let each one return to his seat; I have a
proposition to make to you. Considering that it was
his first attempt, Machecourt has behaved most brill-
iantly; he is in a position to measure himself against
the most murderous of barbers, provided the latter will
yield him the sword and keep the scabbard. I propose
that we name him fencing-master; only on this condition will I consent to let him live; and, if you indorse
my opinion, I will even force myself to offer him my
left hand, inasmuch as he has disabled the other."

"Benjamin is right," cried a multitude of voices.
"Bravo, Benjamin. Machecourt must be made fencing-
master."

And each one ran to his seat, and Benjamin ordered
a second dessert.

Meanwhile the news of this accident had spread to
Clamecy. In passing from mouth to mouth, it had
grown marvellously, and, when it reached my grandmother, it had taken on the gigantic proportions of a
murder committed by her husband upon the person of
her brother.

My grandmother, in a body that was less than five
feet long, had a character that was full of firmness and
energy. She did not go screaming and crying to her

neighbors, to have them apply salts to her nose. With that presence of mind which sorrow imparts to strong souls, she saw at once what she must do. She put her children to bed, took all the money there was in the house, and the few jewels that she possessed, in order to supply her husband with means to leave the country, if that should be necessary; made up a bundle of linen for bandages and of lint to stanch the wounds of the injured man in case he should be still alive; took a mattress from her bed, and asked a neighbor to follow on with it; and then, wrapping herself in her cloak, she started without faltering for the fatal tea-garden. On entering the faubourg, she met her husband, whom they were bringing back in triumph, crowned with corks. Benjamin, on whose left arm he was supported, was crying at the top of his voice: "Know all men by these presents, that Monsieur Machecourt, verger to his Majesty, has just been appointed fencing-master, in reward" . . .

"Dog of a drunkard!" cried my grandmother, on seeing Benjamin; and, unable to resist the emotion that had been stifling her for an hour, she fell upon the pavement. They had to carry her home on the mattress which she had intended for her brother.

As for the latter, he remembered his wound only the next morning when he was putting on his coat; but his sister had a high fever. She was dangerously ill for a week, and during the entire time Benjamin did not leave her bedside. When at last she could listen to him, he promised her that henceforth he would lead a more regular life, and said that he was seriously thinking of paying his debts and marrying.

My grandmother soon recovered. She charged her husband to be on the lookout for a wife for Benjamin.

Sometime after that, one evening in November, my grandfather came home, splashed to the chin, but radiant.

"I have found something far better than we expected," cried the excellent man, pressing the hand of his brother-in-law; "now, Benjamin, you are rich; you can eat as many matelotes as you like."

"But what have you found, then?" asked my grandmother and Benjamin at the same time.

"An only daughter, a rich heiress, the daughter of Minxit, with whom we celebrated Saint Yves a month ago."

"What, that village doctor who consults urines?"

"Precisely; he accepts you unreservedly; he is charmed with your wit; he believes that you are well fitted, by your manners and your eloquence, to aid him in his industry."

"The devil!" said Benjamin, scratching his head, "I am not anxious to consult urines."

"Oh, you big booby! Once you are father Minxit's son-in-law, you can dismiss him and his vials, and bring your wife to Clamecy."

"Yes, but Mlle. Minxit has red hair."

"She is only blonde, Benjamin; I give you my word of honor."

"She is so freckled that one would say a handful of bran had been thrown in her face."

"I saw her this evening. I assure you that she is scarcely freckled at all."

"Besides, she is five feet three inches tall. I really should be afraid of spoiling the human race. We should have children as tall as bean-poles."

"Oh, these are only stupid jokes," said my grandmother; "I met your tailor yesterday, and he absolutely insists on being paid; and you know very well that your barber will not dress your hair again."

"So you wish me, my dear sister, to marry Mlle. Minxit? But you do not know what that means, *Minxit*. And you, Machecourt, do you know?"

"To be sure I know; it means father Minxit."

"Have you read Horace, Machecourt?"

"No, Benjamin."

"Well, Horace says: *Num minxit patrios cineres.* It is that devil of a preterit at which I rebel; besides, my dear sister is no longer sick. M. Minxit, Mme. Minxit, M. Rathery Benjamin Minxit, little Jean Rathery Minxit, little Pierre Rathery Minxit, little Adèle Rathery Minxit. Why, in our family there will be enough to turn a mill. And then, to be frank about it, I am scarcely anxious to marry. You know there is a song that says:

> ... 'qu'on est heureux
> Dans les liens du mariage!'

But this song does not know what it sings. It must have been written by a bachelor.

> ... 'qu'on est heureux
> Dans les liens du mariage!'

That would be all right, Machecourt, if a man were free to choose a companion for himself; but the necessities of social life always force us to marry in a ridiculous way and contrary to our inclinations. Man marries a dowry, woman a profession. Then, after all the fine Sundays of their honeymoon, they return to the solitude of their household, only to see that they do not suit each other. One is avaricious and the other prodigal, the wife is coquettish and the husband jealous, one likes the north wind and the other the south wind; they would like to be a thousand miles apart, but they have to live in the circle of iron within which they have confined themselves, and remain together *usque ad vitam æternam.*"

"Is he drunk?" whispered my grandfather to his wife.

"What makes you think so?" answered the latter.

"Because he is talking sense."

Nevertheless they made my uncle listen to reason, and it was agreed that on the next day, which was Sunday, he should go to see Mlle. Minxit.

CHAPTER III

HOW MY UNCLE MEETS AN OLD SERGEANT AND A POODLE
DOG, WHICH PREVENTS HIM FROM GOING TO
M. MINXIT'S.

THE next day, at eight o'clock in the morning, my uncle was dressed in clean linen, and needed in order to start only a pair of shoes which were to be brought him by Cicero, the famous town-crier of whom we have already spoken, and who combined the profession of shoemaker with that of drummer.

Cicero was not slow in arriving. In those days of frankness it was the custom, when a workman brought work to a house, not to let him go away without first making him drink several glasses of wine. It was a bad habit, I admit; but these kindly ways tended to offset class distinctions; the poor man was grateful to the rich man for his concessions, and was not jealous of him. Consequently during the Revolution there was seen an admirable devotion of servants to their masters, of farmers to their landlords, of laborers to their employers, which certainly could not be found in the present day of insolent arrogance and ridiculous pride.

Benjamin asked his sister to go and draw a bottle of white wine, that he might drink with Cicero. His sister drew one, then two, then three, and even seven.

"My dear sister, I beg of you, one more bottle."

"But do you not know, you wretch, that you are at the eighth?"

"You know very well, dear sister, that we keep no accounts together."

"But you know very well that you have a journey to make."

"Just this last bottle, and I start."

"Yes, you are in a fine condition to start! Suppose anyone should send for you now to visit a patient?"

"How little you appreciate, my good sister, the effects of wine! It is easy to see that you drink only the limpid waters of the Beuvron. Have I to start? My centre of gravity is always in the same place. Have I to bleed some one. . . . But, by the way, my sister, I must bleed you; Machecourt advised it when he went out. You were complaining this morning of a severe headache; a bleeding will do you good."

And Benjamin took out his case of instruments, and my grandmother armed herself with the tongs.

"The devil! You make a very rebellious patient. Well, let us compromise: I will not bleed you, and you shall go to draw us an eighth bottle of wine."

"I will not draw you a single glass."

"Then I will draw it myself," said Benjamin; and, taking the bottle, he started for the cellar.

My grandmother, seeing no better way of stopping him, seized his cue; but Benjamin, without paying any attention to this incident, went to the cellar with a step as firm as if there had been only a bunch of onions hanging to his cue, and came back with his bottle full.

"Well, my dear sister, it was well worth while for two of us to go to the cellar for a paltry bottle of white wine; but I must warn you that, if you persist in these bad habits, you will force me to cut off my cue."

Nevertheless Benjamin, who but a short time before had looked upon the journey to Corvol as a disagreeable duty, was now obstinately bent on starting. My grandmother, to make it impossible for him to do so, had locked up his shoes in the closet.

" I tell you that I will go."

" And I tell you that you shall not go."

" Do you wish me to carry you clear to M. Minxit's hanging to the end of my cue ? "

Such was the dialogue in progress between brother and sister when my grandfather arrived. He put an end to the discussion by declaring that the next day he must go to La Chapelle, and that he would take Benjamin with him.

My grandfather was up before daylight. When he had scribbled off his writ and written at the foot: " The cost of which is six francs four sous and six deniers," he wiped his pen on the sleeve of his coat, carefully put away his glasses in their case, and went to wake Benjamin. The latter was sleeping like the Prince de Condé (provided the Prince was not pretending sleep) on the eve of a battle.

" Hello, there, Benjamin, get up; it is broad daylight."

" You are mistaken," answered Benjamin, with a grunt, and turning over toward the wall, " it is pitch dark."

" Lift up your head, and you will see the sunlight on the floor."

" I tell you that it is the light of the street lamp."

" Oh, then, you do not want to go ? "

" No, I have dreamed all night of hard bread and

sour wine, and if we start some misfortune will happen
to us."

"Well, I declare to you that, if in ten minutes you
are not up, I will send your dear sister to you. If, on
the other hand, you are up, I will open that quarter-
cask of old wine you know so well."

"You are sure that it is from Pouilly, are you?"
said Benjamin, sitting up in bed; "you give me your
word of honor?"

"Yes, upon my word as a summons-server."

"Then go open your quarter-cask; but I warn you
that, if we meet with any accident on our way, you will
have to answer for it to my dear sister."

An hour later my uncle and my grandfather were
on their way to Moulot. At some distance from the
town they met two little peasants, of whom one was
carrying a rabbit under his arm and the other had two
hens in his basket. The former said to his companion:

"If you will tell M. Cliquet that my rabbit is a
warren rabbit, and that you saw him taken in the trap,
you shall be my comrade."

"Willingly," answered the latter, "but on condition
that you will tell Mme. Deby that my hens lay twice
a day and that their eggs are as big as ducks' eggs."

"You are two little thieves," said my grandfather;
"I will have your ears pulled one of these days by the
commissary of police."

"And I, my friends," said Benjamin, "I beg you each
to accept this twelve-denier piece."

"Well, that's generosity well placed," said my grandfather, shrugging his shoulders; "you will undoubtedly

give the flat of your sword to the first poor honest man that you meet, since you prostitute your money on these two scamps."

"Scamps to you, Machecourt, who see only the surface of things; but to me they are two philosophers. They have just invented a machine which, well organized, would make the fortune of ten honest people."

"And what machine is that, pray," said my grandfather, with an air of incredulity, "which has just been invented by these two philosophers, whom I would thrash soundly if we had the time to stop?"

"It is a simple machine," said my uncle; "this is how it works. We are ten friends who, instead of meeting for breakfast, meet to make our fortunes."

"That is something worth meeting for," interrupted my grandfather.

"All ten of us are intelligent, adroit, and, if need be, shrewd. We have loud voices and are wonderful debaters. We handle words with the same skill with which a juggler handles his balls. As for morality, we are all capable in our professions, and well-meaning persons may say, without seriously compromising themselves, that we are superior to our rivals. We form, with the most honorable intentions, a society to puff each other, to inflate our little merits and make them froth and foam."

"I understand," said my grandfather: "one sells 'Rough on Rats' and has only a big drum, the other Swiss tea and has only a pair of cymbals. You unite your means of making a noise, and " . . .

"That's it exactly," interrupted Benjamin. "You see that, if the machine works properly, each of the members has about him nine instruments that make a frightful uproar.

"There are nine of us who say: Page, the lawyer, drinks too much; but I believe that this devil of a man steeps leaves from the common-law book in his wine, and that he has bottled up logic. All the cases that he wants to win, he wins; and the other day he got a verdict of heavy damages for a gentleman who had beaten a peasant.

"The process-server, Parlanta, is a little crafty; but he is the Hannibal of process-servers. His arrests for debt are inevitable; his debtor could only escape him if he had no body at all. He would lay his hand on the shoulder of a duke and peer.

"As for Benjamin Rathery, he is a careless fellow, who mocks at everything and laughs in the face of fever, a man, if you will, of the plate and the bottle; but it is precisely for that reason that I prefer him to his rivals. He has not the air of those sinister doctors whose register is a cemetery. He is too gay and digests too well to have many death certificates to answer for.

"Thus each of the members finds himself multiplied by nine."

"Yes," said my grandfather, "but will that give you nine red coats? Nine times Benjamin Rathery, what does that make?"

"That makes nine hundred times Machecourt," replied Benjamin, quickly. "But let me finish my demonstration; you shall joke afterward.

"Here are nine living advertisements, who insinuate themselves everywhere, who repeat to you to-morrow under another form what they have told you to-day; nine placards that talk and take passers-by by the arm; nine signs that promenade through the town, that discuss, that make dilemmas and enthymemes, and mock at you if you are not of their opinion.

"As a result, the reputation of Page, Rapin, and Rathery, which was dragging painfully along within the precincts of their little town, like a lawyer in a vicious circle, suddenly takes an astonishing flight. Yesterday it had no feet; to-day it has wings. It expands like gas when the bottle in which it was confined has been opened. It spreads throughout the province. Clients come to these people from all parts of the bailiwick; they come from the South and from the North, from the dawn and from the sunset, as in the Apocalypse the elect come to the city of Jerusalem. After five or six years Benjamin Rathery is the owner of a handsome fortune, which he expends, with great noise of glasses and bottles, in breakfasts and dinners; you, Machecourt, are no longer a server of writs; I buy you the office of bailiff. Your wife is covered with silks and laces like a holy queen; your eldest son, who is already a choir-boy, enters the ecclesiastical seminary; your second son, who is sickly and as yellow as a canary bird, studies medicine; I give him my reputation and my old clients, and I keep him in red coats. Of your youngest son, we make a lawyer. Your eldest daughter marries a man of letters. We marry the youngest to a fat *bourgeois*, and the day after the wedding we put the machine away in the attic."

"Yes, but your machine has one little defect; it is not for the use of honest people."

" Why so ? "

" Because."

" Because what ? "

" Because the effect is immoral."

" Can you prove me that by *now* and by *then ?* "

" To the devil with your *nows* and *thens*. You are an educated man, and you reason with your mind; but I, who am a poor server of writs, I feel with my conscience. I maintain that any man who acquires his fortune by other means than his labor and his talents is not a legitimate possessor."

" What you say is very good, Machecourt," cried my uncle; "you are perfectly right. Conscience is the best of all logics, and charlatanism, under whatever form it may disguise itself, is always a swindle. Well, we will break our machine and say no more about it."

While chattering thus, they were approaching the village of Moulot; they saw in front of a vineyard gate a sort of soldier half buried in brambles, the brown and red tufts of which, touched by the frost, fell in confusion like a disordered head of hair. This man had on his head a piece of a cocked hat without a cockade; his dilapidated face had a stony tint, that yellow tint which old monuments have in the sunlight. The two halves of a huge white moustache encircled his mouth, like two parentheses. He was dressed in an old uniform. Across one of the sleeves stretched an old and worn strip of gold lace.

The other sleeve, deprived of its ensign, was nothing but a rectangle distinguished from the rest of the material by a newer wool and a deeper shade. His bare legs, swollen by the cold, were red as beets. He was letting a few drops of brandy drip from a gourd on some old pieces of black bread. A poodle dog of the larger type was sitting in front of him, and following all his movements, like a dumb servant listening with his eyes to the orders given him by his master.

My uncle would sooner have passed by a tavern without stopping than by this man. Halting on the side of the road, he said:

"Comrade, that's a bad breakfast you have there."

"I have eaten many a worse one, but Fontenoy and I have good appetites."

"Who is Fontenoy?"

"My dog, that poodle that you see there."

"The devil! but that is a fine name for a dog. But then, glory is a good thing for kings; why shouldn't it be for poodle dogs?"

"That's his fighting name," continued the sergeant; "his family name is Azor."

"Well, why do you call him Fontenoy?"

"Because at the battle of Fontenoy he made an English captain prisoner."

"Hey, how is that?" exclaimed my uncle, greatly astonished.

"In a very simple way, by hanging to one of the skirts of his coat until I could lay my hand on his shoulder. Fontenoy, just as he is, has been made a member of the order of the army, and has had the honor to be presented to Louis XV., who condescended to say to me: 'Sergeant Duranton, you have a fine dog there.'"

"Well, that was a king who was very sociable with quadrupeds: I am astonished that he did not issue a

patent of nobility to your poodle.   How does it happen
that you have abandoned the service of so good a
king ? "

"Because they have done me a wrong," said the sergeant, his eyes glaring and his nostrils swelling with
anger ; "I have had these golden rags on my arms for
ten years; I have been through all the campaigns of
Maurice de Saxe, and I have more scars on my body
than would be required for two periods of service.
They had promised me the epaulette ; but to make a
weaver's son an officer would have been a scandal
calculated to horrify all the pigeon wings of France and
of Navarre.   They promoted over my body a sort of
little knight just hatched from his page's shell.   He
will find a way to get himself killed, of course; for
they are brave, there is no denying that.   But he does
·not know how to say : 'Eyes, . . . right ! ' "

At this drill command, strongly accented by the sergeant, the poodle turned his eyes to the right in a truly
military fashion.

"Very fine, Fontenoy," said his master, "you forget
that we have retired from the service."   And he continued : "I could not forgive the very Christian king
for that; I have been out with him ever since, and
I asked him for my furlough, which he graciously
granted."

"You have done well, brave man," cried Benjamin,
slapping the old soldier on the shoulder, an imprudent
gesture that came very near causing the poodle to devour him.   "If my approval is of any value to you, I
give it to you without reserve ; the nobles have never
stood in the way of my advancement, but that does not
prevent me from hating them with all my heart."

"In that case it is a purely platonic hatred," interrupted my grandfather.

"Say rather a purely philosophical hatred, Machecourt. Nobility is the most absurd of all things. It is a flagrant revolt of despotism against the Creator. Did God make the grasses of the prairie higher one than the other? Did he engrave escutcheons upon the wings of birds and the skins of wild beasts? What signify these superior men which a king makes by letters patent, as he makes an exciseman or a huckster? Dating from to-day, you will recognize Mr. So-and-so as a superior man. Signed Louis XVI., and lower down Choiseul. Oh, that's a fine way to establish superiority.

"A villein is made a count by Henri IV., because he has served that majesty with a nice goose; if he had served a capon with the goose, he would have been made a marquis; it would have taken no more ink or parchment. Now the descendants of these men have the privilege of beating us, whose ancestors never had an opportunity of offering a fowl's wing to a king.

"And see on what a little thing greatness depends in this world! If the goose had been cooked a little more or a little less, if they had put on it one more pinch of salt or one less pinch of pepper, if a little soot had fallen into the dripping-pan or a little cinder upon the slices of bread, or if the bird had been served a little sooner or a little later, there would have been one less noble family in France. And the people bow their heads before such greatness! Oh! I could wish, as Caligula wished of the Roman people, that France had but a single pair of cheeks that I might slap its face.

" But tell me, imbecile people, what value do you
find then in the two letters that these people place before their names? Do they add an inch to their stature? Have they more iron than you in their blood,
more cerebral marrow in the bony box of their heads?
Could they handle a sword heavier than yours? Does
this marvellous *de* cure scrofula? Does it preserve its
possessor from the colic when he has dined too heavily,
or from intoxication when he has drunk too much?
Do you not see that all these counts, these barons, these
marquises, are capital letters which, in spite of the place
that they occupy in the line, are never of more importance than the small letters? If a duke and peer and
a woodcutter were together on an American prairie or
in the middle of the great desert of Sahara, I should
like to know which of the two would be the nobler.

" Their great-great-grandfather wielded the shield,
and your father made cotton caps; what does that
prove for them or against you? Do they come into
the world with their ancestor's shield at their side?
Have they his scars marked on their skin? What is
this greatness that is transmitted from father to son,
like a new candle which we light from a candle that is
going out? Are the toadstools which arise from the
ruins of a dead oak, oaks on that account?

" When I learn that the king has created a noble
family, it seems to me that I see a farmer planting in his
field a big booby of a poppy, which will infect twenty
furrows with its seed and yield every year only four
big red leaves. Nevertheless, as long as there shall be
kings, there will be nobles.

" The kings make counts, marquises, dukes, that ad-

miration may rise to them by degrees. Nobles, rela-
tively to them, are the bagatelles of the gate, the pa-
rade that gives the idlers a foretaste of the magnificence
of the spectacle. A king without nobility would be a
salon without an ante-chamber; but this dainty pride
will cost them dear. It is impossible that twenty millions of men should consent forever to be nothing in
the State that a few thousand courtiers may be something; who sows privileges will reap revolutions.

"The time is not far off perhaps when all these
brilliant escutcheons will be dragged in the gutter, and
when those who now adorn themselves with them will
need the protection of their *valets.*"

"What!" you say to me, "your uncle Benjamin
said all that?"

"Why not?"

"All in one breath?"

"To be sure. What is there in that that is astonishing? My grandfather had a jug that held a pint and
a half, and my uncle emptied it at one draught: he
called that making tirades."

"And his words? How were they preserved?"

"My grandfather wrote them down."

"Then he had there, in the open air, all the necessary
writing materials?"

"How stupid! Wasn't he a summons-server?"

"And the sergeant? Did he have anything more to
say?"

"Certainly; it was very necessary that he should
speak in order that my uncle might reply."

Now then, the sergeant said:

"I have been on the road for three months; I go

from farm to farm, and I stay as long as they are willing to keep me. I play with the children, I tell the story of our campaigns to the men, and Fontenoy amuses the women with his frolics. I am in no hurry, for I don't exactly know where I am going. They send me back to my fireside, and I have no fireside. My father's stove was long ago staved in, and my arms are hollower and rustier than two old gun-barrels. Nevertheless I think that I shall return to my village. Not that I expect to be better off there than anywhere else. The ground is as hard there as elsewhere, and they do not drink brandy in the roads. But what difference does it make? I shall go there just the same. It is a sort of sick man's whim. I shall be the garrison of the neighborhood. If they do not wish to support the old soldier, they will have at least to bury him, and," he added, "they will certainly be kind enough to place upon my grave a little soup for Fontenoy, until he shall die of sorrow; for Fontenoy will not let me go away alone. When we are alone and he looks at me, he promises me that, this good Fontenoy."

"So that is the fate that they have made for you?" answered Benjamin. "Truly, kings are the most selfish of all beings. If the serpents, of which our poets speak so ill, had a literature, they would make kings the symbol of ingratitude. I have read somewhere that, when God had made the heart of kings, a dog ran off with it, and that, not wishing to begin his work again, he put a stone in its place. That seems to me very likely. As for the Capets, perhaps they have a lily-root in place of a heart; I defy anyone to prove the contrary.

"Because these people had a cross made on their foreheads with oil, their persons are august, they are majesties, they are WE instead of I; they can do no wrong; if their *valet de chambre* should scratch them in putting on their shirt, it would be a sacrilege. Their little ones are highnesses, these brats, which a woman carries in her hand, and whose cradle could be held in a hen-coop; they are very lofty heights, most serene mountains. We would willingly gild their nurses' nipples. If such is the effect of a little oil, how much we ought to respect the anchovies that are pickled in oil till we eat them!

"In the caste of sires, pride goes to the point of madness. They are compared to Jupiter holding a thunderbolt, and they do not consider themselves too highly honored by the comparison. Leave out the thunderbolt, and they would be offended. Nevertheless, Jupiter has the gout, and it takes two *valets* to lead him to his table or to bed. The rhymester Boileau has, by his private authority, ordered the winds to be silent, inasmuch as he was about to speak of Louis XIV.:

> 'Et vous, vents, faites silence,
> Je vais parler de Louis.'

"And Louis XIV. looked on this as very natural; only it has never occurred to him to order the commanders of his vessels to speak of Louis in order to still the tempests.

"All these poor madmen believe that the space of earth over which they reign is theirs; that God has given it to them, soil and sub-soil, to be enjoyed, without disturbance or hindrance, by them and their de-

scendants. Let a courtier tell them that God made the
Seine expressly to supply the great basin of the Tuil-
eries, and they will look on him as a man of wit. They
regard these millions of men around them as their property, the title to whom cannot be disputed on the
penalty of hanging; some have come into the world to
supply them with money; others to die in their quarrels; some, who have the clearest and reddest blood, to
beget mistresses for them. All this evidently results
from the cross which an old arch-bishop, with his withered hand, has laid upon their brows.

"They take a man in the strength of his youth, they
put a gun in his hands and a knapsack on his back,
they adorn his head with a cockade, and they say to
him: 'My brother of Prussia has wronged me; you are
to attack all his subjects. I have warned them by my
process-server, whom I call a herald, that on the first of
April next you will have the honor to present yourself
at the frontier to strangle them, and that they should
be ready to give you a warm welcome. Between monarchs these are considerations which we owe each other.
You will think perhaps at first sight that our enemies
are men; I warn you to the contrary; they are Prussians; you will distinguish them from the human race
by the color of their uniform. Try to do your duty
well, for I shall be there sitting on my throne to watch
you. If you bring victory with you when you return
to France, you will be led beneath the windows of my
palace; I shall appear in full uniform, and say to you:
"Soldiers, I am content with you." If you are one
hundred thousand men, you will have for your share a
hundred-thousandth of these six words. In case you

should remain on the battle-field, which may very easily happen, I will send your death certificate to your family, that they may weep for you and that your brothers may inherit your property. If you lose an arm or a leg, I will pay you what they are worth, but if you have the good or ill fortune, whichever you may think it, to escape the bullet, when you have no longer strength enough to carry your knapsack, I will give you your furlough, and you can go to die where you like; that will no longer concern me.' "

" That's just the way it is," said the sergeant; " when they have extracted from our blood the phosphorus of which they make their glory, they throw us aside as the wine-grower throws on the muck-heap the skin of the grape after squeezing out the liquor, or as a child throws into the gutter the stone of the fruit which he has just eaten."

" That is very wrong of them," said Machecourt, whose mind was at Corvol, and who longed to see his brother-in-law there.

" Machecourt," said Benjamin, looking at him askance, " be more careful of your expressions; this is no laughing matter. Yes, when I see these proud soldiers, who have made the glory of their country with their blood, obliged, like that poor old Cicero, to spend the rest of their life on a cobbler's bench, while a multitude of gilded puppets monopolize the public revenues, and prostitutes have cashmeres for their morning wrappers, a single thread of which is worth the entire wardrobe of a poor house-wife, I am exasperated against kings; if I were God, I would put a leaden uniform on their bodies, and condemn them to a thousand years of military service in the moon, with all their iniquities in their knapsacks. The emperors should be corporals."

After having recovered his breath and wiped his brow, for he was sweating, my worthy great-uncle, with emotion and wrath, he took my grandfather aside, and said to him :

" Suppose we invite this brave man and this glorious poodle to breakfast with us at Manette's ? "

" Hum ! hum ! " objected my grandfather.

" The devil ! " replied Benjamin, " one does not meet every day a poodle who has made an English captain prisoner, and every day political banquets are given to people who are not worth this honorable quadruped."

" But have you any money ? " said my grandfather ; " I have only a thirty-sou piece, which your sister gave me this morning because, I believe, it is imperfectly coined, and she urgently recommended me to bring her back at least half."

" For my part, I have not a sou, but I am Manette's physician, just as she from time to time is my tavern-keeper, and we give each other credit."

" Manette's physician only ? "

" What's that to you ? "

" Nothing ; but I warn you that I will not stay more than an hour at Manette's."

So my uncle extended his invitation to the sergeant. The latter accepted without ceremony, and joyfully placed himself between my uncle and my grandfather, walking in what soldiers call lock-step.

They met a bull, which a peasant was driving to pasture. Offended undoubtedly by Benjamin's coat, he suddenly started for him. My uncle dodged his

horns, and, as he had joints of steel, he cleared at a
bound, with no more effort than if he had cut a caper,
a broad ditch that separated the road from the fields.
The bull, who was undoubtedly determined to make a
slash in the red coat, tried to follow my uncle's example; but he fell into the middle of the ditch. "Good
enough for you!" said Benjamin, "that's what you get
by seeking a quarrel with people who are not dreaming
of you." But the quadruped, as obstinate as a Russian
mounting to an assault, was not discouraged by this
failure; planting his hoofs in the half-thawed ground,
he tried to climb the slope. My uncle, seeing that,
drew his sword, and, while he was pricking the enemy's
snout to the best of his ability, he called the peasant,
and cried: "My good man, stop your beast; else I warn
you that I will pass my sword through his body." But,
as he said the words, he let his sword fall into the ditch.
"Take off your coat, and throw it to him as quickly as
you can," cried Machecourt. "Hide among the vines,"
said the peasant. "Sic him! sic him! Fontenoy," said
the sergeant. The poodle leaped at the bull, and, as if
he knew his enemy, bit him on the ham-string. The
animal then turned his wrath against the dog; but,
while he was making havoc with his horns, the peasant came up and succeeded in passing a noose around
the bull's hind legs. This skilful manœuvre was perfectly successful, and put an end to the hostilities.

Benjamin returned to the road. He thought that
Machecourt was going to laugh at him, but the latter
was as pale as a sheet and trembled on his legs.

"Come, Machecourt, brace up," said my uncle; "else
I shall have to bleed you. And you, my brave Fonte-

noy, you have made to-day a prettier fable than that of
La Fontaine, entitled : 'The Dove and the Ant.' You
see, gentlemen, a good deed is never lost. Generally
the benefactor is obliged to give long credit to the
beneficiary, but he, Fontenoy, has paid me in advance.
Who the devil would have thought that I would ever
be under obligations to a poodle ? "

Moulot is hidden among a clump of willows and
poplars on the left bank of the Beuvron river, at the
foot of a big hill, up which runs the road to La Chapelle.
A few houses of the village had already gone up by the
side of the road, as white and as spick and span as
peasant women when they go into a place frequented
by society ; among them was Manette's wine-shop. At
sight of the frost-covered sign that hung from the attic-
window, Benjamin began to sing with his stentorian
voice :

> " Amis, il faut faire une pause,
> J'aperçois l'ombre d'un bouchon."

On hearing this familiar voice, Manette ran blushing
to the threshold of her door.

Manette was really a very pretty person, plump,
chubby, and white, but perhaps a little too pink; her
cheeks would have reminded you of a pool of milk, on
the surface of which a few drops of wine were floating.

"Gentlemen," said Benjamin, "permit me first of all
to kiss our pretty hostess, as an appetizer for the good
breakfast which she is going to prepare for us directly."

"Indeed, Monsieur Rathery ! " exclaimed Manette,
starting back, "you are not made for peasant women ;
go and kiss Mademoiselle Minxit."

"It seems," thought my uncle, "that the report of

my marriage has already spread through the country.
No one but M. Minxit can have spoken of it; hence he
must be determined to have me for a son-in-law; so, if
he should not receive my visit to-day, that would not
be a reason for breaking off the negotiations."

"Manette," he added, "Mlle. Minxit is not in question here; have you any fish?"

"There are plenty of fish," said Manette, "in M.
Minxit's fish pond."

"Again I ask you, Manette," said Benjamin, "have
you any fish? Be careful what you answer."

"Well," said Manette, "my husband has gone fish-
ing, and he will soon return."

"Soon does not meet our case; put on the gridiron
as many slices of ham as it will hold, and make us an
omelette of all the eggs in your hen-house."

The breakfast was soon ready. While the omelette
was leaping in the frying-pan, the ham was broiling.
Now, the omelette was almost as soon despatched as
served. It takes a hen six months to lay twelve eggs,
a woman a quarter of an hour to convert them into an
omelette, and three men five minutes to absorb the
omelette. "See," said Benjamin, "how much more
rapid is decomposition than recomposition; countries
covered with a numerous population grow poorer every
day. Man is a greedy infant who makes his nurse
grow thin; the ox does not restore to the fields all the
grass that he takes from it; the ashes of the oak that
we burn do not return as an oak to the forest; the
zephyr does not carry back to the rose-bush the leaves
of the bouquet that the young girl scatters around her;
the candle that burns in front of us does not fall back

in waxen dew upon the earth; rivers continually
despoil continents, and lose in the bosom of the sea the
matter which they take from their banks; most of the
mountains have no verdure left upon their big bald
craniums; the Alps show us their bare and jagged
bones; the interior of Africa is nothing but a lake of
sand; Spain is a vast moor, and Italy a great charnel-
house where there remains only a bed of ashes.
Wherever great peoples have passed, they have left
sterility in their tracks. This earth, adorned with verdure and with flowers, is a consumptive whose cheeks
are red, but whose life is condemned. A time will
come when it will be nothing but an inert, dead, icy
mass, a great sepulchral stone upon which God will
write: 'Here lies the human race.' Meantime, gentlemen, let us profit by the blessings which the earth gives
us, and, as she is a tolerably good mother, let us drink
to her long life."

They came then to the ham. My grandfather ate
from a sense of duty, because man must eat to maintain his health and must have blood in order to serve
writs; Benjamin ate for amusement; but the sergeant
ate like a man who sits down to table for no other purpose, and he did not utter a word.

At table Benjamin was famous; but his noble
stomach was not exempt from jealousy, a base passion
which dims the most brilliant qualities.

He watched the sergeant with the vexed air of a
man outdone, as Cæsar would have watched, from the
height of the Capitol, Bonaparte winning the battle
of Marengo. After having contemplated his man for
some time in silence, he thought fit to address these
words to him:

"Drinking and eating are two beings that resemble each other; at first sight you would take them for own cousins. But drinking is as much above eating as the eagle who alights upon the mountain peak is above the raven who perches on the tree-top. Eating is a necessity of the stomach; drinking is a necessity of the soul. Eating is only a common workman, while drinking is an artist. Drinking inspires poets with pleasant ideas, philosophers with noble thoughts, musicians with melodious strains; eating gives them only indigestion. Now, I flatter myself, sergeant, that I could drink quite as well as you; I even think that I could drink better; but, when it comes to eating, I am the merest novice beside you. You could cope with Arthus in person; I even think that on a turkey you could go him one wing better."

"You see," answered the sergeant, "I eat for yesterday, to-day, and to-morrow."

"Permit me then to serve you for day after-to-morrow this last slice of ham."

"Thank you very much," said the sergeant, "there is an end to everything."

"Well, the Creator who has made soldiers to pass suddenly from extreme abundance to extreme want has given to them, as to the camel, two stomachs; their second stomach is their knapsack. Take this ham, which neither Machecourt nor I want, and put it in your knapsack."

"No," said the soldier, "I do not need to lay up provisions; I always get food enough; permit me to offer this ham to Fontenoy; we are in the habit of sharing everything together, on days of feast as on days of fast."

" You have there, indeed, a dog who deserves to be
well taken care of," said my uncle; "will you sell him
to me?"

" Monsieur!" exclaimed the sergeant, quickly placing
his hand upon his poodle.

" Pardon me, worthy man, pardon me; I am distressed at having offended you; I spoke only in jest;
I know very well that to propose to a poor man to sell
his dog is like proposing to a mother to sell her child."

" You will never make me believe," said my grandfather, " that one can love a dog as much as a child; I,
too, once had a poodle, a poodle that was well worth
yours, sergeant,— be it said without offence to Fontenoy,— save that he has taken prisoner nothing but the
tax-collector's wig. Well, one day, when I had lawyer
Page to dinner, he ran off with a calf's head, and that
very night I passed him under the mill-wheel."

" What you say proves nothing; you have a wife and
six children; it is quite work enough for you to love
all these people without forming a romantic affection
for a poodle; but I am talking of a poor devil isolated
among men and with no relative but his dog. Put a
man with a dog in a desert island, in another desert
island put a woman with her child, and I will wager
that in six months' time the man will love the dog, provided the dog is amiable, as well as the woman will love
her child."

" I can conceive," answered my grandfather, " that a
traveller may like a dog to keep him company, that an
old woman that lives alone in her room may like a pug
with which to babble all day long. But that a man
should love a dog with real affection, that he should

love him as a Christian, that is what I deny, that is what I deem impossible."

"And I tell you that under certain circumstances you would love even a rattlesnake; the loving fibre in man cannot remain entirely inert. The human soul abhors a vacuum; observe attentively the most hardened egoist, and at last you will find, like a little flower among the stones, an affection hidden under a fold of his soul.

"It is a general rule, to which there is no exception, that man must love something. The dragoon who has no mistress loves his horse; the young girl who has no lover loves her bird; the prisoner, who cannot in decency love his jailer, loves the spider that spins its web in the window of his cell, or the fly that comes down to him in a ray of sunlight. When we find nothing animate to absorb our affections, we love material objects, —a ring, a snuff-box, a tree, a flower; the Dutchman feels a passion for his tulips, and the antiquary for his cameos."

Just then Manette's husband came in with a fat eel in his basket.

"Machecourt," said Benjamin, "it is noon,—that is to say, dinner-time; suppose we make a dinner of this eel?"

"It is time to go," said Machecourt, "and we shall dine at M. Minxit's."

"And you, sergeant? Suppose we eat this eel?"

"For my part," said the sergeant, "I am in no hurry; as I am not going anywhere in particular, I spend every night at home."

"Very well said! And the respectable poodle, what is his opinion on this point?"

The poodle looked at Benjamin and wagged his tail two or three times.

"Well, silence gives consent: so, Machecourt, there are three of us against you ; you must bow to the will of the majority. The majority, you see, my friend, is stronger than the rest of the world. Put ten philosophers on one side and eleven fools on the other, and the fools will carry the day."

"The eel is indeed a very fine one," said my grandfather, "and, if Manette has a little fresh bacon, it will make an excellent matelote. But, the devil! what about my writ? That must be served."

"Mark this," said Benjamin ; "it will undoubtedly be necessary for some one to lend me his arm to escort me back to Clamecy. If you shirk this pious duty, I will no longer own you as my brother-in-law."

Now, as Machecourt was very anxious to continue as Benjamin's brother-in-law, he remained.

The eel being ready, they sat down at table again. Manette's matelote was a *chef-d'œuvre ;* the sergeant did not tire of admiring it. But the *chefs-d'œuvre* of the cook are ephemeral ; we scarcely give them time to cool. There is only one thing in the arts that can be compared to culinary products; I refer to the products of journalism ; and even a stew can be warmed over, a terrine of *foie gras* may keep a whole month, and a ham may see its admirers gather about it many times; but a newspaper article has no to-morrow ; before we reach the end, we have forgotten the beginning, and, when we have finished it, we throw it on our desk, as we throw our napkin on the table after we have dined. Consequently I do not understand how a man of literary value can consent to waste his talents in the obscure works of journalism ; how he who might write on parchment can make up his mind to scribble on the blotting-paper of a journal; certainly it must occasion him no small heart-break to see the leaves upon which he has placed his thought fall noiselessly with those thousand other leaves which the immense tree of the press shakes daily from its branches.

Meanwhile the hand of the cuckoo clock kept moving on, while my uncle philosophized. Benjamin did not notice that it was dark until Manette placed a lighted candle on the table. Then, without waiting for the observations of Machecourt, who for that matter was scarcely in a condition to observe anything, he declared that they had had enough for one day, and that it was time to return to Clamecy.

The sergeant and my grandfather went out first. Manette stopped my uncle at the threshold.

" Monsieur Rathery," said she, " see here."

" What is this scrawl ? " said my uncle. " ' August 10, three bottles of wine with a cream cheese ; September 1, with M. Page, nine bottles and a plate of fish.' God forgive me, I believe it is a bill."

" Undoubtedly," said Manette ; " I see clearly that it is time to balance our accounts, and I hope that you will send me yours very soon."

" For my part, Manette, I have no account to render. It is an agreeable duty indeed to touch the plump white arm of a pretty woman like yourself."

" You say that to laugh at me, Monsieur Rathery," exclaimed Manette, thrilling with delight.

"I say it because it is true, because I think it," answered my uncle. "As for your bill, my poor Manette, it comes at a fatal moment; I am obliged to declare to you that I haven't the smallest coin at the present hour; but, stay, here is my watch; you shall keep it until I have paid you. It is in the best possible condition; it hasn't been going since yesterday."

Manette began to weep, and tore up the bill.

My uncle kissed her on the cheek, on the forehead, on the eyes, and wherever he could find a place to kiss her.

"Benjamin," said Manette to him, leaning over to whisper in his ear, "if you need money, tell me so."

"No, no, Manette," my uncle answered quickly, "I do not need your money. The devil! that would be getting serious. To make you pay for the happiness you give me! Why, that would be an indignity; I should be as vile as a prostitute!" And he kissed Manette as he had done before.

"Oh, do not embarrass yourself, Monsieur Rathery," said Jean-Pierre, who just then came in.

"What, you were there, Jean-Pierre? Are you jealous, then? I warn you that I have a profound aversion for jealous people."

"Well, it seems to me that I have a good right to be jealous."

"Imbecile! you always take things wrong. These gentlemen have charged me to testify to your wife their satisfaction for the excellent matelote which she has made for us, and I was fulfilling the commission."

"There was a good way, it seems to me, to testify your satisfaction to Manette; and that was by paying her, do you understand?"

"In the first place, Jean-Pierre, we are not dealing with you: it is Manette who keeps this tavern; as for paying you, rest easy, I charge myself with the bill; you know that no one ever loses anything by me; and besides, if you are afraid of waiting too long, I will straightway pass my sword through your body. Does that suit you, Jean-Pierre?"

And with these words he went out.

Up to this time Benjamin had only been over-excited; he contained all the elements of intoxication, without yet being intoxicated. But, on leaving Manette's wine-shop, the cold seized upon his brain and legs.

"Hello, there, Machecourt, where are you?"

"Here I am, holding on to the lappel of your coat."

"You hold me, that's good, that does me honor, you flatter me. You mean to say thereby that I am in a condition to sustain both my hypostasis and your own. At another time, yes; but now I am as weak as the most ordinary of men when he has remained too long at dinner. I have engaged your arm, I call upon you to offer it to me."

"At another time, yes," said Machecourt; "but there is a difficulty in the way; I cannot walk myself."

"Then you have forfeited your honor, you have failed in the most sacred of duties; I had engaged your arm, you were to save yourself for both of us; but I forgive your weakness. *Homo sum*, . . . that is to say, I forgive you on one condition: that you go directly for the town constable and two peasants carrying torches to escort me back to Clamecy. You shall take one of the officer's arms, and I the other."

"But the constable has but one arm," said my grandfather.

"Then the valid arm belongs to me. The best that
I can do for you is to allow you to hang on to my cue,
and you must take care not to untie the ribbon. Or,
if you prefer, get on the poodle's back."

"Gentlemen," said the sergeant, "why look so far
for what is close at hand? I have two good arms,
which fortunately the bullet has spared, and I place
them at your disposition."

"You are a brave man, sergeant," said my uncle,
taking the old soldier's right arm.

"An excellent man," said my grandfather, taking
his left arm.

"I charge myself with your future, sergeant."

"And I too, sergeant, I charge myself with it, although, to tell the truth, any charge at the present
moment " . . .

"I will teach you to pull teeth, sergeant."

"And I, sergeant, will teach your poodle to be a
bailiff's keeper."

"In three months you will be able to be a fakir at
the fairs."

"In three months your poodle, if he behaves himself,
will be able to earn thirty sous a day."

"The sergeant shall serve his apprenticeship by practising on you, Machecourt; you have some decayed old
stumps that torment you; we will pull them out, one
every two days, in order not to fatigue you, and when
we have finished with the stumps, we will pull out your
gums."

"And I will put my bailiff's keeper at the service of

your creditors, old dead-beat. I will proceed to tell
you in advance of the duties you will have to fulfil
toward him. You must give him, in the morning, bread
and cheese, or, in the season, a bunch of little radishes;
for dinner, soup and boiled beef, and for supper a roast
and a salad, though the salad may be replaced by a
glass of wine. You will take care that he does not pine
away in your hands, for nothing does so much honor to
a debtor as a good fat keeper. On his·side he must behave properly toward you; he has no right to disturb
you in your occupations, to play, for instance, the clarinette, or sound the hunting horn."

" Meantime I offer the sergeant a residence at the
house; you do not disapprove, do you, Machecourt?"

" Not exactly, but I am very much afraid that your
dear sister will disown you."

" Oh, gentlemen," said the sergeant, "let us understand each other. Do not expose me to insult; for, I
warn you, one or the other of you will have to answer
for it."

" Rest easy, sergeant," said my uncle; "and, if the
case occurs, you will have to address yourself to me;
for Machecourt doesn't know how to fight, except when
his adversary gives him the sword and keeps the
scabbard."

While thus philosophizing, they reached the door of
the house. My grandfather was not anxious to enter
first, and my uncle preferred to enter second.

To settle the matter, they entered both together,
knocking against each other like two gourds carried
at the end of a stick.

The sergeant and the poodle, whose intrusion made

the cat growl like a royal tigress, brought up the
rear.

"My dear sister," said Benjamin, " I have the honor
to introduce to you a pupil in surgery and a " . . .

" Benjamin is beginning to talk nonsense to you,"
interrupted my grandfather; "don't listen to him.
Monsieur is a soldier sent us to be lodged and whom
we met at the door."

My grandmother was a good woman, but something
of a shrew; she thought that to talk very loud added
to her importance. She had the greatest desire in the
world to get angry, and all the more desire because she
had the right. But she prided herself on her good
breeding, being a descendant of a lawyer ; and the presence of a stranger restrained her.

She offered the sergeant some supper. The latter
having declined and for good reason, she bade one of
her children take him to the neighboring tavern, with an
order that breakfast be given him in the morning before
his departure.

My grandfather always bent like a rush,— peace-
able, worthy man that he was,— when he saw a conjugal
storm brewing. Up to a certain point this weakness
was perhaps excusable in him, inasmuch as he was
always in the wrong.

He had clearly seen the clouds massing on his wife's
wrinkled brow ; and so the sergeant had hardly reached
the threshold when he had gained his bed, into which
he found his way as best he could. As for Benjamin,
he was incapable of such cowardice. A sermon in five
points, like a game of *écarté*, would not have sent him
to bed a minute before his time. He was willing that

his sister should scold him, but he could not consent to fear her. He awaited the tempest that was about to burst forth, with the indifference of a rock, his hands in his pockets and his back resting against the mantel-shelf, and humming between his lips:

> "Malbrough s'en va-t-en guerre,
> Mironton, mironton, mirontaine,
> Malbrough s'en va-t-en guerre,
> Savoir s'il reviendra."

My grandmother had scarcely conducted the sergeant to the door, when, impatient for the fray, she came back to confront Benjamin.

"Well, Benjamin, are you satisfied with your day's work? Do you like the situation in which you are? Or must I go and draw a bottle of white wine for you?"

"Thank you, dear sister. As you have said very elegantly, my day's work is done."

"A fine day's work, indeed! It would take many of that sort to pay your debts. Have you at least reason enough left to tell me how M. Minxit received you?"

"*Mironton, mironton, mirontaine*, dear sister," said Benjamin.

"Ah! *mironton, mironton, mirontaine*," cried my grandmother; "just wait, and I will give you *mironton, mirontaine*."

And she seized the tongs. My uncle took three steps backward and drew his sword.

"Dear sister," said he, putting himself on guard, "I hold you responsible for all the blood that is about to be shed here."

But my grandmother, although she was descended

from a lawyer, had no fear of a sword. She dealt her
brother a blow with the tongs that struck him on the
thumb and made him drop his sword.

Benjamin hopped about the room, squeezing his
wounded thumb in his left hand. As for my grandfather, although he was good among the best, he was
bursting with laughter under the bed-clothes. He
could not help saying to my uncle:

"Well, how do you like that thrust? This time you
had both the scabbard and the sword. You cannot say
that the weapons were not equal."

"Alas! no, Machecourt, they were not; for that, I
ought to have had the shovel. All the same, your wife
— for I can no longer say my dear sister — deserves to
wear at her side, instead of a distaff, a pair of tongs.
With a pair of tongs she would win battles. I am conquered, I confess, and I must submit to the law of the
conqueror. Well, no, we did not go to Corvol; we
stopped at Manette's."

"Always at Manette's, a married woman! Are you
not ashamed, Benjamin, of such conduct?"

"Ashamed! And why, dear sister? As soon as a
tavern-keeper gets married, must one no longer breakfast at her establishment? That is not my way of
looking at it; to a true philosopher a tavern has no
sex. Isn't that so, Machecourt?"

"When I meet her at the market, your Manette, I
will treat the wench as she deserves."

"Dear sister, when you meet Manette at the market,
buy her as many cream cheeses as you like, but if you
insult her" . . .

"Well, if I should insult her, what would you do?"

"I would leave you, I would go away to the islands, and I would take Machecourt with me, I warn you."

My grandmother understood that all these transports would end in nothing, and she at once decided upon her course.

"You shall follow the example of that drunkard in bed yonder," said she; "you need to lie down as much as he. But to-morrow I shall take you myself to M. Minxit's, and we shall see if you will stop on the way."

"*Mironton, mironton, mirontaine*," hummed Benjamin, as he started off for bed.

The idea of the morrow's proceedings disturbed my uncle's usually peaceful, deep, and sound slumbers; he dreamed aloud, and this is what he said:

"You say, sergeant, that you have dined like a king. That is not the word; you use the rhetorical figure known as the *litotes*. You have dined better than an emperor. Kings and emperors, in spite of all their power, cannot have anything extra, and you have had something extra. You see, sergeant, everything is relative. This matelote is certainly not worth a truffled partridge. Nevertheless, it has tickled the nerves of your palate more agreeably than a truffled partridge would tickle the king's. Why is that? Because his majesty's palate is *blasé* in the matter of truffles, whereas yours is not accustomed to matelotes.

"My dear sister tells me: 'Benjamin, do something to get rich. Benjamin, marry Mlle. Minxit that you may have a good dowry.' What good would that do me? Does the butterfly take the trouble to build a nest for the two or three months of fine days allotted it for its life? I am convinced that enjoyments are

relative to position, and that at the end of the year the
beggar and the rich man have had the same amount of
happiness.

"Each individual becomes accustomed to his situation, be it good or bad. The cripple no longer per
ceives that he walks with a crutch, or the rich man
that he has a carriage. The poor snail who carries his
house on his back enjoys a day of perfume and sunshine as much as the bird who chirps above him in the
branches. It is not the cause that is to be considered,
but the effect that it produces. Is not the journeyman
sitting on his bench in front of his cottage as comfortable as the king on the eider-down cushion of his arm-
chair? Does not the peasant eat his soup of cabbage
with as much pleasure as the king eats his soup of
crabs? And does not the beggar sleep as well in the
straw as the great lady under her silk curtains and
between the perfumed linen of her bed? The child
who finds a sou is happier than the banker who has
found a louis, and the poor peasant who inherits an
acre of ground is as triumphant as the king whose
armies have conquered a province and who makes his
people strike up a *Te Deum*.

"Every evil here below is compensated by a good,
and every good that parades itself is attenuated by an
invisible evil. God has a thousand ways of making
compensations. If he has given good dinners to one, .
to another he gives a little better appetite, and that
re-establishes the equilibrium. To the rich man he has
given the fear of losing and the care of keeping, and to
the beggar carelessness. In sending us into this place
of exile he has laden us all with an almost equal bag-

gage of misery and comfort. If it were otherwise, he would not be just, for all men are his children.

"And why, then, in fact, should the rich man be happier than the poor man? To be sure, he does no work; but he has not the pleasure of resting.

"He has fine clothes; but all the charm of them is enjoyed by those who look at him. When the church-warden makes a saint's toilet, does he do it for the saint or for his adorers? For the rest, does not a hump-back show as plainly under a velvet coat as under a linsey-woolsey?

"The rich man has two, three, four, ten *valets* in his service. My God! why proudly add this quantity of useless members to one's body, when it needs but four to serve our person? The man accustomed to be served is an unfortunate, crippled in all his members, who has to be fed.

"This rich man has a city mansion and a country house; but of what use is the country house when the owner is in the mansion, or the mansion when he is in the country house? What boots it that his lodgings consist of twenty rooms, when he can occupy only one at a time?

"Adjoining his country house, he has for his dreamy promenades an immense park, enclosed by a wall of lime and sand ten feet high; but, in the first place, suppose he has no dreams? and then is not the open country, enclosed only by the horizon and belonging to all, as beautiful as his great park?

"In the middle of the aforesaid park, a canal fed by a little stream drags along its greenish and sickly waters, to the surface of which adhere, like plasters,

the broad leaves of the water-lily; but is not the river
that flows freely through the open country clearer and
more liquid than his canal?

"Dahlias of one hundred and fifty varieties line his
walks; grant it; I give you four per cent. additional,
which makes one hundred and fifty-six varieties; but
is not the elm-shaded road that winds through the grass
like a serpent well worth his walks? And the hedges
festooned with wild roses and sprinkled with hawthorn,
the hedges which mingle with the wind their tufts of
many colors and scatter flowers by the wayside,— are
they not well worth those dahlias whose merits can
only be appreciated by the horticulturist?

"The aforesaid park belongs to him exclusively, you
say : you are mistaken; it is only the purchase-deed
locked up in his secretary of which he has the exclusive
ownership, and he only has that on condition that the
ticks do not eat it.

"His park belongs to him much less than to the birds
that build their nests there, the rabbits who browse
amid the wild thyme, and the insects who rustle under
the leaves. .

"Can his watchman keep the serpent from coiling in
the grass, or the toad from nestling under the moss?

"The rich man gives parties; but are not the dances
under the old lindens of the promenade, to the sound
of the bag-pipe, parties also?

"The rich man has a carriage. He has a carriage,
the unfortunate! But is he then a cripple or a paralytic? There is a woman yonder carrying one child in
her arms, while another gambols about her, running
after the butterflies and flowers. Which of the two

little ones is in the more agreeable situation? A carriage! But that is an infirmity; let a wheel break, or your horse cast a shoe, and there you are a cripple. Those grandees who, in the time of Louis XIV., had themselves carried to the ball-room on a litter, poor people who had legs to dance and none to walk,—how much they must have suffered from the fatigue of those who carried them !

"You think that to go in a carriage is an enjoyment of the rich man; you are mistaken; it is only a sort of slavery which his vanity imposes upon him. If it were otherwise, why should this gentleman and this lady, who are as thin as a bundle of thorns and whom an ass could carry with the greatest ease, harness four horses to their coach?

"For my part, when I am on the greensward, in moss up to my ankles; when I am wandering at will along a beautiful cross-road, with hands in my pockets, dreaming and leaving behind me, like one of the damned passing, the blue smoke from my blackened pipe; or when I follow slowly, in the beautiful moonlight, the white road festooned on one side by the shadow of the hedges, I should very much like to see anyone have the insolence to offer me a carriage."

With these words, my uncle awoke.

"What!" you say; "your uncle dreamed that? And out loud?"

Why, what is there that's astonishing in that? Did not Madame George Sand make the reverend father Spiridion dream aloud a whole chapter in one of her novels? Has not M. Golbéry dreamed aloud in the Chamber, for a whole hour, of a proposition on the report of the parliamentary debates? And have not we ourselves been dreaming for the last thirteen years that we have made a revolution? When my uncle had not had time to philosophize during the day, he philosophized while dreaming, to make up for it. That is how I explain the phenomenon the result of which I have just related to you.

CHAPTER IV

HOW MY UNCLE PASSED HIMSELF OFF FOR THE WANDERING JEW.

MEANWHILE my grandmother had put on her shot-colored silk dress, which she took from her drawer only on grand and solemn festival occasions; she had fastened over her round cap, in the form of a head-band, the finest of her ribbons, a cherry-red ribbon as broad as one's hand and broader; she had got ready her short cloak of black taffeta trimmed with lace of the same color, and she had taken from its box her new lynx muff, a present which Benjamin had made her on her birthday, and for which he still owed the furrier. When she was thus dressed up, she ordered one of her children to go after M. Durand's ass, a fine little animal, which at the last fair at Billy had cost three pistoles, and was let for thirty-six deniers more than ordinary asses.

Then she called Benjamin. When the latter came down, M. Durand's ass, with his two baskets hanging over his flanks and between them a large and very white pillow, was fastened before the door eating his provision of bran that had been served him in a basket on a chair.

Benjamin first anxiously inquired whether Machecourt was there to drink a glass of white wine with him. His sister having told him that he had gone out, he added:

"I hope at least, my good sister, that you will be

friendly enough to take a little glass of ratafia with
me." For my uncle's stomach knew how to put itself
within the reach of all stomachs.

My grandmother did not dislike ratafia, on the contrary; she accepted Benjamin's proposition, and permitted him to go after the carafe. Finally, after having warned my father, who was the oldest child, not
to beat his brothers, and Premoins, who was indisposed,
to ask in case he felt certain needs, and after having
set Surgie her stint of knitting work, she mounted the
little ass.

Long live the earth and the sun! The neighbors
had gathered in their door-ways to see her start; for in
those days to see a woman of the middle class dressed
up on any other day than Sunday was an event of which
everyone who witnessed it tried to penetrate the causes,
and upon which he built a system.

Benjamin, cleanly shaven and superabundantly powdered, and as red moreover as a poppy spreading in the
morning sun after a stormy night, followed on behind,
uttering from time to time a vigorous "Gee-hup" in a
chest C, and pricking the animal with the point of his
rapier.

M. Durand's ass, thus pricked in the loins by my
uncle's sword, went very well; he went too well even
to suit my grandmother, who bobbed up and down on
her pillow like a shuttlecock on a battledore. But at
some distance from the spot where the road to Moulot
separates from the road to La Chapelle to go on to its
humble destination, she perceived that the gait of her
ass slackened, like a jet of molten metal which thickens
and moves slower the farther it gets from the furnace;

his bell, which up to that time had kept up a proud and very pronounced jingling, now gave forth only spasmodic sighs, like a voice in the hour of the death agony. My grandmother turned around to seek an explanation from Benjamin; but the latter had disappeared, melted like a ball of wax, conjured away, lost like a midge in space; no one could give any news of him. You can imagine the vexation that my grandmother felt at Benjamin's sudden disappearance. She said to herself that he did not deserve the trouble that they took to secure his happiness; that his indifference was incurable; that he would always stagnate there; that he was a marsh whose waters could not be made to flow. For a moment she felt a desire to abandon him to his destiny, and even to no more plait his shirts; but her queenly character came uppermost; she had begun, and she must finish. She swore that she would find Benjamin again and take him to M. Minxit's, even though she had to fasten him to the tail of her ass. It is by such firmness of resolution that great enterprises are carried to their conclusion.

A little peasant, who was tending his sheep at the fork of the two roads, told her that the red man whom she had lost had gone down toward the village nearly a quarter of an hour before. My grandmother urged on her ass in that direction, and such was the ascendency that her indignation gave her over this quadruped that he began to trot of himself, out of pure deference to his rider, as if he desired to do homage to her grand character.

The village of Moulot seemed· to be in an extraordinary commotion; the Moulotats, generally so sedate and in whose brains there was never more fermentation than in a cream cheese, seemed all to be in transports. The peasants were hurrying down from the neighboring hillsides; the women and children were running and calling each other; all spinning-wheels were abandoned, and all distaffs at rest. My grandmother inquired the cause of this commotion. They told her that the Wandering Jew had just arrived at Moulot, and was breakfasting in the market-place. She understood at once that this pretended Wandering Jew was no other than Benjamin, and, indeed, she was not slow in perceiving him from the height of her ass, in the middle of a circle of idle bystanders.

Above this moving ribbon of black and white heads, the gable of his three-cornered hat rose with great majesty, like the slate-colored steeple of a church amid the moss-clad roofs of a village. They had set for him in the market-place itself a little table where he had been served a half-bottle of wine and a little loaf of bread, and before which he was passing to and fro with the gravity of a great sacrificer, now taking a swallow of white wine, now breaking a bit from his little loaf.

My grandmother urged her ass into the crowd and soon found herself in the front rank.

"What are you doing here, you wretch?" said she to my uncle, shaking her fist at him.

"You see, Madame, I wander; I am Ahasuerus, commonly called the Wandering Jew. As in the course of my travels I have heard much said of the beauty of this little village and the amiability of its inhabitants, I resolved to breakfast here."

Then, approaching her, he said in a low voice:

"In five minutes I follow you, but not a word more, I beg of you; the evil might be irreparable; these imbeciles would be capable of killing me, if they should discover that I am making sport of them."

The eulogy of Moulot, which Benjamin had succeeded in interpolating into his reply to his sister, repaired or rather prevented the check which her imprudent rebuke would otherwise have caused him to suffer, and a thrill of pride ran through the assembly.

"Monsieur Wandering Jew," said a peasant in whose mind still lingered some doubt, "who, then, is this lady who just now shook her fist at you?"

"My good friend," answered my uncle, not at all disconcerted, "she is the Holy Virgin, whom God has ordered me to escort on a pilgrimage to Jerusalem on that little ass. She is really a good woman, but a little talkative; she is ill-humored this morning because she has lost her rosary."

"And why is not the infant Jesus with her?"

"God did not wish her to take him along, because just now he has the small-pox."

Then the objections fell upon Benjamin as thick as hail; but my uncle was not a man to be frightened by the dolts of Moulot; danger electrified him, and he parried with admirable dexterity all the thrusts that were made at him, which did not prevent him from now and then wetting his whistle with a swallow of white wine, and, to tell the truth, he was already at his seventh half-bottle.

The village schoolmaster, as the learned man of the neighborhood, was the first to enter the lists.

"How does it happen, then, Monsieur Wandering

Jew, that you have no beard? It is said in the Brussels lament that you are heavily bearded, and everywhere you are represented with a great white beard which reaches down to your girdle."

"It soiled too easily, Monsieur schoolmaster. I asked the good God's permission to discard that great ugly beard, and he has passed it into my cue."

"But," continued the teacher, "how do you manage to shave, since you cannot stop?"

"God has provided for that, my dear Monsieur schoolmaster. Every morning he sends me the patron of the barbers in the shape of a butterfly, who shaves me with the edge of his wing, while hovering around me."

"But, Monsieur Jew," the schoolmaster continued, "the good God has been very stingy with you in placing at your disposition only five sous at a time."

"My friend," rejoined my uncle, crossing his arms over his breast and bowing profoundly, "let us bless the decrees of God; it is probably because that was all the money he had in his pocket."

"I should very much like to know," said the old tailor of the neighborhood, "how they succeeded in taking your measure for your coat,— which, by the way, fits you like a glove,— since you are never at rest?"

"You should have noticed, you who are of the trade, respectable *pique-prune*, that this coat was not made by the hand of man; every year, on the first of April, there grows on my back a light coat of red serge, and on All Saints' Day a heavy coat of red velvet."

"Then," said a youngster, over whose waggish face

hung tresses of light hair, "you must wear it out very fast; it is not a fortnight now since All Saints' Day, and your coat is already threadbare and white along the seams."

Unfortunately the father of the little philosopher was standing beside him. "Go back to the house and see if I'm there," he said to him, giving him a kick; and he begged my uncle to excuse the impertinence of this little fellow, whose schoolmaster neglected to teach him his religion.

"Gentlemen," cried the schoolmaster, "I call you all to witness, and Monsieur Wandering Jew also, that Nicolas attacks my reputation; he continually assails the village authorities; I am going to take him by his tongue."

"Yes," said Nicolas, "there's a fine authority for you; attack me when you like; I shall find no difficulty in proving the truth of what I say; the bailiff shall question Charlot. The other day I asked him which was Jacob's most remarkable son, and he answered Pharaoh; mother Pintot is my witness."

"Oh! gentlemen," said my uncle, "do not quarrel on my account; I should be grieved if my arrival in this beautiful village should be the occasion of a lawsuit among you; the wool of my coat has not yet fully grown, as we are now only at St. Martin's Day; that is what led little Charlot into error. Monsieur schoolmaster was unaware of this circumstance, and consequently could not teach it to his pupils; I hope that M. Nicolas is satisfied with this explanation."

CHAPTER V

MY UNCLE WORKS A MIRACLE.

My uncle was about to break up the meeting, when he noticed a pretty peasant girl trying to make a passage for herself through the crowd; as he loved young girls at least as well as Jesus Christ loved little children, he signalled to the bystanders to allow her to approach.

"I should very much like to know," said the young Moulotate with her finest bow, the bow that she made to the bailiff when, going to carry him cream, she met him on her way, "whether what old Gothon says is the pure truth: she pretends that you work miracles."

"Undoubtedly," answered my uncle, "when they are not too difficult."

"In that case, could you by a miracle cure my father, who has been sick since morning with a disease with which nobody is familiar?"

"Why not?" said my uncle; "but first of all, my pretty child, you must permit me to kiss you; otherwise the miracle will amount to nothing."

And he kissed the young Moulotate on both cheeks, damned sinner that he was.

"What!" exclaimed in his rear a voice which he knew well, "does the Wandering Jew kiss women?"

He turned around and saw Manette.

"Undoubtedly, my beautiful lady: God permits me to kiss three a year; that is the second one that I have kissed this year, and, if you like, you shall be the third."

The idea of working a miracle fired Benjamin's ambition; to pass himself off for the Wandering Jew, even at Moulot, was much, was immense, was enough to make all the brilliant wits of Clamecy jealous. He took rank immediately among the famous jokers, and lawyer Page would no longer dare to speak to him so often of his hare changed into a rabbit. Who would dare to compare himself, in audacity and resources of imagination, with Benjamin Rathery, when once he had worked a miracle? And who knows? Perhaps the future generation would take the matter seriously. If he were to be canonized; if they should make of his person a big saint of red wood; if they should give him an office, a niche, a place in the almanac, an *Ora pro nobis* in the litanies; if he should become the patron saint of a good parish; if every year they should celebrate his birthday with incense, crown him with flowers, decorate him with ribbons, and place a ripe grape in his hands; if they should enshrine his red coat in a reliquary; if he should have a church-warden to wash his face every week; if he should cure of the pest or of hydrophobia! The only thing necessary was to carry out this miracle successfully; if he had only seen a few performed! But how should he go about it? And if he failed, he would be scoffed at, jeered, vilified, possibly beaten; he would lose all the glory of the hoax so well begun. . . . "Oh! nonsense!" said my uncle, pouring a large glass of wine for inspiration, "Providence will provide: *Audaces fortuna juvat*, and besides, a miracle asked for is a miracle half performed."

So he followed the young peasant girl, dragging in his train, like a comet, a long tail of Moulotats; having entered the house, he saw lying on the bed a peasant with his mouth askew, who seemed to be trying to eat his ear; he inquired how this accident had happened, and whether it was not the result of a yawn or an outburst of laughter.

"It happened this morning at breakfast," answered his wife, "as he was trying to break a walnut with his teeth."

"Very well," said my uncle, his face lighting up, "and did you call anybody?"

"We sent for M. Arnout, who declared that it was an attack of paralysis."

"You could not have done better. I see that Doctor Arnout knows paralysis as well as if he had invented it; and what did he prescribe?"

"The medicine in this vial."

My uncle, having examined the drug, saw that it was an emetic, and threw the vial into the street. His assurance produced an excellent effect.

"I see clearly, Monsieur Jew," said the good woman, "that you are capable of performing the miracle that we ask of you."

"Of such miracles as this," answered Benjamin, "I could work a hundred a day, if I were supplied with them."

He had them bring him an iron spoon, the handle of which he wound with several thicknesses of fine linen; he introduced this improvised instrument into the patient's mouth, raised the upper jaw, which was protruding over the lower jaw, and put it back in its place; for the only disease from which this Moulotat suffered was a dislocated jaw, which my uncle, with his gray eye that penetrated everything, as if it were a nail, had perceived at once. The paralytic of the morning declared that he was completely cured, and he began to eat ravenously of a cabbage soup prepared for the family dinner.

The report spread among the crowd with the rapidity of lightning that father Pintot was eating cabbage soup. The sick and all those whose forms nature had more or less altered implored my uncle's protection. Mother Pintot, very proud to think that the miracle had been performed in her family, introduced to my uncle one of her cousins who had a left shoulder that looked like a ham, and asked him to reduce it; but my uncle, who did not wish to compromise his reputation, answered that the best that he could do would be to pass the hump from the left shoulder to the right; that moreover it was a very painful miracle, and that out of ten hump-backs of the common sort he had scarcely found two who had had the strength to endure it.

Then he declared to the inhabitants of Moulot that he was grieved that he could not stay with them longer, but that he did not dare to keep the Holy Virgin waiting; and he went to join his sister, who was warming her feet in the village tavern and had had time to have the ass fed.

My uncle and my grandmother had the greatest difficulty in the world in getting rid of the crowd, and the village bell was rung as long as they were in sight. My grandmother did not scold Benjamin; after all, she was more pleased than vexed; the way in which Benjamin had extricated himself from this difficult situation flattered her pride as a sister, and she said that a man like Benjamin was well worth Mlle. Minxit, even with an income of two or three thousand francs thrown in.

The description of the Wandering Jew and the Holy Virgin, and even that of the ass, had already reached La Chapelle. When they entered the town, the women were kneeling in their doorways, and Benjamin, who always knew what to do, gave them his blessing.

CHAPTER VI

MONSIEUR MINXIT extended a very cordial welcome to my uncle and my grandmother. M. Minxit was a doctor, I know not why. He had not spent the beautiful days of his youth in the society of corpses. The science of medicine had sprouted in his head one fine day, like a mushroom: if he knew medicine, it was because he had invented it. His parents had never dreamed of giving him a liberal education; all the Latin he knew was on his bottles, and even there, if he had depended on the labels, he would often have given parsley for hemlock. He had a very fine library, but he never poked his nose into his books. He said that, since his books were written, the temperament of man had changed. Some even pretended that all these precious works were only imitations of books made out of pasteboard, on the backs of which he had placed in gilt letters names celebrated in medicine. What confirmed them in this opinion was that, whenever any one asked M. Minxit to let him see his library, he had lost the key. However, M. Minxit was a man of wit, he was endowed with a large share of intelligence, and, in default of printed knowledge, he had much knowledge of every-day life. As he knew nothing, he understood that to succeed he must persuade the multitude that he knew more than his rivals, and he made a specialty of the divination of urines. After twenty years' study of this science, he had succeeded in distinguishing those that were turbid from those that were clear, which did not prevent him from telling every one who came to him that he could tell a great man, a king, or a cabinet minister, by his urine. As there were no kings, or cabinet ministers, or great men, in the vicinity, he did not fear that any one would take him at his word.

M. Minxit had an incisive manner. He talked loud, a great deal, and incessantly; he divined those words which are likely to have an effect on peasants and knew how to make them prominent in his phrases. He had the faculty of deceiving the multitude, a faculty which consists of I know not what impalpable quality, impossible to describe, teach, or counterfeit; an inexplicable faculty by which a simple operator causes a shower of pennies to fall into his cash-box, and by which the great man wins battles and founds empires; a faculty which in some has taken the place of genius, which Napoleon of all men possessed in a supreme degree, and which in all cases I call simply charlatanism. It is not my fault if the instrument with which they sell Swiss tea is the same as that with which they build a throne. Throughout the neighborhood no one was willing to die except by the hand of M. Minxit. The latter, however, did not abuse this privilege; he was no more of a murderer than his rivals, only he made more money with his vials of many colors than they did with their aphorisms. He had acquired a very handsome fortune, and had, moreover, the faculty of spending his money to the purpose; he seemed to give everything as if it had cost him nothing, and the clients that came to him always found open table at his house.

For the rest my uncle and M. Minxit were bound to be friends as soon as they should meet. These two natures resembled each other exactly; they were as near alike as two drops of wine or, to use an expression less offensive to my uncle, as two spoons cast in the same mould. They had the same appetites, the same tastes, the same passions, the same way of looking at things, the same political opinions. Both concerned themselves little about those thousand little accidents, those thousand microscopic catastrophes, which the rest of us, fools that we are, consider as great misfortunes. He who has no philosophy amid the miseries of this world is like a man bareheaded in a shower. The philosopher, on the contrary, has over his head a good umbrella, which shelters him from the storm. Such was their opinion. They regarded life as a farce, and they played their parts in it as gayly as possible. They had a sovereign contempt for those ill-advised people who make their life one long sob. They wished theirs to be a fit of laughter. Age had produced no difference between them, beyond a few wrinkles. They were like two trees of the same species, one of which is old and the other in the full vigor of its sap, but both of which are adorned with the same flowers and bear the same fruits. Consequently the future father-in-law had formed a prodigious friendship for his son-in-law, and the son-in-law professed for the father-in-law a high esteem, barring his vials. Nevertheless my uncle accepted M. Minxit's alliance only in self-defence, by an effort of reason and that he might not displease his dear sister.

M. Minxit, because he loved Benjamin, found it very

natural that he should be loved by his daughter. For
every father, however good he may be, loves himself in
the person of his children; he regards them as beings
who ought to contribute to his comfort; if he chooses
a son-in-law, he does so first largely for himself, and
then a little for his daughter. When he is avaricious,
he puts her into the hands of a miser; when he is a
noble, he welds her to an escutcheon; if he is fond
of chess, he gives her to a chess-player, for he must
have some one to play with him in his old age. His
daughter is an undivided property which he possesses
with his wife. Whether the property is enclosed by a
flowering hedge or by a great ugly wall built of dry
stones, whether it is made to produce roses or rape-
seed, that does not concern her. She has no advice to
give to the experienced agriculturist who cultivates
her. She is unskilled in selecting the seed best suited
to her. Provided these good parents in their soul and
conscience find their daughter happy, that is enough.
It is for her to accommodate herself to her condition.
Every night the wife when making her curl papers and
the good man when putting on his nightcap congratulate themselves on having married their child so well.
She does not love her husband, but she will accustom
herself to love him : with patience one can accomplish
anything. They do not know what it is to a woman
to have a husband that she does not love. It is like a
burning cinder that cannot be expelled from the eye,
or a toothache that does not give one a moment's rest.
Some allow themselves to die in pain; others go elsewhere in search of the love which they cannot procure
with the corpse to which they have been attached.

The latter gently slip into their fortunate husband's soup a pinch of arsenic, and have it inscribed upon his tombstone that he leaves an inconsolable widow. Such is the result of the pretended infallibility and the disguised egoism of the good parents.

If a young girl wanted to marry a monkey who had been naturalized as a man and a Frenchman, the father and mother would not willingly consent, and it certainly would be necessary for the jocko to serve on them the required legal papers. You say: Those are good parents; they do not wish their daughter to make herself unhappy. But I say: Those are detestable egoists. Nothing is more ridiculous than to put your way of feeling in the place of another's: it is like trying to substitute your organization for his. Such a man wishes to die; he probably has good reasons for that. This young girl wishes to marry a monkey; she probably prefers a monkey to a man. Why refuse her the faculty of being happy in her own way? If she thinks herself happy, who has a right to maintain that she is not? This monkey will scratch her in caressing her. What's that to you? She probably would rather be scratched than caressed. Besides, if her husband scratches her, it is not her mamma's cheek that will bleed. Who disapproves the dragon-fly of the marshes for hovering over the reeds rather than among the garden rose-bushes? Does the pike reproach the eel, its god-mother, for staying continually in the mud at the bottom, instead of rising to the flowing water which ripples at the surface of the river?

Do you know why these good parents refuse their blessing to their daughter and her jocko? The father refuses because he desires a son-in-law who can be a voter, and with whom he can talk literature or politics; the mother refuses because she needs a handsome young man to give her his arm, take her to the play, and go to walk with her.

M. Minxit, after having uncorked some of his best bottles with Benjamin, took him into his house, into his cellar, into his barn, into his stables; he walked him through his garden, and forced him to make the circuit of a large meadow watered by a living spring and planted with trees, which stretched away in the rear of the house and at the end of which the stream formed a fish-pond. All this was very desirable; unhappily fortune gives nothing for nothing, and in exchange for all this comfort it was necessary to marry Mlle. Minxit.

After all, Mlle. Minxit was as good as another; she was only two inches too tall; she was neither dark nor light, nor blonde nor red, nor stupid nor witty. She was a woman like twenty-five out of every thirty. She knew how to talk very pertinently of a thousand insignificant little things, and she made very good cream cheeses. It was much less against her than against marriage in general that my uncle rebelled, and if at the very first she had displeased him, it was because he had regarded her in the form of a heavy chain.

"There is my estate," said M. Minxit; "when you shall be my son-in-law, it will be ours, and indeed, when I am no longer here" . . .

"Let us understand each other," said my uncle, "are you very sure that Mlle. Arabelle is not at all reluctant to marry me?"

"And why should she be? You do not do justice to yourself, Benjamin. Are you not the handsomest of young fellows, are you not amiable when you like and as much as you like, and are you not a man of wit in the bargain?"

. "There is some truth in what you say, M. Minxit, but women are capricious, and I have allowed myself to say that Mlle. Arabelle had an inclination for a gentleman of this neighborhood, a certain de Pont-Cassé."

"A country squire," said M. Minxit, "a sort of musketeer who has squandered on fine horses and embroidered coàts the fine domains that his father left him. He has, in truth, asked me for Arabelle, but I rejected his proposal most decidedly. In less than two years he would have devoured my fortune. You can see that I could not give my daughter to such a being. Besides, he is a furious duellist. By way of compensation, one of these days he would have rid Arabelle of his noble person."

"You are right, M. Minxit, but then, if this being is loved by Arabelle" . . .

"Nonsense, Benjamin! Arabelle has in her veins too much of my blood to be smitten with a viscount. What I need is a child of the people, a man like you, Benjamin, with whom I can laugh, drink, and philosophize; a shrewd physician to exploit my clients with me and to supply by his science what the divination of urines may fail to reveal to us."

"One moment," said my uncle, "I warn you, Monsieur Minxit, that I will not consult urines."

"And why, Monsieur, do you not wish to consult urines? Come, Benjamin, he was a very sensible man, that emperor who said to his son : ' Do these gold pieces smell of urine?' If you knew how much presence of mind, imagination, perspicacity, and even logic are required for the consultation of urines, you would not want to follow any other profession all your life long; perhaps you will be called a charlatan, but what is a charlatan? A man who has more wit than the multitude; and I ask you, is it from lack of desire or lack of wit that most doctors do not impose upon their patients? Stay, there comes my fifer, probably to announce the arrival of some vial. I am going to give you a sample of my art."

"Well, fifer," said M. Minxit to the musician, " what's new ? "

" A peasant has come to consult you," he answered.

" And has Arabelle made him talk ? "

" Yes, Monsieur Minxit; he brings you his wife's urine, she having fallen on a flight of steps and rolled down four or five of them. Mlle. Arabelle doesn't remember the exact number."

" The devil!" said M. Minxit, "that is very stupid on Arabelle's part; all the same, I will remedy that. Benjamin, go wait for me in the kitchen with the peasant; you shall know what a doctor who consults urines is."

M. Minxit entered his house through the little garden door, and five minutes afterward came into the kitchen with an harassed and over-fatigued air, holding a riding-whip in his hand and wearing a cloak splashed up to the collar.

" Oh!" said he, throwing himself upon a chair, " what abominable roads! I am worn out; I have travelled more than fifteen leagues this morning; take off my boots immediately and warm my bed."

"Monsieur Minxit, I beg of you!" said the peasant, presenting his vial.

"To the devil," said M. Minxit, "with your vial; you see well enough that I can do no more. That's just like you all; you always come to consult me just as I come in from the country."

"My father," said Arabelle, "this man too is tired; do not force him to come again to-morrow."

"Well, let me see the vial then," said M. Minxit, with an air of extreme vexation; and approaching the window, he added: "This is your wife's urine, isn't it?"

"You are right, Monsieur Minxit," said the peasant.

"She has had a fall," added the doctor, examining the vial again.

"You could not have divined more accurately."

"On a flight of steps, was it not?"

"Why, you are a sorcerer, Monsieur Minxit."

"And she rolled down four of them."

"This time you are wrong, Monsieur Minxit; she rolled down five."

"Nonsense, it is impossible; go count your flight of steps again, and you will see that there are only four in all."

"I assure you, Monsieur, that there are five, and that she did not miss a single one."

"It is astonishing," said M. Minxit, examining the vial again; "there certainly are but four steps in this. By the way, did you bring me all the urine that your wife gave you?"

"I threw a little on the ground, because the vial was too full."

"I am no longer surprised that I did not find the full number; that is the cause of the deficit: it was the fifth step that you poured out, you stupid fellow! So we will treat your wife as having rolled down a flight of five steps."

And he gave the peasant five or six little packages and as many vials, all labelled in Latin.

"I should have thought," said my uncle, "that you would first have practised an abundant bleeding."

"If it had been a fall from a horse, a fall from a tree, or a fall in the road, yes; but a fall on a flight of steps should always be treated in this way."

After the peasant came a young girl.

"Well! how is your mother?" asked the doctor.

"Much better, Monsieur Minxit; but she cannot regain her strength, and I came to ask you what she should do."

"You ask me what she must do, and I will bet that you haven't a sou with which to buy medicines!"

"Alas! no, my good Monsieur Minxit, for my father has had no work for a week."

"Then why the devil does your mother take it into her head to be sick?"

"Rest easy, Monsieur Minxit; as soon as my father gets work, you will be paid for your visits; he charged me to tell you so."

"Indeed! more nonsense! Is your father mad that he expects to pay me for my visits when he has no bread? For what does your imbecile of a father take me? You will go this evening with your ass to get a sack of wheat at my mill, and you will carry away with you from here a basket of old wine and a quarter of mutton; that is what your mother immediately needs. If her strength does not return within two or three days, you will let me know. Now go, my child."

"Well!" said M. Minxit to Benjamin, "what do you think of the practice of medicine by the consultation of urines?"

"You are a brave and worthy man, Monsieur Minxit; that is your excuse; but, the devil! you will never get me to treat a patient who has fallen down stairs otherwise than by bleeding."

"Then you are only a raw recruit in medicine; are you not aware that peasants must have drugs? Otherwise they think that you are neglecting them. Well, then, you shall not consult urines; but it's a pity, for you would have been a famous hand at it."

CHAPTER VII

THE dinner-hour arrived. Although M. Minxit had invited but a few persons besides those known to us,— the priest, the tabellion, and one of his confrères in the neighborhood,— the table was loaded down with a profusion of ducks and chickens, some lying in stately integrity in the midst of their sauce, others symmetrically spreading their disjointed members on the ellipsis of their platter. The wine, for the rest, was from a certain hillside of Trucy, whose vines, in spite of the levelling which has passed over our vineyards as over our society, have maintained their aristocracy, and still enjoy a deserved reputation.

"But," said my uncle to M. Minxit, at sight of this Homeric abundance, "you have a whole poultry-yard here. There is enough to satisfy a company of dragoons after field-day exercises. Or perhaps you expect our friend Arthus?"

"In that case I would have spitted one fowl more," answered M. Minxit, laughing. "But if we do not succeed in disposing of all this, it will be easy to find people to finish our task; and my officers,— that is, my musicians,— and the clients who will come to me to-morrow with their vials, have I not to think of them? I adopt it as a principle that he who has dinner prepared only for himself is not fit to dine."

"It is just," replied my uncle. And after this philosophical reflection, he began to attack M. Minxit's chickens as if he had a personal spite against them.

The guests were suited to each other. For that matter, my uncle was suited to everybody, and everybody was suited to him. They enjoyed frankly and very noisily M. Minxit's copious hospitality. "Fifer," said the latter to one of the table-waiters, "bring in the Burgundy, and tell the musicians to come hither with arms and baggage; those who are drunk are not exempt." The musicians came in at once and, arranged themselves around the room. M. Minxit, having uncorked a few bottles of Burgundy, solemnly lifted his full glass, and said: "Gentlemen, to the health of M. Benjamin Rathery, the first doctor of the bailiwick; I present him to you as my son-in-law, and pray you to love him as you love me. Let the music play." Then an infernal noise of bass drum, triangle, cymbals, and clarinette burst forth in the dining room, and my uncle was obliged to ask mercy for the guests. This announcement, a little too official and premature, caused Mlle. Minxit to sulk and make wry faces. Benjamin, who had something else to do than criticise what was going on around him, noticed nothing; but this mark of repugnance did not escape my grandmother. Her pride was deeply wounded; for, if Benjamin was not to everybody the handsomest young fellow in the country, he was such at least to his sister. After having thanked M. Minxit for the honor that he did her brother, she added, biting each syllable as if she had the poor Arabelle between her teeth, that the principal, the only reason that had determined Benjamin to solicit M. Minxit's alliance was the lofty consideration enjoyed by M. Minxit in all the country round.

Benjamin, thinking that his sister had made a mess of it, hastened to add: "And also the graces and charms of every sort with which Mlle. Arabelle is so abundantly provided, and which promise to the happy mortal who shall be her husband days spun of gold and silk." Then, as if to quiet the remorse which this sad compliment caused him,— the only one that he had yet expended on Mlle. Minxit and which his sister had obliged him to commit,— he began to furiously devour a chicken's wing, and emptied a huge glass of Burgundy at one swallow.

There were three doctors present; they were bound to talk medicine, and they did.

"You said just now, M. Minxit," said Fata, "that your son-in-law was the first doctor of the bailiwick. I do not protest in my own behalf,— although I have made certain cures; but what do you think of Doctor Arnout, of Clamecy?"

"Ask Benjamin," said M. Minxit; "he knows him better than I do."

"Oh, M. Minxit," answered my uncle, "a rival!"

"What difference does that make? You do not need to depreciate your rivals, do you? Tell us what you think of him, just to oblige Fata."

"Since you insist, I think that Doctor Arnout wears a superb wig."

"And why," said Fata, "is not a doctor who wears a wig as good as a doctor who wears a cue?"

"The question is the more delicate because you yourself wear a wig, Monsieur Fata. But I will try to explain myself without wounding the pride of anyone whomsoever. Here is a doctor who has his head full of knowledge, who has ransacked all the old medical books ever written, who knows from what Greek words come the five or six hundred diseases that afflict our poor humanity. Well, if he has only a limited intelligence, I would not like to trust him to cure my little finger; I would give the preference to an intelligent mountebank, for his science is a lantern that is not lighted. It has been said: The value of the man measures the value of his land; it would be quite as true to say: The value of the man measures the value of his knowledge; and that is especially true of medicine, which is a conjectural scieoce. There one must divine causes by equivocal and uncertain effects. The pulse that is dumb under the finger of a fool confides marvellous secrets to the man of wit. Two things above all are necessary to success in medicine, and these two things are not to be acquired: they are perspicacity and intelligence."

"You forget," said M. Minxit, laughing, "the cymbals and the bass drum."

"Oh," said Benjamin, "speaking of your bass drum, I have an excellent idea; does there happen to be a vacancy in your orchestra?"

"For whom?" said M. Minxit.

"For an old sergeant of my acquaintance and a poodle," answered Benjamin.

"And on what instrument can your two *protégés* play?"

"I do not know," said Benjamin; "probably on any instrument you like."

"At any rate we can have your old sergeant groom my four horses until my music-master has familiarized him with some instrument or other, or else he shall pound my drugs."

"By the way," said my uncle, "we can use him to still better advantage; he has a face as brown as a chicken just from the spit; one would think that he had spent his whole life in simply crossing and recrossing the equator; you would take him for the good man Tropic in person; besides, he is as dry as an old burnt bone: we will give it out that from his body we extracted the grease of which we make our pomatum: that will sell better than bear's grease; or else we will pass him off for an old Nubian of one hundred and forty years, who has prolonged his days to this extraordinary age by the use of an elixir of long life, the secret of which he has transmitted to us in consideration of a life pension. Now, we will sell this precious elixir for the mere bagatelle of fifteen sous a bottle. Then no one can afford to be without it."

"Thunder!" said M. Minxit, "I see that you understand the practice of medicine on the grand orchestra plan; send me your man as soon as you like; I will take him into my service, whether as a Nubian or as a dried-up old man."

At this moment a domestic entered the dining-room in a great fright, and told my uncle that a score of women were tugging at his ass's tail, and that, when he had tried to disperse them with a whip, they had come very near tearing him to pieces with their sharp finger-nails.

"I see how it is," said my uncle, bursting with laughter: "they are pulling hairs from the Holy Virgin's beast to keep as relics."

M. Minxit asked for an explanation of this allusion.

"Gentlemen," he cried, when my uncle had finished his story, "we are impious men if we do not worship Benjamin; pastor, you must make a saint of him."

"I protest," said Benjamin; "I do. not wish to go to Paradise, for I should not meet any of you there."

"Yes, laugh, gentlemen," said my grandmother, after having laughed herself; "but that doesn't make me laugh; Benjamin's practical jokes always end in some such way; M. Durand will make us pay for his ass, unless we restore the animal as we received it."

"At any rate," said my uncle, "he cannot make us pay for more than the tail. Would a man who had cut off my cue,— and my cue may surely be said, without flattering it, to be worth as much as the tail of M. Durand's ass,— be as guilty in the eyes of justice as if he had killed me entirely?"

"Certainly not," said M. Minxit, "and if you want to know my opinion, I should not esteem you one obole less."

Meanwhile the yard was filling with women who maintained a respectful attitude, such as is maintained around a too small chapel in which divine service is in progress, and many of whom were kneeling.

"You will have to rid us of these people," said M. Minxit to Benjamin.

"Nothing easier," answered the latter; then he went to the window and told the throng that they would have plenty of time to see the Holy Virgin, that she proposed to remain two days at M. Minxit's, and that the next Sunday she would not fail to attend high mass. On the strength of this assurance the people withdrew satisfied.

"Such parishioners," said the priest, " do me little honor; I must tell them so on Sunday in my sermon. How can any one be so limited in capacity as to take the dirty tail of an ass for a sacred object?"

"But, pastor," responded Benjamin, "you who are so philosophical at table, have you not in your church two or three bones as white as paper, which are under glass and which you call the relics of Saint Maurice?"

" Those are exhausted relics," said M. Minxit: "it is more than fifty years since they worked miracles. My friend the priest would do well to get rid of them and sell them to be made into animal black. I would take them myself to make album græcum, if he would let me have them at a reasonable price."

"What is album græcum?" asked my grandmother, innocently.

" Madame," answered M. Minxit, with a bow, "it is Greek white: I regret that I cannot tell you more about it."

" For my part," said the tabellion, a little old man in a white wig, whose eye was full of mischief and vivacity, "I do not reproach the pastor for the honorable place which he has given in his church to the shin-bones of Saint Maurice: Saint Maurice undoubtedly had shin-bones when he was alive. Why should they not be here as well as anywhere? I am even astonished at one thing,— that the vestry does not possess our patron saint's Hessian boots. But I could wish that the pastor in his turn might be more tolerant and might not rebuke his parishioners for their faith in the Wandering Jew. Not to believe enough is as sure a sign of ignorance as to believe too much."

"What!" replied the priest quickly, "you, Monsieur tabellion, you believe in the Wandering Jew?"

"Why, then, should I not believe in him as well as in Saint Maurice?"

"And you, Monsieur doctor," said he, addressing Fata, "do you believe in the Wandering Jew?"

"Hum! hum!" said the latter, taking a huge pinch of snuff.

"And you, respectable Monsieur Minxit" . . .

"I," interrupted M. Minxit, "agree with my confrère, except that, instead of a pinch of snuff, I take a glass of wine."

"You, at least, Monsieur Rathery, who pass for a philosopher, I really hope that you do not honor the Wandering Jew with belief in his eternal peregrinations."

"Why not?" said my uncle; "you believe in Jesus Christ."

"Oh! that's different," answered the priest, "I believe in Jesus Christ because neither his existence nor his divinity can be called in question; because the evangelists who have written his history are men worthy of faith; because they could not have been mistaken; because they had no motive to deceive their neighbor, and because, even if they had desired it, the fraud could not have been carried out.

"If the facts recorded by them were manufactured, if the Gospel were, like 'Télémaque,' only a sort of philosophical and religious novel, on the appearance of that fatal book which was to spread trouble and division over the surface of the earth; which was to separate husband from wife, children from their fathers; which

rehabilitated poverty; which made the slave the equal
of the master; which conflicted with all received ideas;
which honored everything that up to that time had
been received, and threw as rubbish into the fire of hell
everything that had been honored; which overturned
the old religion of the Pagans, and on its ruins established, in the place of altars, the gibbet of a poor carpenter's son " . . .

"Monsieur priest," said M. Minxit, "your period is
too long; you must cut it with a glass of wine."

The priest, having drunk a glass of wine, continued:

"On the appearance of that book, I say, the Pagans
would have uttered an immense cry of protest, and the
Jews, whom it accused of the greatest crime that a
people can commit, a deicide, would have followed it
with their eternal denunciations."

"But," said my uncle, "the Wandering Jew is supported by an authority no less powerful than that of
the Gospel,— the lament of the *bourgeois* of Brussels in
Brabant, who met him at the gates of the city and
regaled him with a pot of fresh beer.

"The evangelists are men worthy of faith; grant it.
But in fact, inspiration aside, what were these evangelists?   Tramps, men who had neither fire nor shelter,
who paid no taxes, and whom the authorities to-day
would prosecute as vagabonds.   The *bourgeois* of Brussels, on the contrary, were established men, house-
holders; several, I am sure, were syndics or church-
wardens.   If the evangelists and the Brussels *bourgeois*
could have a discussion before the bailiff, I am very sure
that the magistrate would defer to the oath of the
Brussels *bourgeois*.

"The Brussels *bourgeois* could not have been mistaken; for a *bourgeois* is not a puppet, a man of gingerbread, and it is no more difficult to distinguish a man over seventeen hundred years old from a modern than to distinguish an ordinary old man from a child of five.

"The Brussels *bourgeois* had no motive to deceive their fellow-citizens: it was of little importance to them whether there was or was not a man who travels on forever; and what honor could they derive from sitting at table in a brewery with the superlative of vagabonds, with one of the damned, so to speak, a hundred times more despicable than a galley-slave, to whom I myself would not like to take off my hat, and from having drunk fresh beer with him? And, looking at the matter rightly, they even acted, in publishing their lament, rather against their interest than for it; for that bit of poetry is not calculated to give a high opinion of their poetic value. And the tailor Millot-Rataut, whose 'Grand Noël' I have many a time surprised around a bit of Brie cheese, is a Virgil in comparison with them.

"The Brussels *bourgeois* could not have deceived their fellow-citizens, even had they wished to do so. If the facts celebrated in their lament were manufactured, on the appearance of that document the inhabitants of Brussels would have protested; the police would have consulted their registers to see if a certain Isaac Laquedem had spent such a day in Brussels, and they would have protested. The shoemakers, whose venerable brotherhood has been forever dishonored by the brutal conduct of the Wandering Jew, himself a knight of the awl, would not have failed to protest; in short, there would have been a concert of protests sufficient to crumble the towers of the capital of Brabant.

"Besides, in the matter of credibility, the lament of the Wandering Jew has notable advantages over the Gospel; it did not fall from heaven like a meteoric stone; it has a precise date. The first copy was deposited in the royal library, well and duly signed with the name of the printer and the street and number of his domicile. The lament of Brussels is accompanied by a portrait of the Wandering Jew in a three-cornered hat, polonaise coat, Hessian boots, and carrying a huge cane; no medallion, however, has come down to us bearing the effigy of Jesus Christ. The lament of the Wandering Jew was written in an enlightened, investigating century, more disposed to shorten its creed than to lengthen it; the Gospel, on the contrary, appeared suddenly like a torch, lighted no one knows by whom, amid the darkness of a century given over to gross superstitions, and among a people plunged in the deepest ignorance, and whose history is only a long series of acts of superstition and barbarism."

"Permit me, Monsieur Benjamin," said the notary; "you have said that the Brussels *bourgeois* could not have been mistaken as to the identity of the Wandering Jew; yet the inhabitants of Moulot took you this morning for the Wandering Jew; you yourself, in that capacity, have worked an authentic miracle in presence of the entire people of Moulot; your demonstration fails therefore in one point, and your rules regarding historical certainty are not infallible."

"The objection is a strong one," said Benjamin,

scratching his head; "I admit that it is impossible for me to answer it; but it applies as well to Monsieur's Jesus Christ as to my Wandering Jew."

"But," interrupted my grandmother, who always wanted to come down to facts, "I hope that you believe in Jesus Christ, Benjamin?"

"Undoubtedly, my dear sister, I believe in Jesus Christ. I believe in him the more firmly because without believing in the divinity of Jesus Christ one cannot believe in the existence of God, as the only proofs of the existence of God are the miracles of Jesus Christ. But then that does not prevent me from believing in the Wandering Jew, or, to explain myself more clearly, shall I tell you how I view the Wandering Jew?

"The Wandering Jew is the effigy of the Jewish people, sketched by some unknown poet of the people, on the walls of a cottage. This myth is so striking that only a blind man could fail to recognize it.

"The Wandering Jew has no roof, no fireside, no legal and political domicile: the Jewish people have no country.

"The Wandering Jew is obliged to travel on without rest, without stopping, without taking breath, which must be very fatiguing to him with his Hessian boots. He has already been seven times around the world. The Jewish people are not firmly established anywhere; everywhere they live in tents; they go and come incessantly like the waves of the ocean, and they too, like foam floating on the surface of the nations, like a straw borne by the current of civilization, have already been many times around the world.

"The Wandering Jew always has five sous in his

pocket. The Jewish people, continually ruined by the exactions of the feudal nobility and by the confiscations of the kings, always came back to a prosperous condition, as a cork reascends from the bottom to the surface of the water. Their wealth sprang up of itself.

"The Wandering Jew can spend only five sous at a time. The Jewish people, obliged to conceal their wealth, have become stingy and parsimonious; they spend little.

"The torment of the Wandering Jew will last forever. The Jewish people can no more reunite as a national body than the ashes of an oak struck by lightning can reunite as a tree. They are scattered over the surface of the earth until the centuries shall be no more.

"To speak seriously, it is doubtless a superstition to believe in the Wandering Jew, but I will say to you as it is said in the Gospel: let him who is free from all superstition cast the first sarcasm at the inhabitants of Moulot. The fact is that we are all superstitious, some more, others less, and often he who has a wen on his ear as big as a potato makes sport of him who has a wart on his chin.

"There are not two Christians who have the same beliefs, who admit and reject the same things. One fasts on Friday and does not go to church on Sunday; another goes to church on Sunday and eats meat on Friday. This lady mocks at Friday and Sunday alike, and would consider herself damned if she should be married outside of a church.

"Let religion be a beast with seven horns. He who believes only in six of its horns mocks at him who believes in the seventh; he who grants it but five horns mocks at him who recognizes six. Then comes the deist who mocks at all who believe that religion has horns, and finally passes the atheist who mocks at all the others, and yet the atheist believes in Cagliostro and consults the fortune-tellers. In short, there is only one man who is not superstitious,— namely, he who believes only in that which is demonstrated."

It was dark and more than dark when my grandmother declared that she wished to start.

"I will let Benjamin go only on one condition," said M. Minxit, "that he promises me to take part on Sunday in a grand hunting party which I decree in his honor: he must become familiar with his woods and the hares within them."

"But," said my uncle, "I do not know the first elements of hunting. I could readily distinguish a hare stew from a stewed rabbit, but may Millot-Rataut sing me his 'Grand Noël' if I am capable of distinguishing a hare on the run from a running rabbit."

"So much the worse for you, my friend; but that is one reason more why you should come: one should know a little of everything."

"You will see, Monsieur Minxit, that I shall do something awful; I shall kill one of your musicians."

"Oh! be careful not to do that, at least; I should have to pay his bereaved family more than he is worth. But, to avoid any accident, you shall hunt with your sword."

"Well, I promise," said my uncle.

And thereupon he took his leave of M. Minxit, accompanied by his dear sister.

"Do you know," said Benjamin to my grandmother

when they were on their way home, "that I would rather marry M. Minxit than his daughter?"

"One should desire only what he can have, and whatever one can have he should desire," answered my grandmother, dryly.

"But" . . .

"But . . . look out for the ass, and do not prick him with your sword, as you did this morning; that is all I ask of you."

"You are out of sorts, my sister; I should like to know why."

"Well, I will tell you; because you drank too much, debated too much, and did not say a word to Mlle. Arabelle. Now, leave me in peace."

CHAPTER VIII.

HOW MY UNCLE KISSED A MARQUIS.

THE following Saturday my uncle slept at Corvol.

They started the next morning at sunrise. M. Minxit was accompanied by all his people and several friends, among whom was his confrère Fata. It was one of those splendid days that gloomy winter, like a smiling jailer, occasionally gives the earth; February seemed to have borrowed its sun from the month of April; the sky was clear, and the South wind filled the atmosphere with a soft warmth; the river was steaming in the distance among the willows; the white frost of the morning hung in little drops from the branches of the bushes; the little shepherds were singing in the meadows for the first time in the year, and the brooks that ran down the mountain of Flez, awakened by the warmth of the sun, babbled at the foot of the hedges.

"Monsieur Fata," said my uncle, "this is a fine day. Shall we pass under the wet branches of the woods?"

"I don't care to, my confrère," said the latter. "If you will come to my house, I will show you a four-headed child which I have sealed in a bottle. M. Minxit offers me three hundred francs for it."

"You will do well to let him have it," said my uncle, "and put some currant wine in its place."

Nevertheless, as he had a good pair of legs, and as it was only two short leagues from there to Varzy, he decided to follow his confrère. So Fata and he left the main body of the huntsmen, and plunged into a cross-path that ran through the meadow. Soon they found themselves opposite Saint-Pierre du Mont. Now, Saint-Pierre du Mont is a big hill situated on the road from Clamecy to Varzy. At its base it is surrounded with meadows and streaming with water-courses, but at its summit it is shorn and bare. You would take it for a huge ball of earth raised on the plain by a gigantic mole. On its bare and scurvy cranium there was then the remnant of a feudal castle; to-day that is replaced by an elegant country-house, in which a cattle-raiser lives, for thus it is that the works of man, like those of nature, insensibly decompose and recompose.

The walls of the castle were dismantled and its battlements toothless in many spots; the towers seemed to have been broken off in the middle, and they were reduced to the condition of trunks; its moats, half dried up, were encumbered by tall grasses and a forest of reeds, and its drawbridge had given place to a stone bridge; the sinister shadow of this old feudal ruin saddened the entire neighborhood; the cottages had moved back from it: some had gone to the neighboring hill to form the village of Flez, while others had gone down into the valley and grouped themselves as a hamlet along the road.

The master of this old establishment at that time was a certain Marquis de Cambyse. M. de Cambyse was tall, stout, heavily built, and had a giant's strength. You would have thought him an old suit of armour made of flesh. He was of a violent, passionate, excessively irascible nature, and was moreover spoiled by his nobility, and imagined that the Cambyse family was a work unparalleled in creation.

At one time he had been an officer of musketeers, of I know not what color; but he was ill at ease at court, his will there was repressed, his violence could not give itself vent, and moreover he was stifled amid that dust of country squires which sparkled and whirled around the throne. He had returned to his estate, and lived there like a little monarch. Time had taken away one by one the old privileges of the nobility; but he had actually kept them, and exercised them to the full. He was still absolute master, not only of his domains, but also of all the country round about. Barring the buckler, he was a veritable feudal lord. He cudgelled the peasants, took their wives from them when they were pretty, invaded their lands with his hounds, trampled their crops under the feet of his *valets*, and subjected to a thousand annoyances the *bourgeois* who allowed themselves to meet him in the vicinity of his mountain.

He practised despotism and violence from caprice, for entertainment, and especially through pride. In order to be the most eminent personage in the vicinity, he wished to be the wickedest. He knew no better way of showing his superiority to people than to oppress them. To be famous he made himself wicked. Except in size, he was like the flea who cannot make you aware of his presence among your bed-clothes except by pricking you. Although rich, he had creditors. But he made it a point of honor not to pay them. Such was the terror of his name that you could not have found a sheriff's officer in the country willing to serve a paper on him. A single one, father Ballivet, had dared to serve a writ on him with his own hand and speaking in his own

person, but he had risked his life in doing it.   Honor
then to generous father Ballivet, the royal process-
server, who served writs everywhere and two leagues
beyond, as the wags of the neighborhood said in order
to dim the glory of this great process-server.

This was how he managed it.   He wrapped his document in a half-dozen envelopes treacherously sealed, and
presented it to M. de Cambyse as a package coming
from the castle of Vilaine.   While the Marquis was
unwrapping the document, he ran away noiselessly,
reached the main gate, and mounted his horse, which
he had fastened to a tree at some distance from the
castle.   When the Marquis found out what the package contained, furious at having been the dupe of a
process-server, he ordered his domestics to follow in his
tracks ; but father Ballivet was beyond their reach, and
mocked at them with a gesture which I cannot repro-
duce here.

Moreover, M. de Cambyse felt scarcely greater scruple about discharging his gun at a peasant than at a fox.
He had already maimed two or three, who were known
in the neighborhood as the cripples of M. de Cambyse,
and several quasi-notable inhabitants of Clamecy had
been the victims of his wicked practical jokes.   Although
he was not yet very old, there had already been in the
life of this honorable lord enough bloody tricks to en-
title him to two life-sentences ; but his family stood
well at court, and the protection of his noble relatives
secured him against prosecution.   And in fact each one
takes his pleasure where he finds it.   The good King
Louis XV., while engaged in such gentle and merry
sports at Versailles, and while giving parties to the

gentlemen of his court, did not wish his gentlemen in the provinces to grow weary on their estates, and he would have been very much vexed had there been any lack of peasants for them to whip until they howled or of *bourgeois* for them to insult. Louis, called the Well-Beloved, was determined to deserve the love that his subjects had awarded him. So then it is understood that the Marquis de Cambyse was as inviolable as a constitutional king, and that for him there was neither justice nor marshalsea.

Benjamin was fond of declaiming against M. de Cambyse. He called him the Gessler of the neighborhood, and had often manifested a desire to find himself face to face with this man. His wishes were fulfilled only too soon, as you will now see.

My uncle, in his capacity of philosopher, stood in contemplation before the old battlements, black and notched, that rent the azure of the sky.

"Monsieur Rathery," said his confrère to him, pulling him by the sleeve, "it does no one any good to stay around this castle, I warn you."

"What, Monsieur Fata, you too are afraid of a Marquis?"

"But, Monsieur Rathery, you know I am a doctor with a wig."

"That's the way with all of them!" cried my uncle, giving free course to his indignation; "there are three hundred common people against one gentleman, and they allow the gentleman to walk over their bellies. Furthermore, they flatten themselves as much as they can for fear this noble personage may stumble!"

"What do you expect, M. Rathery, against force?"

"But it is you who have the force, poor fellow! You resemble the ox who lets a child lead him from his green meadow to the slaughter-house. Oh, the people are cowards, cowards! I say it with bitterness, as a mother says that her child has a wicked heart. They always abandon to the executioner those who have sacrificed themselves for them, and, if a rope is lacking with which to hang them, they undertake to furnish it. Two thousand years have passed over the ashes of the Gracchi, and seventeen hundred and fifty years over the gibbet of Jesus Christ, and they are still the same people. They sometimes have spurts of courage, and fire issues from their mouths and nostrils; but slavery is their normal condition, and they always return to it, as a tamed canary always returns to its cage. You watch the passing of the torrent swollen by a sudden storm, and you take it for a river. You pass again the next day, and you find nothing but a sheepish thread of water hiding under the grasses of its banks, and which has left, from its passage of the day before, only a few straws on the branches of the bushes. They are strong when they wish to be; but look out, their strength lasts only a moment: those who rely upon them build their house upon the icy surface of a lake."

Just at that moment a man dressed in a rich hunting costume crossed the road, followed by barking dogs and a long train of *valets*. Fata turned pale.

"M. de Cambyse," said he to my uncle; and he bowed profoundly; but Benjamin stood straight and covered like a Spanish grandee.

Now, nothing was more calculated to offend the terrible Marquis than the presumption of this villein who refused him the ordinary homage on the verge of his domains and in front of his castle. It was, moreover, a very bad example, which might become contagious.

"Clodhopper," said he to my uncle, with his gentleman's air, "why do you not salute me?"

"And you," answered my uncle, surveying him from head to foot with his gray eye, "why did you not salute me?"

"Do you not know that I am the Marquis de Cambyse, lord of all this country?"

"And are you ignorant of the fact that I am Benjamin Rathery, doctor of medicine, of Clamecy?"

"Really," said the Marquis, "so you are a sawbones? I congratulate you upon it; it is a fine title that you have."

"It is as good a title as yours! To acquire it, I had to follow long and serious studies. But what did that *de* which you put before your name cost you? The king can make twenty marquises a day, but I defy him, with all his power, to make a doctor; a doctor has his usefulness; later perhaps you will recognize it; but what is a marquis good for?"

The Marquis de Cambyse had breakfasted well that morning. He was in good humor.

"Well," said he to his steward, "this is an original wag; I would rather have met him than a deer. And this one," he added, pointing his finger at Fata, "who is he?"

"M. Fata, of Varzy, Monsieur," said the doctor, making a second genuflection.

"Fata," said my uncle, "you are a poltroon; I suspected as much; but you shall account to me for this conduct."

"So," said the Marquis to Fata, "you are acquainted with this man?"

"Very slightly, Monsieur Marquis, I swear it: I know him only from having dined with him at M. Minxit's; but from the moment that he fails in the respect that he owes to nobility, I know him no more."

"And I," said my uncle, "am just beginning to know him."

"What, Monsieur Fata of Varzy," continued the Marquis, "do you dine with that queer fellow Minxit?"

"Oh, by chance, Monseigneur, one day when I was passing through Corvol. I know very well that this Minxit is not a man to associate with; he is a hare-brained fellow, a man spoiled by his wealth, and who thinks himself as good as a gentleman. Hi! hi! who gave me that kick from behind?"

"I did," said Benjamin, "in behalf of Monsieur Minxit."

"Now," said the Marquis, "you have nothing more to do here, Monsieur Fata; leave me alone with your travelling companion. So then," he added, addressing my uncle, "you persist in not saluting me?"

"If you salute me first, I will salute you second," said Benjamin.

"And that is your last word?"

"Yes."

"You have carefully considered what you are do-ing?"

"Listen," said my uncle: "I wish to show deference for your title, and to prove to you how accommodating I am in everything that concerns etiquette."

Then he took a coin from his pocket, and, tossing it in the air, said to the Marquis:

"Heads or tails? Gentleman or doctor, he whom fortune shall designate shall be the first to salute, and from this there shall be no appeal."

"Insolent fellow," said the fat, chub-faced steward, "do you not see that you are most scandalously lacking in respect to Monseigneur. If I were in his place, I would have beaten you long ago."

"My friend," answered Benjamin, "attend to your figures. Your lord pays you to rob him, not to give him advice."

Just then a game-keeper passed behind my uncle, and with the back of his hand knocked off his three-cornered hat, which fell in the mud. Benjamin had extraordinary muscular strength: as he turned round, there was still on the game-keeper's lips the broad smile which his trick had excited. My uncle, with one blow of his iron fist, sent the man head over heels, half into the ditch, half into the hedge that lined the road. The man's comrades wanted to extricate him from the amphibious position in which he thus found himself, but M. de Cambyse would not allow it. "The rogue must learn," said he, "that the right of insolence does not belong to common people."

Really I do not understand why my uncle, generally so philosophical, did not yield with good grace to necessity. I know very well that it is vexing to a proud citizen of the people, who feels his worth, to be obliged to salute a Marquis. But when we are under the sway of force, our free will is gone; it is no longer an act performed, it is a result produced. We are nothing but a machine that is not responsible for its acts; the man who does us violence is the only one who can be reproached for whatever is shameful or guilty in our action. Consequently I have always looked upon the invincible resistance of martyrs to their persecutors as an obstinacy scarcely worthy of being canonized. You wish, Antiochus, to throw me into boiling oil, if I refuse to eat pork? I must first call your attention to the fact that we do not fry a man as we do a gudgeon; but, if you persist in your demands, I eat your stew, and I even eat it with pleasure if it is well-cooked; for to you, to you alone, Antiochus, will the digestion be dangerous. You, Monsieur de Cambyse, you demand, with your gun levelled at my breast, that I salute you? Well, Marquis, I have the honor to salute you. I know very well that after this formality you will be worth no more and I no less. There is only one case in which we ought, whatever may happen, to stand up against force, and that is when they try to make us commit an act prejudicial to the nation, for we have no right to set our personal interest before the public interest.

But then, such was not the opinion of my uncle. As he stood firm in his refusal, M. de Cambyse had him seized by his *valets* and ordered them to return to the castle. Benjamin, pulled in front and pushed behind, and entangled with his sword, protested nevertheless with all his might against the violence to which they subjected him, and still found a way to distribute a few blows right and left. There were some peasants at work in the neighboring fields: my uncle appealed to them for help; but they were careful not to allow the justice of his appeals, and even laughed at his martyrdom in order to toady to the Marquis.

When they had reached the castle yard, M. de Cambyse ordered that the gate be closed. He had the bell rung to summon all his people; they brought two armchairs, one for him and one for his steward, and he began with this man a semblance of deliberation as to the fate of my poor uncle. He, in presence of this parody of justice, maintained a steadily firm attitude, and even kept his scornful and jeering air.

The worthy steward favored twenty-five lashes and forty-eight hours in the old dungeon; but the Marquis was in good humor, and even seemed to be slightly under the influence of wine.

"Have you anything to say in your defence?" said he to Benjamin.

"Come with me," answered the latter. "with your sword, to a distance of thirty paces from your castle, and I will acquaint you with my methods of defence."

Then the Marquis rose and said:

"Justice, after having deliberated, condemns the individual here present to kiss Monsieur the Marquis de Cambyse, lord of all this neighborhood, ex-lieutenant of musketeers, master of the wolf-hounds of the bailiwick of Clamecy, etc., etc., etc., in a spot which my aforesaid Lord de Cambyse is about to make known to him."

And at the same time he lowered his breeches. The flunkeys understood his intention, and began to applaud with all their might and to cry: "Long live the Marquis de Cambyse!"

As for my poor uncle, he roared with fury; he said later that he feared a stroke of apoplexy at the time. Two game-keepers stood with guns levelled, and they

had received an order from the Marquis to fire at his
first signal.

" One, two," said the latter.

Benjamin knew that the Marquis was a man to execute his threat, he did not wish to run the risk of a gun-
shot, and . . . a few seconds later the justice of the
Marquis was satisfied.

" All right," said M. de Cambyse, " I am content
with you ; now you can boast of having kissed a Marquis."

He had him escorted by two armed game-keepers to
the carriage entrance.   Benjamin fled like a dog to
whose tail a mischievous urchin has fastened a tin can ;
as he was on the road to Corvol, he did not give himself time to change his direction, and went straight to
M. Minxit's.

CHAPTER IX

M. MINXIT PREPARES FOR WAR.

Now, M. Minxit had been informed, I know not by whom,— by rumor doubtless, which meddles with everything,— that Benjamin was held a prisoner at Saint-Pierre du Mont; he knew no better way of delivering his friend than to take the castle of the Marquis by assault and then level it to the ground. Let those who laugh find me in history a war more just. Where the government does not know how to make the laws respected, the citizens must do justice themselves.

M. Minxit's yard resembled a camp-ground; the musicians, on horseback and armed with guns of all sorts, were already arranged in line of battle; the old sergeant, who had lately entered the doctor's service, had taken command of this picked body. From the middle of the ranks rose a large flag made out of a window-curtain, on which M. Minxit had inscribed in printed letters, that no one might fail to see them: THE LIBERTY OF BENJAMIN OR THE EARS OF M. DE CAMBYSE. This was his ultimatum.

In the second line came the infantry, represented by five or six farm-hands carrying their picks on their shoulders, and four slaters of the neighborhood each equipped with his ladder.

The barouche represented the baggage; it was loaded with fagots with which to fill up the moats of the castle, which time itself had filled in several places. But

M. Minxit was bound to do things regularly; he had
taken the further precaution of putting his case of
instruments and a big flask of rum in one of the pockets
of the carriage.

The warlike doctor, with feathers in his hat and a
naked sword in his hand, wheeled about his troops and
hastened the preparations for departure with a voice of
thunder.

It is customary for an army, before entering on a
campaign, to be harangued. M. Minxit was not a man
to fail in this formality. Now, this is what he said to
the soldiers:

"Soldiers, I will not say to you that Europe has its
eyes fixed upon you, that your names will be handed
down to posterity, that they will be engraved in the
temple of glory, etc., etc., etc., because these phrases
are the empty and barren seeds thrown to nincompoops;
but this is what I have to say:

"In all wars soldiers fight for the benefit of the sovereign; generally they have not even the advantage of
knowing why they die; but you are going to fight in
your own interest and in the interest of your wives and
children,— those of you who have any. M. Benjamin,
whom you all have the honor to know, is to become my
son-in-law. In this capacity he will reign with me over
you, and when I shall be no more, he will be your
master; he will be under infinite obligation to you on
account of the dangers which you are to incur on his
account, and he will reward you generously.

"But it is not only to restore liberty to my son-in-
law that you have taken up arms: our expedition also
will result in the deliverance of the country from a

tyrant who oppresses it, who crushes your wheat, who
beats you when he meets you, and who behaves very
badly with your wives.   One good reason is enough to
make a Frenchman fight courageously; you have two:
then you are invincible.   The dead shall have a decent
burial at my expense, and the wounded shall be cared
for in my house.   Long live M. Benjamin Rathery!
Death to Cambyse!   Destruction to his castle!"

"Bravo, Monsieur Minxit!" said my uncle, who had
come in through a back gate, as became a conquered
man. "That was a well-prepared harangue; if you
had delivered it in Latin, I should have thought that
you pillaged it from Titus Livius."

At sight of my uncle a general hurrah went up from
the army.   M. Minxit gave the order "Place rest!"
and took Benjamin into his dining-room.   The latter
gave an account of his adventures in the most circum-
stantial manner, and with a fidelity that statesmen do
not always show in writing their memoirs.

M. Minxit was horribly exasperated at the insult
offered to his son-in-law, and ground all the stumps in
his jaw.   At first he could express himself only in
curses; but, when his indignation had quieted a little,
he said: "Benjamin, you are nimbler than I: you shall
take command of the army, and we will march against
Cambyse's castle; where its turrets were, nettles and
quitch-grass shall grow."

"If you say so," said my uncle, "we will level even
the mountain of Saint-Pierre du Mont; but, saving the
respect that I owe to your opinion, I believe that we
ought to act strategically: we will scale the walls of
the castle by night; we will seize de Cambyse and all

his lackeys plunged in wine and sleep, as Virgil says; and they will all have to kiss us."

"That's a fine idea," answered M. Minxit. "We have a good league and a half to travel before we reach the place, and it will be dark in an hour: run and kiss my daughter, and we will start."

"One moment," said my uncle. "The devil! how you go on! I have eaten nothing to-day, and I should rather like to breakfast before we start."

"Then," said M. Minxit, "I will give the order to break ranks, and a ration of wine shall be distributed to our soldiers to keep them in breath."

"That's right," answered my uncle, "they will have time to finish themselves, while I am taking my refreshment."

Fortunately for the castle of the Marquis, lawyer Page, who was returning from a legal examination, came to ask permission to dine at M. Minxit's.

"You arrive opportunely, Monsieur Page," said the warlike doctor; "I am going to enroll you in our expedition."

"What expedition?" said Page, who had not studied the right to make war.

Then my uncle related his adventure and the way in which he proposed to avenge himself.

"Take care," said lawyer Page; "the thing is more serious than you think. In the first place, as to success, how do you hope with seven or eight cripples to overcome a garrison of thirty domestics commanded by a lieutenant of musketeers?"

"Twenty men and all valid, Monsieur attorney," said M. Minxit.

"Very well," said lawyer Page, coldly; "but the castle of M. de Cambyse is surrounded by walls; will those walls tumble, like those of Jericho, at the sound of cymbals and bass-drum? Suppose, however, that you take the castle of the Marquis by assault: it undoubtedly will be a fine feat of arms; but this exploit is not calculated to win for you the cross of Saint Louis; where you see only a good bit of fun and legitimate reprisals, justice will see a case of breaking and entering, a scaling of walls, a violation of domicile, a night attack, and all these, furthermore, against a Marquis. The least of these things involves the penalty of the galleys, I warn you; you will be obliged therefore after your victory to make up your mind to leave the country, and that to what end? Simply to force a Marquis to kiss you.

"When one can avenge himself without risk and without damage, I admit vengeance; but to avenge one's self to one's own detriment is a ridiculous thing, an act of folly. You say, Benjamin, that you have been insulted; but what is an insult? Almost always an act of brutality committed by the stronger to the prejudice of the weaker. Now, how can another's brutality damage your honor? Is it your fault if this man is a miserable savage, who knows no other right than might? Are you responsible for his cowardice? If a tile should fall on your head, would you run to break it into pieces? Would you think yourself insulted by a dog who had bitten you, and would you challenge him to a single combat, like that of the poodle of Montargis with the assassin of his master? If the insult dishonors anyone, it is the insulting party: all honest people are on the side of the insulted. When a butcher maltreats a sheep, tell me, are we indignant at the sheep?

"If the evil that you wish to do to your insulter would cure you of that which he has done to you, I could understand your thirst for revenge; but if you are the weaker, you will bring down upon yourself new cruelties; if, on the contrary, you are the stronger, you have still to take the trouble to fight your adversary. Thus the man who avenges himself always plays the *rôle* of a dupe. The precept of Jesus Christ which tells us to forgive those who have offended us is not only a fine moral precept, but also sensible advice. From all which I conclude that you will do well, my dear Benjamin, to forget the honor that the Marquis has done you, and to drink with us until night to drown this recollection."

"For my part, I am not at all of cousin Page's opinion. It is always pleasant and sometimes useful to loyally return the evil that has been done us: it is a lesson that we give to the wicked. It is good that they should know that it is at their own risk and peril that they abandon themselves to their mischievous instincts. To leave undisturbed the viper that has bitten you when you might crush it, and to forgive the wicked, is the same thing. Generosity in such a case is not only stupidity, it is a wrong done to society. Though Jesus Christ said: 'Forgive your enemies,' Saint Peter cut off Malchus's ear; these things compensate each other."

My uncle was as obstinate as if he had been the son of a horse and an ass, and for that matter obstinacy is an hereditary vice in our family: nevertheless he agreed that lawyer Page was right.

"I believe, Monsieur Minxit," said he, "that you will

do very well to put your sword back in the scabbard
and your plumed hat in its box. One should make war
only for extremely serious reasons, and the king who
unnecessarily drags a part of his people to those vast
slaughter-houses known as battle-fields is an assassin.
Perhaps you would be flattered, Monsieur Minxit, to
take rank among the heroes; but what is the glory of
a general? Cities in ruins, villages in ashes, countries
ravaged, women abandoned to the brutality of the soldier, children led away captive, casks of wine staved in
in the cellars. Have you not read Fénelon, Monsieur
Minxit? All these things are atrocious, and I shudder
at the very thought of them."

" What are you talking about?" answered Monsieur
Minxit; "this is a question only of a few blows of a
pick-axe at some old crumbling walls."

" Well," said my uncle, "why take the trouble to
knock them down when they are so willing to fall of
themselves? Believe me, restore peace to this beautiful
country; I should be a coward and a wretch if I should
suffer you, in order to avenge an injury wholly personal
to myself, to expose yourself to the manifold dangers
that must result from our expedition."

" But I too," said M. Minxit, "have some personal
injuries to avenge on this country squire; he once sent
me, out of derision, a horse's urine to consult for human
urine."

" A fine reason for risking six years in the galleys!
No, Monsieur Minxit, posterity would not absolve you.
If you will not think of yourself, think of your daughter, of your dear Arabelle: what pleasure would she
take in making such good cream cheeses, if you were
no longer here to eat them?"

This appeal to the paternal feelings of the old doctor had its effect.

"At least," said he, "you promise me that justice shall be done to M. de Cambyse for his insolence; for you are my son-in-law, and from this time forth, where honor is concerned, we are as one man instead of two."

"Oh! rest easy as to that, Monsieur Minxit, I shall always have an eye open for the Marquis. I shall watch him with the patient attention of a cat that watches a mouse; some day or other I shall catch him alone and without an escort; then he will have to cross his noble sword with my rapier, or else I will beat him to my satisfaction. I cannot swear, like the old knights, to let my beard grow or to eat hard bread until I have avenged myself, because one of these things would not be fitting in our profession and the other is contrary to my temperament; but I swear not to become your son-in-law until the insult that has been offered me shall have been gloriously atoned for."

"No, no," answered M. Minxit; "you go too far, Benjamin; I do not accept this impious oath; you must, on the contrary, marry my daughter; you will avenge yourself as well afterward as before."

"Do you think so, Monsieur Minxit? From the moment that I must fight to the death with the Marquis, my life no longer belongs to me; I cannot allow myself to marry your daughter, simply perhaps to leave her a widow on the day after her wedding."

The good doctor tried to shake my uncle's resolution, but, seeing that he could not succeed, he decided to go change his costume and disband his army. Thus ended this great expedition, which cost humanity little blood, but M. Minxit much wine.

CHAPTER X

HOW MY UNCLE MADE THE MARQUIS KISS HIM.

BENJAMIN had slept at Corvol.

The next day, as he was leaving the house with M. Minxit, the first person whom they saw was Fata. The latter, who did not feel a clear conscience, would rather have met two big wolves in his path than my uncle and M. Minxit. Still, as he could not run away, he decided to put the best face he could on the matter, and approached my uncle.

"How do you do, Monsieur Rathery? How is your health, honorable Monsieur Minxit? Well, Monsieur Benjamin, how did you get out of your difficulty with our Gessler? I was terribly afraid that he might serve you a bad trick, and I did not close my eyes all night."

"Fata," said M. Minxit, "keep your obsequiousness for the Marquis when you shall meet him. Is it true that you told M. de Cambyse that you no longer know Benjamin?"

"I do not remember that, my good Monsieur Minxit."

"Is it true that you told the same Marquis that I was not a man to associate with?"

"I could not have said that, my dear Monsieur Minxit; you know how much I esteem you, my friend."

"I affirm on my honor that he said both those things," said my uncle, with the icy *sang-froid* of a judge.

"Very well," said M. Minxit; "then we will settle his account."

"Fata," said Benjamin, "I warn you that M. Minxit desires to flog you. Here, then, is my switch; for the honor of the profession, defend yourself; a doctor cannot allow himself to be beaten like an ass."

"The law is on my side," said Fata; "if he strikes me, every blow will cost him dear."

"I sacrifice a thousand francs," said M. Minxit, making his whip whistle in the air; "take that, *Fata, fatorum*, destiny, providence of the ancients! and that, and that, and that, and that!"

The peasants had come to their door-ways to see Fata flogged; for — I say it to the shame of our poor humanity — nothing is so dramatic as a man ill-treated.

"Gentlemen," cried Fata, "I place myself under your protection."

But no one left his place. For M. Minxit, through the consideration which he enjoyed, had almost the right of administering petty justice in the village.

"Then," continued the unfortunate Fata, "I call you to witness the violence practised on my person; I am a doctor of medicine."

"Wait," said M. Minxit, "I will strike harder, in order that those who do not see the blows may hear them, and that you may have some scars to show to the bailiff."

And in fact he did strike harder, ferocious plebeian that he was.

"Rest easy, Minxit," said Fata, as he went away, "you will have to deal with M. de Cambyse: he will not suffer me to be maltreated because I salute him."

" You will say to Cambyse," said M. Minxit, " that I mock at him, that I have more men than he, that my house is more solid than his castle, and that, if he wishes to come to-morrow to the plateau of Fertiant with his people, I am his man."

Let us say directly, to end with this affair, that Fata had M. Minxit cited before the bailiff to answer for the violence committed on his person; but that he could find no witness to testify to the fact, although the thing had happened in the presence of a hundred individuals.

When my uncle reached Clamecy, his sister handed him a letter postmarked Paris, of the following tenor: —

" *Monsieur Rathery:*

"I have it on good authority that you intend to marry Mlle. Minxit; I expressly forbid you to do so.

"Vicomte de Pont-Cassé."

My uncle sent Gaspard to get a sheet of royal writing paper; he took Machecourt's ink-stand, and straightway answered this missive.

" *Monsieur Vicomte:*

"You may go . . . .

"Accept the assurance of the respectful sentiments with which I have the honor to be

" Your humble and devoted servant,

"B. Rathery."

Whither did my uncle wish to send his vicomte? I do not know. I have made useless inquiries to penetrate the mystery of this reticence; but at any rate I have given you an idea of the firmness, clearness, nerve, and precision of his style when he saw fit to take the trouble to write.

Meanwhile, my uncle had not abandoned his ideas of revenge; quite the contrary. The following Friday, after having visited his patients, he sharpened his sword and put on Machecourt's overcoat over his red coat. As he did not wish to sacrifice his cue, and as he could not put it in his pocket, he hid it under his old wig, and went thus disguised to watch his Marquis. He established his headquarters in a sort of wine-shop situated on the edge of the Clamecy road opposite the castle of M. de Cambyse. The proprietor of the establishment had just broken his leg. My uncle, always prompt to come to the aid of his neighbor when he was fractured, made known his profession and offered the help of his art to the patient. He was authorized by the afflicted family to put back in their proper place the two fragments of the broken shinbone; which he did quickly and to the great admiration of the two grand lackeys in the livery of M. de Cambyse, who were drinking in the wine-shop.

My uncle, when the operation was finished, took up his position in an upper chamber of the tavern, directly above the sign, and began to observe the castle with a spy-glass, which he had borrowed from M. Minxit. He had been waiting there a good hour and had not yet noticed anything by which he could profit, when he saw a lackey of M. de Cambyse descending the hill at full speed. This man came to the door of the wine-shop, and asked if the doctor was still there. Being answered in the affirmative by the servant, he went up to my uncle's room, and, doffing his hat very low, begged him to give attendance on M. de Cambyse, who had just swallowed a fish-bone. My uncle at first was tempted to refuse. But he reflected that this circumstance might favor his project of revenge, and he decided to follow the domestic.

The latter ushered him into the chamber of the Marquis. M. de Cambyse was in his arm-chair, with his head resting on his hands, and his elbows on his knees, and he seemed to be the victim of a violent agitation. The Marquise, a pretty brunette of twenty-five years, stood beside him, trying to reassure him. On the arrival of my uncle, the Marquis raised his head and said :

"At dinner I swallowed a fish-bone, which has stuck in my throat. I had heard that you were in the village, and I have sent for you, although I have not the honor of knowing you, persuaded that you will not refuse me your aid."

"We owe that to everybody," answered my uncle, with an icy *sang-froid;* "to the rich as well as to the poor, to gentlemen as well as to peasants, to the wicked as well as to the just."

"This man frightens me," said the Marquis to his wife, "make him go out."

"But," said the Marquise, "you know very well that no doctor will venture to come to the castle; since you have this one here, try at least to keep him."

The Marquis surrendered to this opinion. Benjamin examined the sick man's throat, and shook his head with an air of anxiety. The Marquis turned pale.

"What is the matter?" said he; "can the trouble be more serious than we had supposed?"

"I do not know what you have supposed," answered Benjamin, in a solemn voice, "but the trouble will indeed be very serious, if the necessary measures are not promptly taken to combat it. You have swallowed a bone from a salmon, and the bone is from the tail, the very place where they are most poisonous."

"That is true," said the astonished Marquise; "but how did you find that out?"

"By inspection of the throat, Madame."

The fact is that he had found it out in a very natural way. In passing by the dining-room, the door of which was open, he had seen on the table a salmon, of which only the tail was missing, and he had inferred that to the tail of this fish had belonged the swallowed fish-bone.

"We have never heard," said the Marquise, in a voice trembling with fright, "that the bones of the salmon were poisonous."

"That does not alter the fact that they are exceedingly so," said Benjamin, "and I should be sorry to have Madame Marquise doubt it, for I should be obliged to contradict her. The bones of the salmon contain, like the leaves of the manchineel tree, a substance so bitter and corrosive that, if this bone should remain a half-hour longer in the throat of Monsieur Marquis, it would produce an inflammation which I could not subdue, and the operation would become impossible."

"In that case, doctor, operate directly, I beg of you," said the Marquis, more and more frightened.

"One moment," said my uncle; "the thing cannot proceed as rapidly as you desire; there is first a little formality to be fulfilled."

"Fulfil it, then, very quickly, and begin."

"But this formality concerns you; you alone must accomplish it."

"Then tell me at least of what it consists, surgeon of misfortune! Do you wish to leave me to die for want of acting?"

"I still hesitate," continued Benjamin, slowly. "How shall I venture such a proposition as that which I have to make to you? With a Marquis! With a man who descends in a direct line from Cambyse, king of Egypt!"

"I believe, wretch, that you are taking advantage of my position to make sport of me," cried the Marquis, the violence of his character coming to the surface.

"Not the least in the world," answered Benjamin, coldly. "Do you remember a man whom three months ago you had dragged to your castle by your myrmidons because he did not salute you, and upon whom you inflicted the most outrageous affront that one man can inflict upon another?"

"A man whom I forced to kiss .... In fact, you are the man. I recognize you by your five feet ten inches."

"Well, the man of five feet ten inches, this man whom you regarded as an insect, as a grain of dust whom you would never meet except under your feet, now demands of you reparation of the insult which you have offered him."

"My God! I ask nothing better; fix the sum at which you value your honor, and I will have it counted out to you directly."

"Do you think, then, Marquis de Cambyse, that you are rich enough to pay for the honor of an honest man?

Do you take me for a lawyer? Do you think that I
would submit to an insult for money? No, no, it is a
reparation of honor that I want. A reparation of
honor! Do you understand, Marquis de Cambyse?"

"Well, so be it," said M. de Cambyse, whose eyes
were fixed on the hands of his clock, and who saw with
terror the fatal half-hour slipping by; "I will declare
in presence of Madame Marquise, I will declare it in
writing, if you say so, that you are a man of honor, and
that I did wrong in offending you."

"The devil! you have a summary way of paying
your debts. Do you think, then, that, when you
have insulted an honest man, you have only to admit
that you were wrong, and that all is mended? To-
morrow you would laugh heartily in the company of
your country squires at the simpleton who had contented himself with this semblance of satisfaction. No,
no, it is the penalty of retaliation to which you must
submit; the weak man of yesterday has become the
strong man of to-day; the worm has turned into a serpent. You shall not escape my justice, as you escape
that of the bailiff; there is no protection that can
defend you against me. I have kissed you; you must
kiss me."

"Have you, then, forgotten, wretch, that I am the
Marquis de Cambyse?"

"You forgot that I was Benjamin Rathery. An insult is like God; all men are equal before it. There is
neither great insulter nor little insulted."

"Lackey," said the Marquis, whose wrath made him
forget the supposed danger that he incurred, "take this
man into the yard, and have him given a hundred
lashes; I want to hear him howl from here."

"Very well," said my uncle, "but in ten minutes the operation will have become impossible, and in an hour you will be dead."

"But can I not send to Varzy by my footman for a surgeon?"

"If your footman finds the surgeon at home, he will arrive just in time to see you die, and bestow his care upon Madame Marquise."

"But it is not possible," said the Marquise, "that you should remain inflexible. Is there not, then, more pleasure in forgiveness than in vengeance?"

"Oh, Madame," replied Benjamin, bowing gracefully, "I beg you to believe that, if it was from you that I had received such an insult, I should harbor no grudge against you."

Madame de Cambyse smiled, and, understanding that there was nothing to be gained with my uncle, she herself urged her husband to submit to necessity, and called his attention to the fact that he had but five minutes left in which to make up his mind.

The Marquis, overcome by terror, made a sign to the two lackeys who were in his room to retire.

"No," said the inflexible Benjamin, "that is not what I desire. Lackey, you will go, on the contrary, to notify the people of M. de Cambyse to gather here in his name. They witnessed the insult; they must witness the reparation. Madame Marquise alone can be permitted to retire."

The Marquis glanced at the clock, and saw that there were but three minutes left. As the lackey did not budge, he said:

"Hurry, Pierre, and execute Monsieur's orders; do

you not see that he alone is master here for the moment?"

The domestics arrived one after another; none were lacking but the steward; but Benjamin, unrelenting to the end, would not begin until he was present.

.　　.　　.　　.　　.　　.　　.　　.　　.　　.

"Well," said Benjamin, "now we are quits, and all is forgotten; therefore I will conscientiously attend to your throat."

He extracted the bone very quickly and well, and placed it in the hands of the Marquis. While the latter was examining it with curiosity, he said:

"I must give you some air."

Then he opened a window, leaped into the yard, and with two or three strides of his long legs reached the carriage-entrance. While he was hurrying down the hillside, the Marquis stood at a window, shouting:

"Stop, Monsieur Benjamin Rathery; pray stop; come back and receive my thanks and those of Madame Marquise. I must pay you for your operation."

But Benjamin was not a man to be caught by these fine words. At the foot of the hill he met the footman of the Marquis.

"Landry," said he to him, "my compliments to Madame Marquise, and reassure M. de Cambyse in regard to salmon bones; they are no more poisonous than those of a pike; only they should not be swallowed. Let him keep his throat wrapped in a poultice, and in two or three days he will be cured."

As soon as my uncle was out of reach of the Marquis, he turned to the right, crossed the meadows of Flez and the thousand brooks which intersected them,

and went to Corvol. He desired to regale M. Minxit
with the first news of his expedition ; he saw him from
a distance standing before his door, and waving his
handkerchief as a sign of triumph, he shouted :

" We are revenged."

The good man ran to meet him, with all the speed
of his short fat legs, and threw himself into his arms
with the same effusion as if he had been his son ; my
uncle said that he even saw two big tears roll down
his cheeks, which he tried to hide. The old doctor,
whose nature was no less proud and irascible than
Benjamin's, was exultant with joy. On reaching the
house he told the musicians, in order to celebrate the
glory of the day, to execute trumpet-flourishes until
night, and then he ordered them to get drunk,—an
order which was punctually executed.

CHAPTER XI

NEVERTHELESS, Benjamin came back to Clamecy a little disturbed at his own audacity. But the next day the footman of the castle delivered to him in behalf of his master, together with a considerable sum of money, a note that read as follows:

"The Marquis de Cambyse begs M. Benjamin Rathery to forget what has passed between them, and to receive, in payment for the operation which he has so skilfully executed, the insignificant sum which he sends him."

"Oh," said my uncle, after reading this letter, "this good lord would like to purchase my discretion; he even has the honesty to pay me in advance; it is a pity that he does not treat all his trades-people in the same way. If I had simply, vulgarly, and without any preliminary extracted the fish-bone that he had planted in his throat, he would have put six francs in my hand and sent me to eat a bite in the kitchen. The moral of this is that *with the great it is better to be feared than to be loved*. May God damn me if during my life I ever fail in this principle!

"Nevertheless, as I have no intention of being discreet, I cannot conscientiously keep the money which he sends me as the wages of my discretion; one should be honest with everybody, or else have nothing to do with them. But let us count the money in this bag;

let us see how much he pays for the operation, and how much he gives for silence : one hundred and fifty francs ! Thunder ! Cambyse is generous ; he will allow only twelve sous, without any guarantee of not being beaten, to the thrasher who swings his flail from three o'clock in the morning until eight o'clock at night, and he pays me one hundred and fifty francs for a quarter of an hour's work : there's magnificence for you !

"For the extraction of this bone M. Minxit would have asked a hundred francs ; but he practises medicine on the grand orchestra and the grand spectacle plan ; he has four horses and twelve musicians to feed. For me, who have to support only my case of instruments and my hypostasis,—an hypostasis, it is true, of five feet nine inches,—two pistoles is all that that is worth. So, taking twenty from one hundred and fifty, there are thirteen pistoles to send back to the Marquis ; I almost feel remorse at taking any of his money. This operation for which I charge him twenty francs I would not have failed to perform for a thousand francs,—a thousand francs to be paid of course after my death. This poor grand lord, how wretched and pitiful he looked with his pale and suppliant face and his salmon-bone in his throat ! How nobility apologized in his person to the people represented in mine ! He would willingly have allowed me to fasten his escutcheon behind his back. If at that time there were in his *salon* any portraits of his ancestors, their brows must still be red with shame. I would like the little spot where he kissed me to be separated from my person after my death, and transferred to the Pantheon . . . when the people have a Pantheon, I mean of course.

"But, Marquis, you are not to be let off in this way: before three days the bailiwick will know your adventure; I even intend to have it related to posterity by Millot-Rataut, our maker of songs; he must manufacture for me on this subject half a handful of Alexandrines. As for these twenty francs, they are money found; I do not wish them to pass through my dear sister's hands. To-morrow is Sunday; to-morrow, then, I give my friends with this money a luncheon such as I have never given them, a luncheon for which I will pay cash. It is well to let them know how a man of wit can avenge himself without recourse to his sword."

The thing thus arranged, my uncle began to write to the Marquis to announce the return of his money. I should be delighted if I could give my readers a new specimen of my uncle's epistolary style. Unhappily, his letter is not to be found among the historical documents which my grandfather has handed down to us; perhaps my uncle the tobacco-merchant made a cornet of it.

While Benjamin was in the act of writing, his tailor came in with a bill in his hand.

"What's that?" said Benjamin, laying his pen on the table; "your bill again, Monsieur Bonteint, forever your eternal bill? My God! you have presented it to me so many times that I know it by heart: six ells of scarlet full width, with ten ells of lining and three sets of carved buttons, isn't that right?"

"That's right, Monsieur Rathery, exactly right; a total of one hundred and fifty francs ten sous six deniers. May I be excluded from Paradise as a rascal if I do not lose at least a hundred francs on this transaction!"

"If that is the case," rejoined my uncle, "why continue to waste your time in scribbling off all these ugly bits of paper? You know very well, Monsieur Bonteint, that I never have any money."

"I see, on the contrary, Monsieur Rathery, that you have some, and that I arrive at an opportune moment. Here on this table is a bag which must contain almost the exact amount of my bill, and if you will permit it" . . .

"One moment," said my uncle, quickly laying his hand on the bag; "this money does not belong to me, Monsieur Bonteint. Here is the very letter of return which I have just written, and on which you have caused me to make a blot. Here," he added, offering the letter to the merchant, "if you wish to read it" . . .

"It is useless, Monsieur Rathery, utterly useless. All that I want to know is at what time you will have some money that belongs to you."

"Alas! M. Bonteint, who can foresee the future? What you ask I would very much like to know myself."

"That being so, Monsieur Rathery, you will not blame me if I go directly to Parlanta to tell him to push the suit that I have begun against you."

"You are in ill-humor, respectable Monsieur Bonteint. What sort of cloth clippings have you been walking on to-day?"

"You must admit, Monsieur Rathery, that I at least have good reason to be ill-humored; for three years you have owed me this money, and you put me off from month to month, on the strength of I know not what epidemic, of the arrival of which I see no sign. You

are the cause of my daily quarrels with Madame Bonteint, who reproaches me with not knowing how to col-
lect my bills, and who sometimes pushes her vivacity to
the point of calling me a blockhead."

"Madame Bonteint is surely a very amiable lady;
you are fortunate, Monsieur Bonteint, in having such a
wife, and I beg you to present her my compliments as
soon as possible."

"I thank you, Monsieur Rathery, but my wife is, as
they say, something of a Greek; she prefers money to
compliments, and she says that, if you had had to deal
with my rival Grophez, you would long ago have been
in the Boutron Hotel."

"The devil take it!" cried my uncle, furious that
Bonteint showed no signs of retreating, "it is your
fault if I have not settled with you; all your rivals
have been or are sick: Dutorrent has had inflammation
of the chest twice this year; Artichaut, the typhoid
fever; Sergifer has the rheumatism; Ratine has had
the diarrhœa for six months. But you enjoy perfect
health; I have had no opportunity of supplying you
any medicine; you have a complexion like one of your
pieces of nankeen, and Madame Bonteint resembles a
statuette made out of fresh butter. You see I have
been deceived; I thought that you would be an honor
to my clientage; if I had known then what I know
now, I would not have given you my custom."

"But, Monsieur Rathery, it seems to me that neither
Madame Bonteint or myself are obliged to be sick in
order to furnish you the means of paying your bills."

"And I declare to you, Monsieur Bonteint, that you
are under precisely that moral obligation. How would

you manage to pay your bills if your customers did
not wear coats? This obstinacy in keeping your health
is an abominable procedure on your part; it is a trap
that you have set for me; you ought at the present
hour to have on my account-book an indebtedness of
one hundred and fifty francs; hence I deduct from
your bill one hundred and thirty francs ten sous six
deniers for the diseases that you ought to have had.
You will admit that I am reasonable. You are very
fortunate in having to pay for the medicine without
having had to have the doctor, and I know many people
who would like to be in your place. So, then, if from
one hundred and fifty francs ten sous six deniers we
take one hundred and thirty francs ten sous six deniers, there is a balance of twenty francs still due you;
if you wish them, there they are; I advise you as a
friend to take them; you will not soon have so good an
opportunity again."

"I will willingly take them," said M. Bonteint, "as
an instalment."

"As a final settlement of the account," insisted my
uncle, "and even then I need all my strength of soul
to make this sacrifice. I intended this money for a
bachelors' breakfast, it was even my design to invite
you, although you are the father of a family."

"This is more of your nonsense, Monsieur Rathery;
I have never been able to get anything else from you.
You know very well, however, that I have a seizure
drawn up against you in good form, and that I might
proceed to execution directly."

"Well, it is precisely that of which I complain, Monsieur Bonteint; you have no confidence in your friends;

why go to these useless expenses? Could you not
come to me and say: 'Monsieur Rathery, it is my intention to have you seized.' I would have answered:
'Seize me yourself, Monsieur Bonteint; you need no
sheriff's officer for that;' I will even serve you as a
bailiff's man, if that will be agreeable to you; and
besides, there is time enough yet; seize me on the instant; do not stand on ceremony; all that I have is at
your disposition; I permit you to pack up, wrap up,
and carry away anything that you like."

"What! Monsieur Rathery, you would be good
enough " . . .

"Why, of course, Monsieur Bonteint, I should be
delighted to be seized by your hands; I will even help
you to seize me."

My uncle then opened an old ruin of a wardrobe, in
which were still hanging on a nail some bits of yellow
copper lining, and, taking two or three old cue-ribbons
from a drawer, he said to M. Bonteint, as he offered
them to him:

"See, you will not lose all; these articles will not
count in the total; I throw them in."

" Indeed!" answered M. Bonteint.

" This red morocco portfolio which you see is my
case of instruments."

As M. Bonteint was about to lay his hand on it,
Benjamin said:

"Softly; the law does not allow you to touch that.
My instruments are the tools of my profession, and I
have a right to keep them."

" But," said M. Bonteint . . .

" Here now is a corkscrew, with an ebony handle inlaid with silver. As for this article," he added, as he put it in his pocket, " I withdraw it from my creditors; and besides, I need it more than you do."

" But," replied M. Bonteint, "if you keep everything that you need more than I do, I shall need no cart in which to carry away my plunder."

" One moment," said my uncle, "you will lose nothing by waiting. Here on this shelf are some old medicine bottles, some of which are cracked: I do not guarantee their integrity; I abandon them to you with all the spiders that are in them. On this other shelf is a large stuffed vulture; that will cost you nothing but the trouble of moving it, and it will make a very good sign for you."

" Monsieur Rathery ! " said Bonteint.

" Here is Machecourt's wedding wig; I don't know how it happens to be here. I do not offer it to you, because I know that you wear only a false forelock."

" What do you know about it, Monsieur Rathery?" cried Bonteint, getting more and more irritated.

" Here in this bottle," continued my uncle, with imperturbable *sang-froid*, "is a tapeworm which I have preserved in spirit of wine. You can use it to make garters for yourself, Madame Bonteint, and your children. I call your attention to the fact, however, that it would be a pity to mutilate this beautiful animal: you can boast of having in your possession the longest being in creation, not excepting the immense boa-constrictor. For the rest, you will estimate it at what value you like."

" Surely you are making sport of me, Monsieur Rathery; all these things have not the slightest value."

"I know that very well," said my uncle, coldly, "but then you have no bailiff's man to pay. Now here, for instance, is an article worth in itself alone the entire amount of your bill: it is the stone that I extracted two or three years ago from the mayor's bladder; you can have it carved into the shape of a snuff-box; put a band of gold about it and add a few precious stones, and it will make a very pretty birthday present for Madame Bonteint."

Bonteint, furious, started for the door.

"One moment," said my uncle, catching hold of the skirt of his coat. "Don't be in such a hurry, Monsieur Bonteint. I have shown you yet only the least of my treasures. Stay, here is an old engraving representing Hippocrates, the father of medicine; I guarantee it a good likeness; furthermore, here are three incomplete volumes of the 'Medical Gazette,' which will entertain you delightfully during these long winter evenings."

"Once more, Monsieur Rathery" . . .

"Oh! do not be angry, papa Bonteint; we have just reached the most valuable article among my possessions."

My uncle then opened an old closet, and took out two red coats, which he threw at M. Bonteint's feet, and from which there arose a cloud of dust that made the good merchant cough, together with a swarm of spiders that scattered about the room.

"There," said he, "there are the last two coats that you sold me! You have outrageously deceived me, Monsieur Fauxteint:* they faded in one morning, like two rose leaves, and my dear sister could not even use

---

* *Bonteint*, good tint; *Fauxteint*, false tint.— *Translator*.

them to color the Easter eggs for her children. You really deserve to have the cost of the coloring material deducted from your bill."

"Oh, really," cried Bonteint, horrified, "that is really too much; never was a creditor more insolently treated. To-morrow morning you shall hear from me, Monsieur Rathery."

"So much the better, Monsieur Bonteint; I shall always be delighted to learn that you are in good health.—By the way, Monsieur Bonteint, you are forgetting your cue-ribbons!"

As Bonteint went out, lawyer Page came in. He found my uncle shouting with laughter.

"What have you been doing to Bonteint?" he said; "I just met him on the stairs, almost red with anger; he was in such a violent crisis of exasperation that he did not bow to me as he passed."

"The old imbecile," said Benjamin, "is angry with me because I have no money. As if that ought not to disturb me more than him!"

"You have no money, my poor Benjamin! So much the worse, doubly so much the worse, for I came to offer you a golden bargain."

"Offer it just the same," said Benjamin.

"The vicar Djhiarcos wishes to get rid of a quarter-cask of Burgundy, which one of his devotees has given him, because he has the catarrh and Doctor Arnout will allow him only mild drinks; as the diet is likely to be long, he is afraid that his wine may spoil. He wants this money to furnish some rooms for a poor orphan who has just lost her last aunt. So it is not only a good bargain, but a good deed that I propose to you."

"Yes," said Benjamin, "but without money it is not so easy to do a good deed; good deeds are expensive, and cannot be done at will. But what is your opinion of the wine?"

"Exquisite," said Page, smacking his lips; "he made me taste it; it is Beaune of the first quality."

"And how much does the virtuous Djhiarcos want for it?"

"Twenty-five francs," said Page.

"I have only twenty francs; if he wants to part with it for twenty francs, it is a bargain. In that case we will lunch on credit."

"His terms are twenty-five francs, take it or leave it. Twenty-five francs to relieve a poor orphan from poverty and preserve her from vice,— you will agree that that is not too much."

"But if you had five francs, Page," replied my uncle, "we could buy it together."

"Alas!" said Page, "it is a good fortnight since I have seen so much money. I believe that specie is afraid of M. de Calonne; it retires" . . .

"It does not always frequent the doctors," said my uncle. "So we must think no more of your quarter-cask."

For sole response, Page heaved a deep sigh.

Just then came in my grandmother, carrying a big roll of linen in her arms, like an Infant Jesus. She placed the cloth enthusiastically on my uncle's knees.

"See, Benjamin," said she, "I have just made a superb bargain; I caught sight of this piece of cloth this morning, as I was making the tour of the fair-grounds. You need shirts, and I thought that it would just suit you. Madame Avril offered seventy-five francs for it; she allowed the merchant to leave her, but I could see from the way in which she eyed him that she had a good mind to call him back. 'Let me see your cloth,' said I then to the peasant. I offered him eighty francs; I did not think that he would part with it for that sum. The linen is worth one hundred and twenty francs if it is worth a sou, and Madame Avril is furious with me for having interfered with her bargain."

"And this linen," cried my uncle, "you have bought, bought?"

"Bought," said my grandmother, who did not understand Benjamin's exasperation; "and there is no way of getting out of it; the peasant is downstairs waiting for the money."

"Well, go to the devil!" cried Benjamin, throwing the roll across the room, "you and . . . That is, forgive me, my dear sister, forgive me, no; do not go to the devil; it is too far; but go carry the cloth back to the merchant: I have no money to pay for it."

"And the money that you received this morning from M. de Cambyse?" asked my grandmother.

"Why, that money is not mine; M. de Cambyse has given me too much."

"Too much? What do you mean?" answered my grandmother, looking at Benjamin in amazement.

"Why, yes, too much, my sister, too much, do you understand? too much. He sends me one hundred and fifty francs for a twenty-franc operation: now do you understand?"

"And you are stupid enough to send him back his money? Well, I should like to see my husband play me such a trick as that."

"Yes, I have been stupid enough for that; what do you expect? Everybody cannot have the wit that you exact of Machecourt; I have been stupid enough for that, and I do not repent of it. I will not be a charlatan to please you. My God! my God! how difficult it is in this world to be an honest man! Your nearest and your dearest are sure to be the first to lead you into temptation."

"But you miserable fellow, you lack everything; you haven't a pair of silk stockings that are presentable, and while I mend your shirts on one side, they fall to pieces on the other."

"And because my shirts fall to pieces on one side while you mend them on the other, must I fail in probity, my dear sister?"

"But your creditors, when will you pay them?"

"When I have the money, that is all; I defy the richest man to do better."

"And the cloth merchant, what shall I tell him?"

"Tell him what you like. Tell him that I don't wear shirts, or that I have three hundred dozen in my closet; he will choose which of these reasons suits him best."

"Oh, my poor Benjamin!" said my grandmother, carrying off the linen, "with all your wit you will never be anything but a fool."

"In fact," said Page, when my grandmother was at the foot of the stairs, "your dear sister is right; you push probity to the point of stupidity."

My uncle rose with vivacity, and, grasping the lawyer's arm so firmly in his iron hand as to make him cry out with pain, he said:

"Page, this is not simply probity, it is noble and legitimate pride; it is respect not only for myself, but also for our poor oppressed class. Would you have me allow this country squire to say that he offered me a sort of *pourboire* and that I accepted it? Do you wish them to hurl back at us, when their escutcheon is only a beggar's badge, that charge of beggary which we have so often made against them? Would you have us give them the right to proclaim that we too receive alms when they are willing to bestow them upon us? Listen, Page, you know whether I love Burgundy; you know, too, from what my dear sister has just said, whether I need shirts; but for all the vineyards of Côte-d'Or and all the hemp-fields of Pays-Bas, I would not have a single face in the bailiwick in presence of which I must hang my head. No, I will not keep this money, though I needed it to purchase my life. It is for us, men of heart and education, to do honor to these people in the midst of whom we were born; they must learn through us that they do not need to be nobles in order to be men; that they may rise through self-esteem from the degradation into which they have fallen; and that they may say at last to the handful of tyrants who oppress them: 'We are as good as you are, and more numerous. Why should we continue to be your slaves, and why should you wish to remain our masters?' Oh, Page, may I live to see that day, if I have to drink sour wine all the rest of my life!"

"That is very fine," said Page, "but all that does not give us Burgundy."

"Rest easy, drunkard, you will lose nothing. Sunday I am going to give you all a luncheon, with these

twenty francs that I have taken from the throat of
M. de Cambyse, and at dessert I will tell you their
story. I am going to write directly to M. Minxit.
I cannot have Arthus, inasmuch as I have only twenty
francs to spend, or else he would have to dine copiously
that day. But if you meet Rapin, Parlanta, and the
others before I do, warn them not to make any other
engagements."

I must say at once that this luncheon was postponed
for a week because M. Minxit could not be there, and
then indefinitely abandoned because my uncle was
obliged to part with his two pistoles.

CHAPTER XII.

SEE how marvellously fertile are the flowers: they scatter their seeds about them like rain; they abandon them to the winds like dust; they send them without stint, like those alms that mount to dark garrets, to the peaks of desolate rocks, among the old stones of cracked walls, amid ruins that fall and hang, and they will find a handful of earth to fertilize them, a drop of rain for their roots to suck, and, after a ray of light to make them grow, another ray to paint them. The departing breezes of the spring carry away the last perfumes of the meadows, and the earth is strewn with fading leaves; but when the autumn breezes shall. pass, shaking their moist wings over the fields, another generation . of flowers will have invested the earth with a new robe, and their feeble perfume will be the last breath of the dying year, which in dying smiles on us still.

In all other respects, women are like flowers; but in the matter of fecundity they bear no resemblance to them. Most women, ladies especially,—and I pray you, *prolétaires* my friends and brothers, to believe that I use this expression only to conform to custom, for to me the truest lady is the woman who is most amiable and the prettiest,—ladies, I say, produce no longer; they become mothers of families as seldom as possible; they are barren for economy's sake. When the clerk's wife has had her little clerk and the notary's wife her little notary, they believe that they have fulfilled their obligation to the human race, and they abdicate. Napoleon, who was very fond of recruits for his armies, said that the woman whom he liked best was the woman who had the most children. Napoleon could very easily say this, having kingdoms instead of domains to give to his sons. The fact is that children are very expensive, and that this expense is not within the reach of everybody: the poor man alone can permit himself the luxury of a numerous family. Are you aware that the months required for the nursing of a child alone cost almost as much as a cashmere dress? Besides, the baby grows fast; then come the swollen accounts of the boarding-school proprietor and the bills of the shoemaker and the tailor; the infant of to-day to-morrow will be a man, his moustache begins to grow, and there he is a bachelor of letters. Then you know not what to do with him. To get rid of him you buy him a fine profession; but you are not slow in perceiving, from the drafts made on you from the four corners of the city, that this profession brings your professor nothing but invitations and visiting cards: you must keep him, till past the age of thirty, in kid gloves, Havana cigars, and mistresses. You will admit that that is very disagreeable. If there were a hospital for young people twenty years old, as there is or used to be for infants, I assure you that it would be crowded.

But in the century when my uncle Benjamin lived, things went differently: that was the golden age of nurses and of midwives. Women abandoned themselves to their instincts without concern and without forethought; they all had children, rich and poor alike, and even those who had no right to have them. But in those days they knew what to do with these children; competition, that ogress with the steel fangs which devours so many little people, had not yet arrived. There was a place for everybody in the beautiful sunshine of France, and in every profession there was plenty of elbow room. Places offered themselves, like fruit hanging from the branch, to men capable of filling them, and the fools themselves found situations, each according to the specialty of his foolishness; glory was as easily achieved, as accommodating a girl, as fortune; it did not take half the wit that is required now to be a man of letters, and with a dozen Alexandrines one was a poet. I do not say that I regret the loss of that blind fertility of the olden time, which produced like a machine without knowing what it did: I find that I have quite neighbors enough as it is; I simply wish to make you understand how it was that at the period of which I speak my grandmother, although she was not yet thirty years old, was already at her seventh child.

So my grandmother was at her seventh child. My uncle absolutely insisted that his dear sister should be present at his wedding, and he had made M. Minxit consent to postpone the marriage until after my grandmother's churching. The wardrobe of the new comer was all white and embroidered, and his entrance upon existence was expected daily. The six other children were all living, and delighted at being in the world. Sometimes they lacked one a pair of shoes, another a cap; now this one was out at the elbows, and now that one was out at the heels; but they had their white starched shirts, and on the whole got along marvellously and flourished in their rags.

My father, however, who was the eldest, was the best and most handsomely dressed of the six: that perhaps was due to the fact that his uncle Benjamin handed over to him his old knee-breeches, in which scarcely any change had to be made in order that Gaspard might wear them as pantaloons, and often no change at all. By the protection of cousin Guillaumot, who was sexton, he had been promoted to the dignity of choir boy, and, I say it with pride, he was one of the best choir boys in the diocese. If he had persisted in the career that cousin Guillaumot had opened for him, instead of the handsome captain of a fire company that he is to-day, he would have made a magnificent priest. It is true that I should still be sleeping in the void, as says the good M. de Lamartine, who sleeps himself sometimes; but sleep is an excellent thing, and besides, to live to be the editor of a country newspaper and the rival of the department of public wit,— is that really worth living for?

However that may be, my father owed to his Levitical functions the advantage of having a superb sky-blue coat. This is how that good fortune came to him: the banner of Saint Martin, patron saint of Clamecy, had been dismissed; my grandmother, with that eagle-eye of hers, had discovered in this holy stuff the wherewithal to make her eldest son a jacket and a pair of pantaloons, and she had succeeded in securing the cast-off banner from the vestrymen at a ridiculous price. The saint was painted in the very middle; the artist had represented him in the act of cutting off a piece of his cloak with his sabre to cover the nakedness of a beggar; but this was not a serious obstacle to my grandmother's plan. She simply turned the material, so that Saint Martin came on the inside, which for that matter was quite immaterial to the saint.

The coat had been finished by a seamstress in the Rue des Moulins: it would have fitted my uncle Benjamin perhaps quite as well as my father; but my grandmother had had it made in such a way that, after having been worn out the first time by the eldest son, it could be worn out a second time by the second son. At first my father strutted about in his sky-blue coat; I even believe that he contributed out of his salary to pay for the making. But he was not slow in finding out that a magnificent garment is often like hair-cloth. Benjamin, to whom nothing was sacred, had nicknamed him the patron saint of Clamecy. This nickname the children had picked up, and it had cost my father many blows. More than once did it happen to him to come home with a piece of the sky-blue coat in his pocket. Saint Martin had become his personal enemy. Often you could have seen him at the foot of the altar plunged in gloomy meditation. Now, of what was he dreaming? Of some way of getting rid of his coat; and one day, to the *Dominus vobiscum* of the officiating clergyman, he responded, thinking that he was talking to his mother: "I tell you that I will never wear your sky-blue coat again."

My father was in this state of mind when, on the Sunday after high mass, my uncle, having to pay a visit to Val-des-Rosiers, proposed to him to accompany him. Gaspard, who preferred playing quoits in the street to

serving as an aid to my uncle, answered that he could
not, because he had a baptism to attend.

"That doesn't hinder," said Benjamin; "another will
serve in your place."

"Yes, but I must go to catechism at one o'clock."

"I thought that you had made your first com-
munion."

"It is true I came very near making it, but you prevented me by forcing me to get drunk the night before
the ceremony."

"And why did you get drunk?"

"Because you were drunk yourself, and threatened
to beat me with the flat of your sword if I did not get
drunk too."

"I was wrong," said Benjamin, "but all the same
you risk nothing by coming with me; we shall not be
long; we shall return before the catechism hour."

"Indeed!" answered Gaspard; "where another would
take only an hour, you need half a day. You stop at
all the taverns; and the priest has forbidden me to go
with you because you set me bad examples."

"Well, pious Gaspard, if you refuse to come with
me, I will not invite you to my wedding; if, on the
contrary, you grant me this favor, I will give you
twelve sous."

"Give them to me now," said Gaspard.

"And why do you wish them now, you scamp? Do
you distrust my word?"

"No, but I am not anxious to be your creditor. I
have heard it said in the village that you pay nobody,
and that they do not wish to seize your effects because
your possessions are not worth thirty sous."

" Well said, Gaspard ! " said my uncle ; " here, there
are fifteen sous, and go tell my dear sister that you are
going with me."

My grandmother went clear to the threshold to advise Gaspard to be very careful of his coat, for, she said,
he must keep it for his uncle's wedding.

" Are you joking?" said Benjamin; " is there any
need of recommending a French choir boy to be careful of the banner of his patron saint?"

" Uncle," said Gaspard, "before we start I warn you
of one thing,— that, if you call me again banner-bearer,
blue bird, or patron saint of Clamecy, I will run away
with your fifteen sous, and come back to play quoits."

On entering the village my uncle met M. Susurrans,
the grocer, very short and very thin, but made, like
gun-powder, out of charcoal and saltpetre. M. Susurrans had a sort of small farm at Val-des-Rosiers; he
was on his way back to Clamecy, carrying under his
arm a keg that he hoped to smuggle in, and at the
end of his cane a pair of capons which Madame Susurrans was waiting for to put on the spit. M. Susurrans knew my uncle and esteemed him, for Benjamin
bought of him the sugar with which he sweetened his
drugs and the powder that he put on his cue. So M.
Susurrans proposed to him to come to the farm to re-
fresh himself. My uncle, to whom thirst was a normal
condition, accepted without ceremony. The grocer and
his customer established themselves at the corner of
the fire, each on a stool; they placed the keg between them; but they did not allow its contents to
turn sour, and when it was not in the hands of one, it
was at the lips of the other.

"Appetite comes by drinking as well as by eating; suppose we eat the chickens," said M. Susurrans.

"In fact," answered my uncle, "that will save you the trouble of carrying them home, and I do not understand how you undertook to load yourself down with such a burden."

"And with what sauce shall we eat them?"

"With that which is quickest made," said Benjamin, "and here is an excellent fire with which to roast them."

"Yes," said M. Susurrans, "but there are no kitchen utensils here save those that are necessary to make an onion soup: we have no spit."

Benjamin, like all great men, was never taken unawares.

"It shall not be said," he answered, "that two men of wit like ourselves were unable to eat a roasted fowl for want of a spit. If you say so, we will spit our chickens on the blade of my sword, and Gaspard here will turn them before the fire."

You would never have thought of this expedient, friendly reader, but my uncle had imagination enough for ten novelists of our day.

Gaspard, who did not often have a chance to eat chicken, went joyfully to work, and in an hour's time the fowls were roasted to a turn. They turned a washtub upside-down, and dragged it up to the fire; on this they placed the plates, knives, and forks, and thus, without leaving their seats, the guests were at table. Glasses were lacking; but the keg was not long left still; they drank out of the bunghole, as in the days of Homer; it was not very convenient, but such was the stoic character of my uncle that he would rather drink good wine thus than sour wine out of crystal glasses. In spite of the difficulties of all sorts which the operation involved, the chickens were soon despatched. For some time the unfortunate birds had been nothing more than stripped carcasses, and still the two friends kept on drinking. M. Susurrans, who was, as we have said, a very small man, whose stomach and brain almost touched each other, was as drunk as well could be; but Benjamin, the great Benjamin, had preserved the major part of his reason, and looked with pity on his weaker adversary; as for Gaspard, to whom they had occasionally passed the keg, he went a little beyond the limits of temperance; filial respect does not allow me to use any other expression.

Such was the moral situation of the guests when they left the wash-tub. It was then four o'clock, and they began to get ready to start. M. Susurrans, who remembered very well that he was to carry some chickens to his wife, looked about for them to place them on the end of his cane; he asked my uncle if he had not seen them.

"Your chickens," said Benjamin; "are you joking? You have just eaten them."

"Yes, you old fool," added Gaspard, "you have eaten them; they were spitted on my uncle's sword, and I turned the spit."

"It is not true," cried M. Susurrans, "for, if I had eaten my chickens, I should not be hungry, and I have appetite enough to devour a wolf."

"I do not deny it," responded my uncle, "but it is none the less true that you have eaten your chickens.

See, if you doubt it, there are the two carcasses ; you can hang them to the end of your cane if you like."

"You are lying, Benjamin ; I do not recognize those as the carcasses of my chickens ; you have taken them from me, and you shall return them to me."

"Very well," said my uncle, "send to my house for them to-morrow, and I will return them to you."

"You shall return them to me directly," said M. Susurrans, rising on tip-toe to grasp my uncle by the throat.

"Ah, there! papa Susurrans!" said Benjamin ; "if you are joking, I warn you that this is carrying the joke too far, and " . . .

"No, you miserable fellow, I am not joking," said M. Susurrans, placing himself in front of the door, "and you shall not leave here, neither you nor your nephew, until you have restored my chickens."

"Uncle," said Gaspard, "would you like me to trip up this old imbecile ?"

"It is useless, Gaspard, useless, my friend," said Benjamin ; "besides, you are a churchman, and it does not become you to intervene in a quarrel. Say there!" he added, "once, twice, M. Susurrans, will you let us go out ?"

"When you have restored my chickens," answered M. Susurrans, making a half turn to the left and presenting the end of his cane at my uncle as if it had been a bayonet.

Benjamin lowered the cane with his hand, and, taking the little man by the middle of the body, he hung him by the waistband to a piece of iron over the door which was used to hang kitchen utensils upon.

Susurrans, thus likened to a saucepan, kicked about like a beetle pinned to a curtain. He screamed and gesticulated, crying now "Fire!" now "Murder!"

My uncle caught sight of a Liège almanac which was lying on the mantel-shelf. Said he:

"Stay, Monsieur Susurrans; study, writes Cicero, is a consolation in all situations of life: amuse yourself in studying until some one comes to take you down; for I have no time to carry on a conversation with you, and I have the honor to wish you good evening."

My uncle had gone only twenty steps when he met the farmer running up, who asked him why his master was crying "Fire!" and "Murder!"

"Probably because the house is burning and someone is killing your master," answered my uncle, tranquilly; and, whistling to Gaspard, who was lingering in the rear, he continued on his way.

The weather had grown milder. The sky, so bright but a little while before, had become a dull and dirty white, like a gypsum ceiling before it is dry. A fine, thick, piercing rain was falling, streaming in little drops along the stripped branches, and making the trees and bushes weep.

My uncle's hat drank in this rain like a sponge, and soon its two corners became two spouts from which black water poured upon his shoulders. Benjamin, anxious about his coat, turned it inside out, and, remembering his sister's injunction, he ordered Gaspard to do the same. The latter, forgetting Saint Martin, conformed to my uncle's command.

A little distance farther on, Benjamin and Gaspard met a troop of peasants returning from vespers. At sight of the saint on Gaspard's coat, with his head down and his horse with all four feet in the air, as if he had fallen from the sky, the rustics first burst into loud shouts of laughter, and then their laughter turned to hisses. You know my uncle well enough to believe that he would not allow such a crowd to make sport of him with impunity. He drew his sword; Gaspard, on his side, armed himself with stones, and, carried away by his ardor, led the attack. My uncle then saw that Saint Martin was the only party wronged in this affair, and he was seized with such a desire to laugh that he was obliged to rest on his sword to keep from falling.

"Gaspard," he shouted, in a choking voice, "patron saint of Clamecy, your saint is upside down, your saint's helmet is falling off."

Gaspard, understanding that he was the object of all this mirth, could not endure this humiliation; he took off his coat, threw it on the ground, and trampled on it with his feet. When my uncle had finished laughing, he tried to force him to pick it up and put it on again: but Gaspard ran away across the fields, and was seen no more. Benjamin pitifully picked up the coat and put it on the end of his sword. In the meantime M. Susurrans came up. He had sobered off a little, and remembered very distinctly that he had eaten his chickens; but he had lost his three-cornered hat. Benjamin, who was much amused at the little man's vivacity, and who wished, as we professors say, people of evil associations and low tone, to get him a little rattled, maintained that he had eaten his hat; but Benjamin's muscular strength had impressed itself so forcibly upon Susurrans that he squarely refused to take offence; he even pushed his obstinacy to the point of making apologies to my uncle.

Benjamin and M. Susurrans returned to Clamecy together. Toward the middle of the faubourg they met lawyer Page.

"Where are you going?" said the latter to my uncle.

"Why, you must see for yourself; I am going to my dear sister's to dine."

"Not at all," said Page; "you are going to dine with me at the Hotel du Dauphin."

"And if I accept, to what circumstance shall I owe this advantage?"

"I will explain that to you in a word. A wealthy wood merchant of Paris, for whom I have won an important case, has invited me to dine with his attorney, whom he does not know. We are in the midst of the carnival; I have decided that you shall be his attorney, and I was on my way to notify you. It is an adventure worthy of us, Benjamin, and I undoubtedly have not presumed too much upon your genius in hoping that you would play a part in it."

"It is, indeed," said Benjamin, "a well-conceived masquerade. But I do not know," he added, laughing, "whether honor and delicacy will permit me to play the part of the attorney."

"At table," said Page, "the most honest man is the man who most conscientiously empties his glass."

"Yes, but suppose your wood merchant should talk to me about his case?"

"I will answer for you."

"And suppose to-morrow he should take it into his head to pay a visit to his attorney?"

"It is to you that I will take him."

"That's all very well, but I haven't an attorney's phiz; at least I so flatter myself."

"You shall assume it; you have already succeeded in passing yourself off for the Wandering Jew."

"And my red coat?"

"Our man is an idler from Paris; we will make him believe that in the provinces a red coat is a part of an attorney's insignia."

"And my sword?"

"If he notices it, you will tell him that you cut your pens with that."

"But who then is your wood merchant's attorney?"

"Dulciter. Would you be so inhuman as to let me dine with Dulciter?"

"I know very well that Dulciter is not amusing; but, if he should know that I had dined in his place, he would sue me for damages."

"I will plead your cause; come, I am sure that dinner is ready; but, by the way, our host urged me to bring with me Dulciter's head clerk: where the devil am I to find a clerk for Dulciter?"

Benjamin burst into a mad laugh.

"Oh!" he shouted, clapping his hands, "I have it! Stay," he added, putting his hand on the shoulder of M. Susurrans, "here is your clerk."

"Oh, fie!" said Page, "a grocer?"

"What difference does that make?"

"He smells of cheese."

"You are not an epicure, Page; he smells of candles."

"But he is sixty years old."

"We will introduce him as the Nestor of the corporation."

"You are rogues and good-for-nothings," said M. Susurrans, his impetuous character coming to the front again; "I am not a bandit, nor a frequenter of wine-shops."

"No," interrupted my uncle; "he gets drunk alone in his cellar."

"Possibly, Monsieur Rathery, but at any rate I do not get drunk at the expense of others, and I will not take part in your filibustering projects."

"But you must at any rate," said my uncle, "take part this evening; otherwise I will tell everybody where I hung you."

"And where then did you hang him?" said Page.

"Imagine," said Benjamin . . .

"Monsieur Rathery," cried Susurrans, putting a finger over his mouth.

"Well, do you consent to come with us?"

"Why, Monsieur Rathery, consider that my wife is waiting for me; they will think me dead, murdered; they will institute a search for me on the road to Valdes-Rosiers."

"So much the better; perhaps they will find your three-cornered hat."

"Monsieur Rathery, my good Monsieur Rathery!" exclaimed Susurrans, clasping his hands.

"Well, then," said my uncle, "don't be childish! You owe me a reparation, and I owe you a dinner; at one stroke we shall cancel our mutual obligations."

"At least let me go tell my wife."

"No," said Benjamin, placing himself between him

and Page; "I know Madame Susurrans from having seen her at her counter. She would put you under lock and key, and I do not wish you to escape us: I would not give you for ten pistoles."

"And my keg," said Susurrans, "what am I going to do with that now that I am an attorney's clerk?"

"It is true," said Benjamin, "you cannot present yourself at our client's with a keg."

They were then in the middle of the Beuvron bridge; my uncle took the keg from the hands of Susurrans and threw it into the river.

"Rascal of a Rathery! knave of a Rathery!" cried Susurrans; "you shall pay me for my keg; it cost me six francs; but you shall know what it will cost you."

"M. Susurrans," said Benjamin, assuming a majestic attitude, "let us imitate the sage who said: *Omnia mecum porto;* that is, everything that hinders me I throw into the river. See, there at the end of this sword is a magnificent coat, my nephew's Sunday coat; a coat which might figure in a museum, and which cost for the making alone thirty times as much as your miserable keg. Well, I sacrifice it without the slightest regret; throw it over the bridge, and we shall be quits."

As M. Susurrans was unwilling to do anything of the kind, Benjamin threw the coat over the bridge, and, taking Page's arm and that of Susurrans, he said:

"Now let us be off; they can raise the curtain; we are ready to go upon the stage."

But man proposes and God disposes. As they were going up the steps of Vieille-Rome, they met Madame Susurrans face to face. Not seeing her husband return, she had started out to meet him with a lantern. When she saw him between my uncle and lawyer Page, both of whom had a suspicious reputation, her anxiety gave place to anger.

"At last, Monsieur, here you are!" she cried; "it is really fortunate; I began to think that you were not coming home to-night; you are leading a pretty life, and setting a fine example to your son."

Then, surveying her husband with a rapid glance, she saw how incomplete he was.

"And your chickens, Monsieur! and your hat, wretch! and your keg, drunkard! What have you done with them?"

"Madame," responded Benjamin, gravely, "we have eaten the chickens; as for the three-cornered hat, he has had the misfortune to lose it in the road."

"What! the monster has lost his three-cornered hat! a three-cornered hat that had just been done over!"

"Yes, Madame, he has lost it, and you are very fortunate, considering the position which he occupied, that he did not lose his wig as well; as for the keg, the customs officials seized it, and they have reported the offence."

As Page could not help laughing, Mme. Susurrans said:

"I see how it is; you have debauched my husband, and you are laughing at us besides. You would be in much better business attending to your patients and paying your debts, Monsieur Rathery."

"Do I owe you anything, Madame?" replied my uncle, proudly.

"Yes, my dear," broke in Susurrans, feeling strong under his wife's protection, "he debauched me; he and his nephew ate my chickens; they took my three-cornered hat and threw my keg into the river; he tried also, infamous man that he is, to force me to go to dine with him at the Dauphin and to play at my age the part of an attorney's clerk."

"Away, base man! I am going at once to warn M. Dulciter that you intend to dine in his place and in that of his clerk."

"You see, Madame," said my uncle, "that your husband is drunk and doesn't know what he is talking about; if you take my advice, you will put him to bed as soon as you reach the house, and give him every two hours a decoction of camomile and lime-tree flowers: while holding him up, I had occasion to feel his pulse, and I assure you that he is not at all well."

"Oh! you rascal! Oh! you knave! Oh! you revolutionist! You dare to tell my wife that I am sick from having drunk too much, whereas it is you who are drunk! Wait, I am going to Dulciter's at once, and you will hear from him directly."

"You must see, Madame," said Page, with the utmost sang-froid, "that this man is talking wildly: you would be false to all your wifely duties if you should not make your husband take camomile and lime-tree flowers, according to the prescription of M. Rathery, who is surely the most skilful doctor in the bailiwick, and who answers this madman's insults by saving his life."

Susurrans was about to renew his curses.

"Come," his wife said to him, "I see that these gentlemen are right: you are so drunk that you cannot talk; follow me directly, or I will lock you out, and you will sleep wherever you can."

"That's right," said Page and my uncle together, and they were still laughing when they reached the door of the Dauphin. The first person whom they met in the yard was M. Minxit, who was mounting his horse to return to Corvol.

"Stay," said my uncle, seizing his horse's bridle, "you shall not leave here to-night, Monsieur Minxit; you are going to sup with us; we have lost one guest, but you are worth thirty of him."

"If that will please you, Benjamin . . . Hostler, take my horse back to the stable, and tell them to prepare a bed for me."

CHAPTER XIII.

HOW MY UNCLE SPENT THE NIGHT IN PRAYER FOR HIS SISTER'S SAFE DELIVERY.

My time is precious, dear readers, and I suppose that yours is no less so; I shall not amuse myself therefore in describing to you this memorable supper; you know the guests well enough to form an idea of the way in which they supped. My uncle left the Hotel du Dauphin at midnight, advancing three steps and retiring two, like certain pilgrims of former times who vowed to go to Jerusalem by that method. On entering the house, he saw a light in Machecourt's chamber; and, supposing that his brother-in-law was scribbling off some writ, he went in with the intention of bidding him good-night. My grandmother was in the pains of child-birth; the midwife, frightened at my uncle's unexpected appearance at this hour, came to officially notify him of the event that was about to take place. Benjamin remembered, through the mists that obscured his brain, that his sister, during the first year of her marriage, had had a very painful delivery which endangered her life: immediately he melted into two tear-spouts.

" Alas!" he cried, in a voice loud enough to waken the entire Rue des Moulins, "my dear sister is going to die; alas! she is going " . . .

" Madame Lalande," cried my grandmother from her bed, "put that dog of a drunkard out doors."

"Retire, Monsieur Rathery," said Madame Lalande, "there is not the slightest danger; the child presents itself by the shoulders, and in an hour your sister will be delivered."

But Benjamin still cried: "Alas! my dear sister is going to die."

Machecourt, seeing that the midwife's remarks had no effect, thought it his duty to intervene.

"Yes, Benjamin, my friend, my good brother, the child presents itself by the shoulders; do me the favor to go to bed, I beg of you."

So spoke my grandfather.

"And you, Machecourt, my friend, my good brother," answered my uncle, "I beg of you, do me the favor to go" . . .

My grandmother, seeing that she could not count on Machecourt to take any decisive step with Benjamin, decided to put him out doors herself.

With lamblike docility my uncle suffered himself to be pushed outside. His mind was soon made up: he decided to go sleep beside Page, who was snoring like a blacksmith's bellows on one of the tables at the Dauphin. But, as he was passing by the church, the idea occurred to him to pray to God for his dear sister's safe delivery; now the weather had grown very cold again, and the temperature was several degrees below freezing. Notwithstanding this, Benjamin knelt on the steps of the church-front, joined his hands as he had seen them do at his dear sister's, and began to mumble some bits of prayer. As he was beginning his second *Ave*, sleep took possession of him, and he began to snore like his friend Page. The next morning at five o'clock,

when the sexton came to ring the "Angelus," he saw
something kneeling like a human form. At first he
imagined in his simplicity that some saint had left his
niche to do penance, and he began to get ready to take
him back into the church; but, on coming closer, the
light of his lantern enabled him to recognize my uncle,
who had an inch of frost on his back and an icicle on
the end of his nose half an ell in length.

"Hello, Monsieur Rathery! Hello!" he shouted in
Benjamin's ear.

As my uncle did not answer, he went calmly to ring
his "Angelus," and, when he had finished and well
finished, he came back to M. Rathery. In case that he
might not be dead, he took him on his shoulders like a
sack and carried him to his sister's. My grandmother
had been delivered two good hours; the neighbors who
had spent the night by her side transferred their cares
to Benjamin. They placed him on a mattress before
the fire, wrapped him in warm towels and blankets, and
placed a hot brick at his feet; in the excess of their
zeal, they would willingly have put him in the oven.
My uncle thawed out gradually; his cue, which was as
stiff as his sword, began to weep on the bolster, his
joints relaxed, the power of speech returned to him, and
the first use that he made of it was to call for hot wine.
They quickly made him a kettleful; when he had
drunk half of it, he was taken with such a sweat that
they thought he was going to liquefy. He swallowed
the rest, went to sleep, and at eight o'clock in the morning was as well as anybody. If the priest had made an
official report of these facts, my uncle would surely have
been canonized. They probably would have given him

to the tavern-keepers for their patron saint; and it may be said, without flattering him, that, with his cue and his red coat, he would have made a magnificent tavern-sign.

More than a week had passed since my grandmother's safe delivery, and already she was thinking of her churching. This sort of quarantine imposed by the canons of the church involved serious inconveniences to her in particular and to the whole family in general. In the first place, when any rather striking event — some bit of scandal, for instance — ruffled the smooth surface of the neighborhood, she could not go to gossip with her neighbor in the Rue des Moulins, which to her was a cruel privation; further, she was obliged to send Gaspard to the market and the butcher's, wrapped in a kitchen-apron. Now, when Gaspard lost the dinner-money playing quoits, or when he brought home a scrag of mutton instead of a leg, or when, on being sent to get a cabbage to put in the kettle, he did not return until after the soup was done, Benjamin laughed, Mache-court swore, and my grandmother whipped Gaspard.

"Why," said my grandfather one day, irritated at being obliged, in consequence of Gaspard's absence, to eat a calf's head without shallots, "do you not do your work yourself?"

"Why! Why!" replied my grandmother; "because I cannot go to mass without paying Mme. Lalande."

"Why the devil, then, dear sister," said Benjamin, "did you not wait till you had some money before giving birth to your child?"

"Ask rather your imbecile brother-in-law why he has not brought me six francs for a month."

"So then," said Benjamin, "if you were to go six months without receiving money, for six months you would remain shut up in your house as in a lazaretto?"

"Yes," replied my grandmother, "because if I should go out before I had been to mass, the priest would denounce me from the pulpit and the people would point their fingers at me in the streets."

"In that case you should call on the priest to send you his housekeeper to perform your household duties; for God is too just to require Machecourt to eat calf's head without shallots simply because you have given him a seventh child."

Happily the six francs so impatiently awaited arrived accompanied by a few others, and my grandmother was able to go to mass.

On re-entering the house with Mme. Lalande, she found my uncle stretched out in Machecourt's leather arm-chair, his heels resting on the andirons and a porringer full of hot wine in front of him; for I must tell you that, since his convalescence, Benjamin, grateful to the hot wine that had saved his life, took enough of it every morning to satisfy two naval officers. To justify this tremendous extra allowance, he said that his temperature was still below zero.

"Benjamin," said my grandmother, "I have a service to ask of you."

"A service!" answered Benjamin, "and what can I do, dear sister, to be agreeable to you?"

"You ought to be able to guess, Benjamin; you must stand godfather to my last child."

Benjamin, who had guessed nothing at all, and whom this proposition took entirely unawares, shook his head and uttered a big: "But" . . .

"What!" said my grandmother, looking at him with flashing eyes, "is it possible that you would refuse me that?"

"No, dear sister, quite the contrary, but" . . .

"But what? You begin to make me impatient with your buts."

"Well, you see, I have never been a godfather, and I should not know how to perform my functions."

"Fine difficulty, that! You will be told what to do; I will ask cousin Guillaumot to give you some lessons."

"I doubt neither the talent nor the zeal of cousin Guillaumot; but, if it is necessary for me to take lessons in the science of being a godfather, I fear that this study is not suited to my style of intelligence; perhaps you would do better to take a well-informed godfather at the start; Gaspard, for instance, who is a choir boy, would suit you perfectly."

"Come, Monsieur Rathery," said Madame Lalande, "you must accept your sister's invitation; it is a family duty from which you cannot be exempted."

"I see how it is, Madame Lalande," said Benjamin; "although I am not rich, I have the reputation of doing things well, and you would as willingly deal with me as with Gaspard, isn't that it?"

"Oh, fie! Benjamin. Oh, fie! Monsieur Rathery," exclaimed my grandmother and Madame Lalande together.

"See, my dear sister," continued Benjamin, "to be frank with you, I am not anxious to be a godfather. I am very willing to behave toward my nephew as if I had held him over the baptismal fonts; I will listen with satisfaction to the compliment that he shall ad-

dress me every year on my birthday, and, though it
should be in the style of Millot-Rataut, I promise to
think it charming. I will permit him to kiss me every
New Year's Day, and I will give him for his present
a punchinello that goes with a spring or a pair of
breeches, just as you prefer. I will even feel flattered
if you name him Benjamin. But to go plant myself
like a big imbecile in front of the baptismal fonts, with
a candle in my hand, oh, no, dear sister, do not ask that
of me; my manly dignity is opposed to it; I should be
afraid that Djhiarcos would laugh in my face. And
besides, how can I declare that the squalling young one
renounces Satan and his works? Do I know whether
he renounces Satan and his works? What proves to
me that he renounces the works of Satan? If the
responsibility of a godfather is only a sham, as some
think, of what use is a godfather, of what use is a god-
mother, of what use are two securities instead of one,
and why have my signature indorsed by another? If,
on the contrary, this responsibility is serious, why
should I incur the consequences? Our soul being the
most precious thing that we have, must not one be
mad to put it in pawn for that of another? And
besides, what makes you in such a hurry to have your
infant baptized? Is it a terrine of *foie gras* or a May-
ence ham which would spoil if it were not salted at
once? Wait until he is twenty-five; then at least he
will be able to answer for himself, and, if he needs a
security, I shall know what I have to do. Until he is
eighteen, your son will not be able to enlist in the
army; until he is twenty-one, he will not be able to
make a civil contract; until he is twenty-five, he will

not be able to marry without your consent and Machecourt's; and yet you expect him at the age of nine days to have sufficient discrimination to choose a religion. Nonsense! you can see for yourself that that is not reasonable."

"Oh, my dear lady," cried the nurse, frightened at my uncle's heterodox logic, "your brother is one of the damned. Take good care not to let him stand godfather to your child; it would bring misfortune."

"Madame Lalande," said Benjamin, in a severe tone, "a course in midwifery is not a course in logic. It would be cowardly on my part to discuss with you; I will content myself with asking you whether Saint John baptized in the Jordan, in consideration of a sesterce and a cornet of dried dates, the neophytes brought him from Jerusalem on their nurses' arms."

"Indeed!" said Madame Lalande, embarrassed by the objection, "I would rather believe it than go there to see."

"What, Madame, you would rather believe it than go there to see! Is that the proper language for a midwife well-informed in her religion? Well, since you take that air, I will do myself the honor to confront you with this dilemma" . . .

"Let us alone with your dilemmas," interrupted my grandmother; "does Madame Lalande know what a dilemma is?"

"What, Madame!" exclaimed the nurse, piqued at my grandmother's observation, "I do not know what a dilemma is? I, the wife of a surgeon, do not know what a dilemma is? Go on, Monsieur Rathery, I am listening to you."

"It is entirely useless," replied my grandmother, dryly; "I have decided that Benjamin shall be godfather, and godfather he shall be; there is no dilemma in the world that can exempt him from it."

"I appeal to Machecourt," cried Benjamin.

"Machecourt has condemned you in advance: he went this morning to Corvol to invite Mlle. Minxit to be godmother."

"So then," cried my uncle, "they dispose of me without my consent; they have not even the honesty to forewarn me. Do they take me for a stuffed man, for a gingerbread man? A fine figure I shall cut with my five feet nine inches beside the five feet three inches of Mlle. Minxit, who, with her flat and calibrated figure, will look like a greased Maypole crowned with ribbons. Do you know that the idea of going to church side by side with her has tormented me for the last six months, and that the repugnance excited in me by this disagreeable duty has almost made me renounce the advantage of becoming her husband?"

"Do you see, Madame Lalande," said my grandmother, "how facetious this Benjamin is? He loves Mlle. Minxit passionately, and yet he must laugh at her."

"Hum!" said the nurse.

Benjamin, who had forgotten Madame Lalande, saw that he had been guilty of a *lapsus linguæ;* to escape his sister's reproaches, he hastened to declare that he consented to anything that they might require of him, and ran away before the nurse had gone.

The baptism was to take place the following Sunday; my grandmother had dressed herself especially for the

ceremony; she had authorized Machecourt to invite all
his friends and those of my uncle to a solemn dinner.
As for Benjamin, he was in a position to meet the expense that the magnificent *rôle* of godfather called for:
he had just received from the government a present of
a hundred francs for the zeal which he had displayed in
propagating inoculation in the country, and in rehabili-
tating the potato, attacked at once by the agriculturists
and the physicians. '

CHAPTER XIV.

ON the following Saturday, the day before the baptismal ceremony, my uncle was cited to appear before the bailiff to hear himself sentenced under penalty of imprisonment to pay Monsieur Bonteint the sum of one hundred and fifty francs ten sous six deniers for merchandise sold to him; so it was expressed in the summons, the cost of which was four francs five sous. Any other than my uncle would have deplored his fate in all the tones of elegy; but the soul of this great man was inaccessible to the buffets of fortune. The whirlwind of misery which society raises about itself, the vapor of tears in which it is enveloped, could not rise to his height; his body was down deep in the mire of humanity: when he had drunk too much, he had a headache; when he had walked too far, he was tired; when the road was muddy, he splashed himself up to his neck; and, when he had no money to pay his score, the inn-keeper charged it on his ledger; but, like the rock whose base is beaten by the waves and whose brow is radiant in the sunlight, like the bird which has its nest in the thickets by the wayside and lives amid the azure of the skies, his soul soared in an upper region, always calm and serene; he had but two needs, — the satisfaction of hunger and thirst, — and, if the firmament had fallen in pieces upon the earth, and had left one bottle intact, my uncle would have calmly emptied it to the resurrection of the crushed human race, standing on a smoking fragment of some star. To him the past was nothing, and the future was nothing as yet. He compared the past to an empty bottle, and the future to a chicken ready for the spit.

"What care I," said he, "what sort of liquor the bottle contained? And as for the chicken, why should I roast myself in turning it round and round before the fire? Perhaps when it is cooked to a turn, when the table is laid, and when I have put my napkin on, some dog will come along and carry away the smoking fowl between his teeth.

> 'Éternité, néant, bassé, sombres abimes!'

cries the poet; for my part, all that I should try to save from the gloomy abyss would be my last red coat if it floated within my reach; life is entirely in the present, and the present is the passing moment; now, what to me is the happiness or the sorrow of a moment? Here is a beggar and there a millionaire; God says to them: 'You have but a minute to remain upon earth'; this minute gone, he grants them a second, then a third, and makes them live on thus to the age of ninety years. Do you think that one is really happier than the other? Man himself is the artisan of all the miseries that afflict him; the pleasures which he contrives are not worth a quarter of the trouble that he takes to acquire them. He is like a hunter who scours the country all day long for an emaciated hare or a partridge's body. We boast of the superiority of our intelligence, but what matters it that we can measure the course of the stars, that we can tell almost to a second at what hour the moon will pass between the earth and the sun, that we can traverse the solitudes of the ocean with wooden boats or hempen sails, if we do not know how to enjoy the blessings which God has placed in our existence. The animals whom we insult with the name of brutes know how to take life much better than we do. The ass rolls about in the grass and eats it, without troubling himself about whether it will grow again; the bear does not go to guard a farmer's flocks in order to have mittens and a fur cap in the winter; the hare does not become the drummer of a regiment in the hope of laying up provisions for his old age; the vulture does not seek a position as a letter-carrier in order to wear a beautiful gold necklace around its bare neck: all are content with what nature has given them, with the bed which she has prepared for them in the grass of the forests, with the roof which she has made for them with the stars and the azure of the firmament.

"As soon as a ray lights on the plain, the bird begins to twitter on its branch, the insect hums around the bushes, the fish leaps to the surface of its pool, the lizard lounges on the warm stones of the ruin it inhabits; if some shower falls from the clouds, each takes refuge in its asylum and sleeps there peacefully while waiting for the morrow's sun. Why does not man do likewise?

"May it not displease the great King Solomon, the ant is the stupidest of animals: instead of enjoying itself during the fine weather in the fields, and getting its share of that magnificent festival which heaven for the space of six months gives the earth, it wastes all its summer in piling one upon another little scraps of leaves; then, when its city is finished, a passing wind sweeps it away with its wing."

So Benjamin got Bonteint's process-server drunk and used the stamped paper of the summons to wrap some ointment in.

The bailiff before whom my uncle was to appear was so important a personage that I must not neglect to give you his portrait. Besides, my grandfather on his death-bed expressly urged me to do so, and for nothing in the world would I fail in this pious duty.

The bailiff, then, was born, like so many others, of poor parents. His first swaddling-clothes were cut out of a *gendarme's* old cloak, and he began his studies in jurisprudence by cleaning his father's big sword and currying his red horse. I cannot explain to you how, from the lowest rank of the judicial hierarchy, the bailiff rose to the highest judicial position in the neighborhood; all that I can tell you is that the lizard as well as the eagle reaches the peaks of the high rocks.

Among other fancies the bailiff had a mania for being a grand personage. The inferiority of his origin was his despair. He could not conceive how it was that a man like himself was not born a gentleman. He attributed it to an error of the Creator. He would have given his wife, his children, and his clerk for the tiniest coat of arms. Nature had been to the bailiff a good mother enough; in truth, she had given him his share of intelligence, neither too much nor too little, but she had added to this a large dose of craft and audacity. The bailiff was neither stupid nor witty. He lingered on the borderland of the two camps: with this differ-

ence, however,— that he had never set foot in that of
the people of wit, whereas he had made frequent excur-
sions into the easy and open territory of the other.
Unable to have the wit of bright men, the bailiff had
contented himself with that of fools: he made puns.
The lawyers and their wives made it a duty to consider
these puns very funny; his clerk was charged with
spreading them among the people, and even with ex-
plaining them to those dull minds which at first failed
to understand their meaning. Thanks to this agreeable
social talent, the bailiff had acquired in a certain circle
a reputation as a man of wit; but my uncle said that
he purchased this reputation with counterfeit coin.

Was the bailiff an honest man? I would not dare to
say the contrary. You know the Code defines robbers,
and society regards as honest people all those who are
outside the definition; now, the bailiff was not defined
by the Code. The bailiff, by dint of intrigue, had succeeded in managing, not only the business, but also the
pleasures of the town. As a magistrate, the bailiff was
a personage not to be highly recommended; he understood the law very well, but, when it went against his
hatreds or his sympathies, he interpreted it to suit him
self. It was charged that one scale of his balance was
gold and the other wood, and, in fact, I know not how
it happened, but his friends were always right and his
enemies always wrong. If they were arraigned for an
offence, the latter incurred the highest penalty of the
law; if he could have added to it, he would have done
so with a good heart. Nevertheless the law cannot always bend: when the bailiff found himself under the
necessity of passing sentence upon a man whom he

feared or from whom he hoped something, he got out of the affair by declining to sit, and thus his impartiality was a boast among his *coterie*. The bailiff aimed at universal admiration: he cordially, but secretly, detested those who obscured him by any superiority whatever. If you pretended to believe in his importance, if you applied to him for protection, you made him the happiest man in the world; but, if you refused to take off your hat to him, this insult buried itself deeply in his memory, and made a wound there, and, if you had lived a hundred years and he also, never would he have forgiven you. So it went hard with the unfortunate fellow who abstained from saluting the bailiff. If any affair brought him before his tribunal, he excited him by some well-planned outrage to fail in respect. Then vengeance became to him a duty, and he put our man in prison, while deploring the fatal necessity which his functions imposed upon him. Often even, to make his grief seem more real, he had the hypocrisy to take to his bed, and on great occasions he went so far as to submit to bleeding.

The bailiff paid court to God as well as to the powers of earth; he was never absent from high mass, and he always placed himself in the very middle of the vestrymen's pew. That brought him every Sunday a share of the blessed bread with the protection of the priest. If he could have established by an official report that he had attended divine service, he undoubtedly would have done so. But these little faults were made up for in the bailiff by brilliant qualities. No one understood better than he how to organize a ball at the expense of the city or a banquet in honor of the Duc de Nivernais. On these solemn occasions he was magnificent in majesty, appetite, and puns; Lamoignon or President Molé would have been very small men beside him. In reward for the eminent services that he rendered to the city, he had hoped for ten years to receive the cross of Saint Louis; and, when Lafayette was decorated after his American campaigns, he loudly protested against the injustice.

Such was the bailiff morally; physically he was a fleshy man, although he had not yet attained his full majesty; his person resembled an ellipse swollen at the bottom; you might have compared him to an ostrich-egg standing on two legs. Perfidious nature, which beneath a fiery sky has given to the manchineel tree a broad and thick shade, had granted to the bailiff the face of an honest man. Consequently he was fond of posing, and it was a fine day in his life when he could go, escorted by the firemen, from the tribunal to the church.

The bailiff always stood as stiff as a statue on a pedestal: if you had not known him, you would have said that he had a plaster of Burgundy pitch or a broad blister between his shoulders: he walked in the street as if he had carried a holy sacrament; his step was as invariable as a yard-stick: a shower of spears would not have made him lengthen it an inch; with the bailiff for his single instrument an astronomer could have measured an arc of the meridian.

My uncle did not hate the bailiff; he did not even deign to despise him; but, in presence of this moral abjection, he felt something like a revolt of his soul, and he sometimes said that this man had the effect upon him of a big toad crouching in a velvet arm-chair.

As for the bailiff, he hated Benjamin with all the energy of his bilious soul. The latter was not ignorant of this; but he cared very little about it.

My grandmother, fearing a conflict between these two natures so diverse, wanted Benjamin to abstain from going to court; but the great man, who had confidence in the strength of his will, had disdained this timid counsel; only, on Saturday morning he abstained from taking his customary allowance of hot wine.

Bonteint's lawyer proved that his client had a right to claim a judgment against my uncle for seizure of his body. When he had entirely finished his demonstration, the bailiff asked Benjamin what he had to say in his defence.

"I have but one observation to make," said my uncle, "but it is worth more than Monsieur's whole speech, for it is unanswerable: I am five feet nine inches above the level of the sea and six inches above the level of the ordinary man; I think" . . .

"Monsieur Rathery," interrupted the bailiff, "however tall a man you may be, you have no right to joke with justice."

"If I had a desire to joke," said my uncle, "it would not be with so powerful a personage as Monsieur, whose justice, moreover, does not joke; but when I affirm that I am five feet nine inches above the level of the sea, I do not perpetrate a joke; I offer a serious defence. Monsieur can have me measured if he doubts the truth of my declaration. I think, then" . . .

"Monsieur Rathery," replied the bailiff quickly, "if you continue in this tone, I shall be obliged to deprive you of the floor."

"It is not worth while," answered my uncle, "for I am done. I think, then," he added, hurrying his syllables one after another, "that the body of a man of my stature is not to be seized for fifty miserable three-franc pieces."

"According to you," said the bailiff, "the seizure of the body could be practised only on one of your arms, one of your legs, or perhaps even on your cue."

"In the first place," answered my uncle, "I will beg Monsieur to observe that my cue is not in question; then I make no pretension to the quality attributed to me by Monsieur; I was born undivided, and I intend to remain undivided all my life; but, as the security is worth at least double the amount of the credit, I beg Monsieur to order that the sentence for seizure of my body shall not be executed until Bonteint shall have furnished me with three more red coats."

"Monsieur Rathery, this is not a tavern; I beg you to remember to whom you are talking; your remarks are as ill-considered as your person."

"Monsieur bailiff," answered my uncle, "I have a good memory, and I know very well to whom I am talking. I have been too carefully brought up by my dear sister in the fear of God and the *gendarmes* to allow me to forget it. As for the tavern, since you have brought up the question of the tavern, it is too highly appreciated by honest people to need to be rehabilitated by me. If we go to the tavern, it is because, when we are thirsty, we have not the privilege of refreshing ourselves at the expense of the city. The tavern is the wine-cellar of those who have none; and the wine-cellar of those who have one is nothing but a

tavern without a sign. It ill becomes those who drink
a bottle of Burgundy and something else for their
dinner to abuse the poor devil who now and then
regales himself at the tavern with a pint of Croix-
Pataux. Those official orgies where they get intoxicated in drinking toasts to the king and to the Duc de
Nivernais are simply, euphony aside, what the people
call drinking bouts. To get drunk at one's table is
more decent, but to get drunk at the tavern is nobler,
and more profitable to the public treasury besides. As
to the consideration that attaches to my person, it is
less extended than that which Monsieur can claim for
his, inasmuch as I enjoy the consideration of honest
people only. But " . . .

" Monsieur Rathery," cried the bailiff, finding no
better and easier answer to the epigrams with which my
uncle was tormenting him, " you are an insolent fellow."

" So be it," replied Benjamin, knocking off a straw
which had attached itself to the facing of his coat, " but
I must in conscience warn Monsieur that I have confined myself this morning within the limits of the
strictest temperance, and that consequently, if he should
try to make me depart from the respect that I owe to
his robe, he would do so at his costs of provocation."

" Monsieur Rathery," exclaimed the bailiff, " your
allusions are insulting to justice; I fine you thirty
sous for contempt."

" There are three francs," said my uncle, putting a
little coin on the judge's green table, " take your pay out
of that."

" Monsieur Rathery," cried the exasperated bailiff,
" leave the room."

" Monsieur bailiff, I have the honor to salute you. My compliments to Madame your wife, if you please."

" I fine you forty sous more," screamed the judge.

" What!" said my uncle, " a fine of forty sous because I present my compliments to Madame your wife."

And he went out.

" That devil of a man!" said the bailiff in the evening to his wife; " never would I have supposed him so moderate. But let him look out; I have issued a warrant for his arrest, and shall ask Bonteint to execute it immediately. He shall learn what it is to defy me. When I invite him to the festivities given by the city, it will be hot, and if I can diminish his practice " . . .

" Oh, fie, Monsieur!" answered his wife, " are those proper sentiments to be uttered by a man who sits in the vestrymen's pew? And besides, what has M. Rathery done to you? He is such a merry, handsome, and amiable man!"

" I will tell you what he has done to me, Madame; he has dared to remind me that your father-in-law was a *gendarme ;* moreover, he is wittier and more honest than I. Do you think that a little matter ?"

The next day my uncle had ceased to think about the warrant issued for his arrest; he started for the church, powdered and solemn, Mlle. Minxit on his right and his sword on his left; he was followed by Page, who presented a smart appearance in his brown coat; by Arthus, whose abdomen was enveloped to a point beyond its diameter by a waistcoat figured with large branches, among which little birds were fluttering; by Millot-Rataut, who wore a brick-colored wig, and whose gridelin tibias were marbled with black; and by a great many others, whose names it does not please me to hand down to posterity. Parlanta alone failed to answer to the call. Two violins squeaked at the head of the procession; Machecourt and his wife brought up the rear. Benjamin, always magnificent, scattered by the way sugar-plums and small coins from the inoculation money. Gaspard, very proud to serve him as a pocket, walked by his side, carrying the sugar-plums in a big bag.

CHAPTER XV.

BUT quite another ceremony was in store for him!
Parlanta had received from Bonteint and the bailiff
express orders to execute the warrant during the ceremony; he had ambushed his assistants in the vestibule
of the court-house, and was awaiting the procession
himself under the portal of the church.

As soon as he saw my uncle's three-cornered hat
emerge from the steps of Vieille-Rome, he went up to
him and summoned him in the name of the king to follow him to prison.

" Parlanta," answered my uncle, " your conduct is
hardly conformable to the rules of French politeness;
could you not wait until to-morrow to effect my confis-
cation, and come to-day to dine with us ? "

" If you are very desirous of it," said Parlanta, " I
will wait; but I warn you that the bailiff's orders are
explicit, and that I run a risk, if I disregard them, of
incurring his resentment in this life and in the other."

" That being the case, do your duty," said Benjamin ;
and he went to ask Page to take his place beside Mlle.
Minxit; then, bowing to the latter with all the grace
that his five feet nine inches would allow, he said :

" You see, Mademoiselle, that I am forced to separate
from you ; I beg you to believe that nothing less than

a summons in the name of His Majesty could induce me to do such a thing. I should have liked, if Parlanta had allowed me, to enjoy the pleasure of this ceremony to the end; but these sheriff's officers are like death: they seize their prey wherever they find it, they tear it violently from the arms of the loved one as a child tears a butterfly by its gauze wings from the calyx of a rose."

"It is as disagreeable to me as to you," said Mlle. Minxit, pouting frightfully: "your friend is a little man and as round as a ball, and he wears a wig *à marteaux;* I shall look like a Maypole beside him."

"What do you expect me to do?" said Benjamin, dryly, wounded at so much egoism; "I cannot make you any shorter, or M. Page any thinner, and I cannot lend him my cue."

Benjamin took leave of the company and followed Parlanta, whistling his favorite air:

"Malbrough s'en va-t-en guerre."

He halted a moment on the threshold of the prison to cast a last glance at the free spaces which were about to close behind him; he saw his sister motionless on the arm of her husband, who was following him with a distressed look; on seeing this, he pulled the door violently after him, and rushed into the prison-yard.

That night my grandfather and his wife came to see him; they found him perched at the top of a flight of steps, throwing to his companions in captivity the balance of his sugar-plums, and laughing like the happiest of men to see them scramble for them.

"What the devil are you doing there?" said my grandfather to him.

"You see for yourself," answered Benjamin, "I am finishing the baptismal ceremony. Do you not find that these men swarming at our feet to pick up insipid sweetmeats faithfully represent society? Is it not in this way that the poor inhabitants of this earth push each other, crush each other, overturn each other, to get the blessings that God has cast in the midst of them? Is it not thus that the strong man tramples the weak man under his feet, thus that the weak man bleeds and cries, thus that he who has taken everything insults by his superb irony him to whom he has left nothing, and thus finally that, when the latter dares to complain, the other kicks him? These poor devils are breathless, covered with sweat; their fingers are bruised, and their faces torn; not one has come out of the struggle without a scratch of some kind. If they had listened to their real interests rather than to their wild instinct of greed, instead of disputing over these sugar-plums as enemies, would they not have shared them as brothers?"

"Possibly," answered Machecourt; "but try not to get too lonesome this evening and to sleep well to-night, for to-morrow morning you will be free."

"How so?" answered Benjamin.

"Because," replied Machecourt, "to get you out of · this difficulty, we have sold our little vineyard."

"And is the contract signed?" inquired Benjamin, anxiously.

"Not yet," said my grandfather, "but we are to meet to-night to sign it."

"Well, you, Machecourt, and you, my dear sister, pay careful attention to what I am going to say: if you sell your vineyard to get me out of Bonteint's clutches, the first use that I shall make of my liberty will be to leave your house, and never in all your life will you see me again."

"Nevertheless," said Machecourt, "the matter must be so arranged; one is a brother or one is not. I cannot allow you to remain in prison when I have in my hands the means of restoring your liberty. You take things as a philosopher, but I am not a philosopher. As long as you remain here, I shall be unable to eat a morsel or drink a glass of white wine for my benefit."

"And I," said my grandmother, "do you think that I can accustom myself to see you no more? Did not our mother recommend you to my care on her death-bed? Have I not brought you up? Do I not look upon you as the eldest of my children? And these poor children, it is pitiable to see them; since you are no longer with us, one would say there was a coffin in the house. They all wanted to come with us to see you, and little Nanette was not willing to touch her pie-crust, saying that she kept it for her uncle Benjamin, who was in prison and had only black bread to eat."

"This is too much," said Benjamin, pushing my grandfather by the shoulders; "go away, Machecourt, and you too, my dear sister, go away, I beg of you, for you will cause me to be guilty of a weakness: but, I warn you, if you sell your vineyard to pay my ransom, never in my life will I set eyes on you again."

"Nonsense, you booby!" answered my grandmother, "is not a brother more valuable than a vineyard? Would you not do for us what we do for you, if opportunity offered? And when you are rich, will you not

aid us to establish our children? With your profession
and your talents you can return us a hundred times
over what we give you to-day. And, my God! what
would the public say of us if we should leave you
behind the bars for a debt of a hundred and fifty francs?
Come, Benjamin, be a good brother, and do not make us
all unhappy by insisting on staying here."

While my grandmother was speaking, Benjamin had
his head hidden in his hands, and was trying to repress
the tears that were gathering under his eyelids.

"Machecourt," he cried suddenly, "I can stand this
no longer; tell Boutron to bring me a little glass of
wine; and come and kiss me. See," said he, pressing
him against his breast until he cried with pain, "you
are the first man that I ever kissed, and these are the
first tears that I have shed since the last time that I
was flogged."

And truly my poor uncle burst into tears. But the
jailer having brought two little glasses, he had no
sooner emptied his than he became as calm and serene
as an April sky after a shower.

My grandmother again tried to move him, but her
words had no more effect upon him than the moon's
rays upon an icicle.

The only thing that troubled him was that the jailer
had seen him weep. So Machecourt had to keep his
vineyard willy-nilly.

CHAPTER XVI.

A BREAKFAST IN PRISON.— HOW MY UNCLE GOT OUT OF PRISON.

THE next morning, as my uncle was promenading in the prison-yard, whistling a well-known air, Arthus entered, followed by three men carrying baskets covered with white linen.

"Good morning, Benjamin," he cried: "we come to breakfast with you, since you can no longer come to breakfast with us."

At the same time Page, Rapin, Guillerand, Millot-Rataut, and Machecourt marched in. Parlanta brought up the rear, looking a little abashed: my uncle went up to him, and, taking him by the hand, said:

"Well, Parlanta, I hope you do not bear me any ill-will for having made you lose a good dinner yesterday."

"On the contrary," answered Parlanta, "I was afraid that you would be angry with me for not allowing you to finish your baptism."

"Understand this, Benjamin," interrupted Page, "we have assessed ourselves to get you out of here; but, as we have no ready cash, we act as if money had not been invented; we give Bonteint our respective services, each according to his profession. I will plead his first case for him; Parlanta will write two summonses for him; Arthus will draw up his will; Rapin will give him two or three consultations that will cost him dearer than he thinks; Guillerand will give his children some grammar lessons of indifferent excellence; Rataut, who is nothing, inasmuch as he is a poet, engages himself upon his honor to buy of him all the coats that he may need for the next two years, which, in my opinion and his, does not engage him to very much."

"And does Bonteint accept?" said Benjamin.

"Accept!" said Page; "why! he receives values amounting to more than five hundred francs. Rapin arranged this affair with him yesterday; it remains but to draw up the documents."

"Well," said my uncle, "I will take my share of this good deed; I engage to treat him, without any bill, during the next two sicknesses with which he may be afflicted. If I kill him with the first, his wife shall inherit the privilege of the second; as for you, Machecourt, I permit you to subscribe a jug of white wine."

Meantime Arthus had had the table set at the jailer's. He took from the baskets the dishes, the contents of which had become somewhat mixed, and placed them in their order on the table.

"Come," he shouted, "let us sit down, and a truce to babbling! I do not like to be disturbed when I am eating; you will have plenty of time to chatter at dessert."

The breakfast did not taste at all of the place in which it was celebrated. Machecourt alone was a little sad, for the arrangement made with Bonteint by my uncle's friends seemed to him like a joke.

"Come, Machecourt," cried Benjamin, "your glass is always in your hand, full or empty; are you the prisoner here, or am I? By the way, gentlemen, do you know that Machecourt came near doing a good deed yesterday? He wanted to sell his good vineyard to pay Bonteint my ransom."

"Magnificent!" cried Page.

"Succulent!" said Arthus.

"I consider it an instance of morality in action," declared Guillerand.

"Gentlemen," interrupted Rapin, "virtue must be honored wherever one is fortunate enough to find it; I propose, therefore, that every time that Machecourt sits down at table with us, he shall be given an arm-chair."

"Adopted!" cried all the guests together, "and here's to Machecourt's health!"

"Indeed!" said my uncle, "I do not know why people are so afraid of prison. Is not this fowl as tender, and this Bordeaux as fragrant, on this side of the grating as on the other?"

"Yes," said Guillerand, "as long as there is grass beside the walls to which it is fastened the goat does not feel its tether; but when the place is stripped, it begins to worry and tries to break its tether."

"To go from the grass that grows in the valley," answered my uncle, "to that which grows on the mountain is the liberty of the goat; but man's liberty is to do only that which befits him. He whose body has been seized but whose power to think at his will has been left him is a hundred times freer than he whose soul has been left captive in the chains of an odious occupation. The prisoner undoubtedly passes sad hours in contemplating through his bars the road that winds along the plain and loses itself beneath the bluish shade of some far-off forest. He would like to be the poor

woman who leads her cow along the road while twirling her distaff, or the poor wood-cutter who goes back
loaded with boughs to his hut smoking above the trees.
But this liberty to be where one likes, to go straight
ahead until one is weary or is stopped by a ditch, to
whom does it belong? Is not the paralytic in prison
in his bed, the merchant in his shop, the clerk in his
office, the *bourgeois* within the limits of his little town,
the king within the limits of his kingdom, and God
himself within that icy circumference which confines
worlds? You go breathless and streaming with sweat
over a road burned with the sun; here are tall trees
that spread beside you their lofty tiers of verdure, and
ironically shake their yellow leaves upon your head;
you would like very much to remain a moment in their
shade, and wipe your feet on the moss that carpets
their roots; but between them and you there is six
feet of wall or the pointed bars of an iron grating.
Arthus, Rapin, and all of you who have only a stomach, who know how only to dine after having break
fasted, I do not know whether you will understand me;
but Millot-Rataut, who is a tailor and makes songs, he
will understand me. I have often desired to follow in
its vagabond peregrinations the cloud driven by the
winds across the sky. Often when, resting my elbows
on my window-sill, I dreamily follow the moon which
seems to look at me like a human face, I would like to
fly away like a bubble of air toward those mysterious
solitudes that pass above my head, and would give all
the world to sit for a moment on one of those gigantic
peaks which rend the white surface of that planet.
Was I not then also a captive on the earth as truly

as the poor prisoner between the high walls of his prison?"

"Gentlemen," said Page, "one thing must be admitted: to the rich man the prison is made too pleasant and too comfortable. It corrects him like a spoiled child, after the fashion of that nymph who whipped Cupid with a rose. If you permit the rich man to carry to his prison his kitchen, his wine-cellar, his library, his parlor, it is not a condemned man whom you punish, it is a *bourgeois* who changes his lodgings. There you are before a good fire, wrapped in your well-lined dressing gown; with your feet on the andirons you digest your food, with stomach redolent with truffles and champagne; the snow-flakes flutter by the bars of your window, while you blow toward the ceiling the white smoke of your cigar. You dream, you think, you build castles in Spain or write poetry. By your side is your newspaper, that friend which we quit, which we recall, and which we finally dismiss when it becomes too tiresome. Tell me, what is there in such a situation that resembles a penalty? Have you not thus passed hours, days, entire weeks, without leaving your house? What, meanwhile, is the judge doing, who has had the barbarity to condemn you to this torture? He is hearing cases from eleven o'clock in the morning, shivering in his black robe and listening to the paternosters of some lawyer who repeats himself. Meanwhile, catarrh with its torpid clutch seizes his lungs, or a chilblain with its sharp tooth bites his toes. You say that you are not free! On the contrary, you are a hundred times freer than in your house; your whole day belongs to you; you get up when you like, go to bed when you like, do what you like, and you are no longer obliged to shave.

"Take Benjamin, for instance, who is a prisoner: do you think that Bonteint has served him such a bad turn in getting him shut up here? He was often obliged to rise before the street lamps went out. With one stocking on wrong side out, he went from door to door, to inspect this one's tongue and feel that one's pulse. When he had finished in one direction, he had to begin again in another; he splashed himself in the cross-roads up to his cue, and his peasant generally had nothing to offer him but curds and black bread. When he had come home at night very tired, had settled himself comfortably in his bed, and was beginning to taste the joys of the early hours of sleep, he was brutally awakened to go to the aid of the mayor choking with indigestion, or of the bailiff's wife in the midst of a miscarriage. Now, here he is, rid of all this bustle. He is as well situated here as a rat in a Dutch cheese. Bonteint has made him a present of a little income, which he eats as a philosopher. He is really the lily of the gospel, which neither bleeds nor purges and yet is well fed, which neither toils nor spins and yet is arrayed in a magnificent red robe. Truly, we are dupes to pity him, and actual enemies of his comfort to try to get him out of here."

"One is comfortable here, I grant," answered my uncle, "but I would quite as willingly be uncomfortable somewhere else. That shall not prevent me from admitting, as Page has shown you, not only that the prison is too comfortable for the rich man, but also that it is too comfortable for everybody. It is undoubtedly hard to cry to the law when it scourges a poor fellow:

'Strike harder; you do not hurt him enough'; but it is very necessary to guard also against that unintelligent and near-sighted philanthropy which sees nothing beyond his misfortune. Real philosophers, like Guillerand, like Millot-Rataut, like Parlanta, in a word, like all of us, should consider men only *en masse*, as we consider a wheat field. A social question should always be examined from the standpoint of the public interest. You have distinguished yourself by a fine feat of arms, and the king decorates you with the cross of Saint Louis; do you think that it is because he wishes you well and in the interest of your individual glory that His Majesty authorizes you to wear his gracious image upon your breast? Alas! no, my poor brave; it is in his own interest first, and then in that of the State; it is in order that those who, like you, have hot blood in their veins, seeing you so generously rewarded, may imitate your example. Now, suppose that, instead of a good deed, you have committed a crime; you have killed, not three or four men who do not wear the same kind of coat-collar that you do, but a good *bourgeois* of your own country. The judge has sentenced you to death, and the king has refused to pardon you. There is nothing left for you now but to draw up your general confession and begin your lamentation. Now, what feeling moved the judge to pass this sentence upon you? Did he wish to rid society of you, as when one kills a mad dog, or to punish you, as when one whips an ugly child? In the first place, if his object had been simply to cut you off from society, a very deep cell with a very thick door and a loop-hole for a window would have been amply sufficient for that.

Then, the judge often condemns to death a man who has attempted to commit suicide, and to prison a poor fellow to whom he knows that the prison will be hospitable. Is it, then, to punish them that he grants these two good-for-nothings precisely what they ask; that he performs for one, to whom existence is a torture, an operation that ends his life, and that he grants to the other, who has neither bread nor roof, a place of refuge? The judge wishes but one thing; he wishes to frighten by your torture those who would be tempted to follow your example.

"'People, take care that you do not kill,' that is all that your sentence means. If you could substitute for yourself under the knife a mannikin who resembles you, it would be all the same to the judge; if even, after the executioner had cut off your head and shown it to the people, he could resuscitate you, I am very sure he would do so willingly; for, after all, the judge is a good man, and he would not like to have his cook kill a chicken before his eyes. They cry very loudly, and you proclaim it yourselves, that it is better to acquit ten guilty men than to condemn one innocent man. That is the most deplorable of the absurdities to which fashionable philanthropy has given birth; it is an anti-social principle. I maintain, for my part, that it is better to condemn ten innocent men than to acquit a single guilty man."

At these words, all the guests raised a great outcry against my uncle.

"No, indeed," cried my uncle, "I am not joking, and this subject is not one to excite laughter. I express a firm, powerful, and long-settled conviction. The whole city pities the innocent man who mounts the scaffold; the newspapers resound with lamentations, and your poets take him for the martyr of their dramas. But how many innocent men perish in your rivers, on your highways, in the depths of your mines, or even in your workshops, torn to pieces by the ferocious teeth of your machines, those gigantic animals that seize a man by surprise and swallow him before your eyes, you unable to render him any aid. Yet their death hardly tears an exclamation from you. You pass by, and a few steps farther on you think no more about it. You even forget to tell your wife of it at dinner. The next day the newspaper buries him in one corner of its pages, throws over his body a few lines of heavy prose, and all is ended. Why this indifference for one and this superabundance of pity for the other? Why ring one's funeral knell with a little bell and the other's with a big one? Is a mistaken judge a more terrible accident than an overturned stage-coach or a disarranged machine? Do not my innocents make as big a hole in society as yours? Do they not leave the wife a widow and the children orphans as well as yours?

" Undoubtedly it is not agreeable to go to the scaffold for another, and I who speak to you admit that, if the thing should happen to me, I should be very much put out. But, in relation to society, what is this little blood that the executioner sheds? A drop of water that oozes from a reservoir, a bruised acorn that falls from an oak. An innocent man condemned by a judge is a consequence of the distribution of justice, as the fall of a carpenter from the top of a house is a consequence of the fact that man shelters himself under a

roof.   Out of a thousand bottles that a workman makes, .
he breaks at least one; out of a thousand sentences that
a judge passes, one at least will be unjust.   It is an evil
that is expected, and for which there could be no possible remedy except the total suppression of justice.
Take an old woman sifting beans; what would you say
of her if, through fear of throwing away a good one,
she should keep all the rubbish which she found with
it?   Would it not be the same with the judge who,
through fear of condemning one innocent man, should
acquit ten guilty?

" Moreover, the condemnation of an innocent man is
a rare thing; it marks an epoch in the annals of justice.
It is almost impossible that a fortuitous concourse of
circumstances should so unite against a man as to over-
whelm him with charges which he cannot disprove.
And even in such a case I maintain that there is in the
attitude of an accused man, in his look, in his gesture,
in the sound of his voice, elements of evidence which
cannot escape the judge.   Besides, the death of an innocent man is only an individual misfortune, while the
acquittal of a guilty man is a public calamity.   Crime
listens at the doors of your court-room; it knows what
goes on inside, it calculates the chances of safety which
your indulgence leaves it.   It applauds you when,
through exaggerated caution, it sees you acquit a guilty
man, for it is crime itself that you acquit.   Justice undoubtedly should not be too severe; but, when it is
too indulgent, it abdicates, it annuls itself.   From that
time forward men predestined to crime abandon themselves without fear to their instincts, and no longer see
in their dreams the sinister face of the executioner; be-

tween them and their victims the scaffold no longer rises; they take your money provided they need it, and your life provided it stands in their way. You applaud yourselves, good people, at having saved an innocent man from the axe, but you have caused twenty to die by the dagger. There is a balance of nineteen murders to be charged to your account.

"And now I come back to the prison. The prison, in order to inspire a healthy terror, must be a place of torture and misery. Nevertheless, there are in France fifteen millions of men who are more miserable in their houses than the prisoner behind his bars. 'Too happy the man of the fields if he knows his happiness,' says the poet. That's all very well in an idyl. The man of the fields is the thistle of the mountain; not a glowing ray of sunlight that does not burn him, not a breath of the north wind that does not bite him, not a shower that he must not undergo; he toils from the morning Angelus till the evening Angelus; he has an old father, and he cannot mitigate the severity of his old age; he has a beautiful wife, and he can give her nothing but rags; he has famishing children continually calling for bread, and often there is not a crumb in the bin. The prisoner, on the contrary, is warmly clad and sufficiently fed; before having a piece of bread to put in his mouth, he is not obliged to earn it. He laughs, he sings, he plays, he sleeps on his straw as long as he likes, and yet he is the object of public pity. Charitable persons organize themselves into societies to make his prison less uncomfortable, and they do this so well that, instead of a penalty, his imprisonment becomes a reward. Beautiful ladies make his kettle simmer, and season his soup; they preach morality to him with white bread

and meat. Surely to the toilsome liberty of the fields
or the shop, this man will prefer the careless and comfortable captivity of the prison. The prison ought to
be the hell of the city; I should like to see it rise in
the middle of the public square, gloomy and clad in
black like the judge; through its little grated windows
it should cast sinister looks at the passers-by; from
within it should arise, instead of songs, the noise of
clanking chains or barking dogs; the old man should
fear to rest under its walls; the child should not dare
to play within its shadow; the belated *bourgeois* should
turn out of his road to avoid it, and separate himself
from it as he separates himself from the graveyard.
Only on this condition will you obtain from the prison
the result that you expect of it."

My uncle perhaps would be discussing still, if M.
Minxit had not arrived to cut short his argument.
The worthy man was streaming with perspiration;
he sucked in the air like a porpoise stranded on the
beach, and was as red as my uncle's coat.

" Benjamin," he cried, mopping his forehead, " I have
come to take you to breakfast with me."

"How so, Monsieur Minxit?" cried all the guests
together.

" Why, because Benjamin is free; that is the whole
of the mystery. Here," he added, pulling a paper
from his pocket and handing it to Boutron, " this is
Bonteint's receipt."

" Bravo, Monsieur Minxit!"

And everybody, rising, glass in hand, drank to M.
Minxit's health. Machecourt tried to rise, but he fell
back on his chair; joy had almost deprived him of his
senses; Benjamin chanced to cast a glance at him.

"What, Machecourt!" he exclaimed, "are you mad? Drink to Minxit's health, or I bleed you on the spot."

Machecourt rose mechanically, emptied his glass at one swallow, and began to weep.

"My good Monsieur Minxit," continued Benjamin, "may I" . . .

"Pshaw!" said the latter, "I see how it is: you are about to thank me; well, I relieve you of that duty, my poor fellow; it is for my own fine eyes and not for yours that I take you out of here; you know very well that I cannot get along without you. You see, gentlemen, in all the actions that seem the most generous there is only egoism. If this maxim is not consoling, it is not my fault, but it is true."

"Monsieur Boutron," said Benjamin, "is Bonteint's receipt in regular form?"

"I see nothing defective about it except a big blot which the honest tailor has doubtless added by way of a flourish."

"In that case, gentlemen," said Benjamin, "permit me to go to my dear sister to announce this good news to her myself."

"I follow you," said Machecourt, "I wish to be a witness of her joy; never have I been so happy since the day when Gaspard came into the world."

"You will permit me," said M. Minxit, sitting down to table. "Monsieur Boutron, another plate. For that matter, gentlemen, I will do as much for you; this evening I invite you to supper at Corvol."

This proposition was welcomed with acclamation by all the guests. After breakfast they retired to the *café* to await the hour for starting.

CHAPTER XVII

A TRIP TO CORVOL.

THE waiter came to tell my uncle that there was an old woman at the door who wanted to speak to him.

"Tell her to come in," said Benjamin, "and give her some refreshment."

"Yes," answered the waiter, "but you see the old woman is not at all inviting. She is ragged, and she is weeping tears as big as my little finger."

"She is weeping!" cried my uncle; "and why, you scamp, didn't you tell me that at once?"

And he hastened out.

The old woman who had called for my uncle was indeed shedding big tears, which she wiped away with an old piece of red calico.

"What is the matter, my good woman?" said Benjamin, in a tone of politeness that he did not assume toward everyone, "and what can I do for you?"

"You must come to Sembert," said the old woman, "to see my sick son."

"Sembert! That village at the top of Monts-le-Duc? Why, that's half way to heaven! All the same, I will call there to-morrow afternoon."

"If you do not come to-day," said the old woman, "to-morrow the priest will come with his black cross, and perhaps it is already too late, for my son is afflicted with a carbuncle."

"That is awkward for your son and for me; but, to

accommodate everybody, could you not apply to my confrère Arnout?"

"I have applied to him; but, as he is acquainted with our poverty and knows that he will not be paid for his visits, he would not disturb himself."

"What!" said my uncle, "you have no money with which to pay your doctor? In that case, it is another matter; that concerns me. I ask you to allow me only time enough to empty a little glass that I have left on the table, and I am with you. By the way, we shall need some Peruvian bark; so here is a little coin; go to Perier's and buy a few ounces; you will tell him that I did not have time to write a prescription."

A quarter of an hour later my uncle was toiling, side by side with the old woman, up those uncultivated and savage slopes that take their roots in the faubourg of Bethléem and terminate in the broad plateau on top of which the hamlet of Sembert is perched.

M. Minxit's guests, for their part, started off in a cart drawn by four horses. The inhabitants of the faubourg of Beuvron had placed themselves in their doorways, candle in hand, to 'see them pass, and it was indeed a more curious phenomenon than an eclipse. Arthus was singing "*Aussitot que la lumière*"; Guillerand, "*Malbrough s'en va-t-en guerre*"; and the poet Millot, whom they had fastened to one of the cart-stakes because he did not seem very solid, struck up his "*Grand Noël*." M. Minxit prided himself on an extraordinary magnificence; he gave his guests a memorable supper, which is to this day a topic of conversation at Corvol. Unfortunately he was so prodigal with his toasts that, when they reached the second course, his guests were

unable to raise their glasses. At this point Benjamin
arrived. He was worn with fatigue and in a humor to
massacre everything, for his patient had died on his
hands, and he had fallen down twice on the road. But
in him no sorrows or vexations could stand before a
white table-cloth adorned with bottles; so he sat down
to table as if nothing had happened.

"Your friends," said M. Minxit, "are novices; I
should have expected more solidity from sheriff's officers, manufacturers, and school-teachers; I shall not
have the satisfaction of offering them any champagne.
And here is Machecourt who doesn't know you, and
Guillerand is offering Arthus his snuff-box instead of
his glass."

"What do you expect?" answered Benjamin;
"everybody is not of your strength, Monsieur Minxit."

"Yes," replied the worthy man, flattered by the
compliment, "but what are we going to do with all
these milksops? I have no beds for them all, and
they are not in a condition to go back to Clamecy to-
night."

"Indeed, you are greatly embarrassed," said my
uncle; "have some straw spread in your barn, and as
fast as they go to sleep, you can send them out on a
litter; you can cover them, lest they may catch cold,
with the big matting that you put over your bed of
little radishes to keep the frost from them."

"You are right," said M. Minxit.

He sent for two musicians commanded by the sergeant, and the plan proposed by my uncle was carried
out to the letter. Millot was not slow in going to
sleep, and the sergeant swung him over his shoulder

and carried him off as if he were a clock-case. The transportation of Rapin, Parlanta, and the others presented no serious difficulties; but, when they came to Arthus, they found him so heavy that they had to let him sleep where he lay. As for my uncle, he emptied his last bumper of champagne, and then started in his turn for the barn to bid them good-night.

The next morning, when M. Minxit's guests rose, they resembled sugar-loaves just taken from their cases, and it required all the domestics of the establishment to rid them of the straw with which they were covered. After having breakfasted off the second course which they had left intact the night before, they started off with their four horses on a brisk trot.

They would have reached Clamecy very happily, but for a little incident that happened on the way; the horses, made impetuous by the whip, overturned the cart into one of the thousand gullies with which the road was lined, and they all fell pell-mell into the mud. The poet Millot, who was always unlucky, had the misfortune to find himself under Arthus.

Benjamin, fortunately for his coat, had remained at Corvol. M. Minxit entertained at dinner that day all the celebrities of the neighborhood, and among others two noblemen. One of these illustrious guests was M. de Pont-Cassé, a red musketeer; the other was a musketeer of the same color, a friend of M. de Pont-Cassé, and whom the latter had invited to spend a few weeks with him in the remains of his castle. Now, M. de Pont-Cassé, into whose confidence we have already taken our readers, would not have been displeased to repair the damages which his own fortune had suffered with that of M. Minxit, and he had his eye on Arabelle, although he óften told his friends that she was an insect born in urine. Arabelle had allowed herself to be taken in by the extravagance of his fine manners; she thought him much handsomer with his faded plumes and much more amiable with his court rubbish than my uncle with his unpretentious wit and his red coat. But M. Minxit, who was a man not only of wit, but of common sense, was not at all of this opinion; though M. de Pont-Cassé had been a colonel, he would not have given him his daughter. He had kept Benjamin to dinner in order that Arabelle might institute a comparison between her two adorers which, in his opinion, could not be to the musketeer's advantage, and also because he relied on my uncle to efface the tinsel of the two noblemen and mortify their pride.

Benjamin, while waiting for dinner, went to take a walk in the village. As he left M. Minxit's grounds, he saw a pair of officers coming down the street, who would not have turned out for a mail-coach, and at whom the peasants were staring in wonder. My uncle was not a man to disturb himself about so small a matter; nevertheless, as he passed by them, he very distinctly heard one of them say to his companion: "Say, that is the queer chap who wants to marry Mlle. Minxit." My uncle's first impulse was to ask them why they thought him so queer; but he reflected that it would be scarcely becoming, although he generally cared very little for the proprieties, to make a spectacle of himself before the inhabitants of Corvol. So he acted as if he had heard nothing, and entered the house of his friend the tabellion.

" I have just met in the street," said he, " two fellows who looked like plumed lobsters, and who almost insulted me; could you tell me to what family of the crustacea these queer fellows belong?"

" Oh, the devil!" said the tabellion, seemingly frightened, "don't try any of your jokes in that direction: one of them, M. de Pont-Cassé, is the most dangerous duellist of our epoch, and of all those who have gone on the duelling-ground with him not one has come back safe and sound."

" We shall see," said my uncle.

The village clock having struck two, he took his friend the tabellion by the arm, and went back with him to M. Minxit's. The company was already gathered in the parlor, and only waiting for them in order to sit down at table.

The two noblemen, who acted in the presence of these countrymen as if they were in a conquered country, monopolized the conversation from the start. M. de Pont-Cassé did not cease twirling his moustache, and talking of the court, of his duels, and of his amorous exploits. Arabelle, who had never heard such magnificent things, took great pleasure in his remarks. My uncle noticed this; but, as Mlle. Minxit was indifferent to him, he thought it none of his concern. M. de Pont-Cassé, piqued at the little effect which he produced upon Benjamin, addressed him some remarks that bordered on insolence; but my uncle, sure of his strength, disdained to pay any attention to them, and occupied himself solely with his glass and his plate. M. Minxit was scandalized at the careless voracity of his champion.

"Don't you understand what M. de Pont-Cassé means?" cried the good man; "of what are you thinking, Benjamin?"

"Of dinner, Monsieur Minxit, and I advise you to do the same; for I believe that is the purpose for which you asked us here."

M. de Pont-Cassé had too much pride to believe that he could be spared. He took my uncle's silence for a confession of his inferiority, and began a more direct attack.

"I have heard you called de Rathery," said he to Benjamin; "I was acquainted, or rather I have seen, for one does not make the acquaintance of such people, a Rathery among the king's hostlers; perhaps he was a relative of yours?"

My uncle pricked up his ears like a horse struck with a whip.

"M. de Pont-Cassé," he answered, "the Ratherys never made themselves servants of the court under any livery whatsoever. The Ratherys have proud souls, Monsieur; they will not eat bread unless they earn it, and they, with a few millions of others, pay the wages of those flunkeys of all colors known as courtiers."

There was a solemn silence among the company, and each one gave my uncle an approving look.

"Monsieur Minxit," he added, "a bit more of that hare-pie, if you please; it is excellent, and I would wager that the hare of which it was made was not a nobleman."

"Monsieur," said the friend of M. de Pont-Cassé, assuming a martial attitude, "what do you mean by your remark about a hare?"

"That a nobleman," answered my uncle coldly, "would not be good in a pie; that was all that I meant."

"Gentlemen," said M. Minxit, "it is understood of course that your discussions should not overstep the limits of pleasantry."

"Understood," said M. de Pont-Cassé; "strictly the remarks of M. *de* Rathery are of a nature to offend two officers of the king, who have not the honor to be, like himself, of the plebeians; nevertheless, from his red coat and his big sword, I at first took him for one of ours, and I still tremble, like the man who has been on the point of taking a serpent for an eel, as I think that I came near fraternizing with him. Nothing but his long cue wriggling over his shoulders undeceived me."

"Monsieur de Pont-Cassé," cried M. Minxit, "I will not allow" . . .

"Let him go on, my good Monsieur Minxit," said my uncle; "insolence is the weapon of those who do not know how to handle the flexible switch of wit. For my part, I have no occasion to reproach myself regarding my conduct toward M. de Pont-Cassé, for I have not as yet paid any attention to him."

"Very well," said M. Minxit.

The musketeer, who prided himself on being a very witty fellow and who knew that in the combats of wit as well as in those of the sword fortune is fickle, did not become discouraged.

"Monsieur Rathery," he continued, "Monsieur surgeon Rathery, do you know that between our two professions there is a closer analogy than you think? I would bet my burnt sorrel horse against your red coat that you have killed more people this year than I did in my last campaign."

"You would win, Monsieur de Pont-Cassé," replied my uncle coldly, "for this year I have had the misfortune to lose a patient; he died yesterday of a carbuncle."

"Bravo, Benjamin! Bravo, the people!" cried M. Minxit, unable longer to contain his joy. "You see, my nobleman, that all the people of wit are not at court."

"You yourself are the best proof of that, Monsieur Minxit," answered the musketeer, disguising the mortification of his defeat under a serene front.

Meantime, all the guests, except the two noblemen, presented their glasses to Benjamin, and touched them cordially against his own.

"To the health of Benjamin Rathery, the avenger of the misunderstood and insulted people!" cried M. Minxit.

The dinner was prolonged far into the evening. My uncle noticed that Mademoiselle Minxit had disappeared some time after M. de Pont Cassé; but he was too much preoccupied with the praises showered upon him to pay any attention to his *fiancée*. Toward ten o'clock he took leave of M. Minxit. The latter escorted him to the limits of the village, and made him promise that the marriage should take place within a week. As Benjamin arrived at a point opposite the Trucy mill, a sound of conversation reached his ears, and he thought he distinguished the voice of Arabelle and that of her illustrious adorer.

Benjamin, out of regard for Mlle. Minxit, did not wish to surprise her at that hour on a country road with a musketeer. He hid beneath the branches of a large walnut-tree, and waited for the two lovers to pass before continuing on his way. He doubtless did not intend at all to steal Arabelle's little secrets, but the wind brought them to him, and, in spite of himself, he had to receive the confidence.

" I know a way," said M. de Pont-Cassé, " of making him pack off: I will send him a challenge."

" I know him," answered Arabelle ; " he is a man of ungovernable pride, and, though he were sure of being killed on the spot, he would accept."

" So much the better ! In that way I shall rid you of him forever."

" Yes, but in the first place I do not want to be an accomplice in a murder ; and in the second place my father loves this man more perhaps than he loves me. his only daughter ; I will never consent that you shall kill my father's best friend."

" You are charming, Arabelle, with your scruples ; I have killed more than one for a word that rang badly in my ear, and this plebeian, whose wit is ferocious, has taken a cruel revenge upon me ; I should not like everybody at court to know what was said to-night at your father's table. Nevertheless, not to go counter to your wishes, I will content myself with crippling him. If, for instance, I should cut the cord of his kneepan, that would be a disqualification sufficient to justify you in refusing him your hand."

" But suppose you, Hector, should fall yourself?" said Mlle. Minxit in her tenderest voice.

" I who have killed the finest swordsmen of the army,— the brave Bellerive, the terrible Desrivières, the formidable Châteaufort,—I fall by a surgeon's rapier! But you insult me, my beautiful Arabelle, when you give voice to such a doubt. Do you not know, then, that I am as sure of my sword as you of your needle? Designate yourself the spot where you would like me to strike him, and I shall be delighted to serve you with this bit of gallantry."

The voices were lost in the distance; my uncle left his hiding-place, and tranquilly resumed his journey to Clamecy, considering what course he should take.

CHAPTER XVIII.

"M. DE PONT-CASSÉ wishes to cripple me; he has promised Mlle. Minxit that he will do so, and a knight of the musketeers is not a man to fail in his word.

"Let me see: what shall I do in this matter? Must I allow myself to be crippled by M. de Pont-Cassé with the docility of a dog under the scalpel, or shall I decline the honor that he condescends to do me? It is for M. de Pont-Cassé's interest that I should go upon crutches; that I know; but I do not exactly see why I should give him that pleasure. I hold very little to Mlle. Minxit, although she is decorated with a dowry of one hundred thousand francs; but I hold very much to the symmetry of my person, and I flatter myself that I am sufficiently good-looking to keep this pretension from seeming ridiculous. You say, a man challenged to a duel must fight; but where do you find that, if you please? Is it in the Pandects, in Charlemagne's Capitularies, in the commandments of God, or in those of the Church? And in the first place, M. de Pont-Cassé, between you and me is the match really equal? You are a musketeer and I am a doctor; you are an artist in the matter of fencing, and I scarcely know how to handle anything but the bistoury or the lancet; you, it seems, feel no more scruple in depriving a man of his limb than in tearing a wing from a fly, whereas I have a horror of blood, and especially of arterial blood.

Would it not be as ridiculous on my part to accept your challenge as if I were to consent to walk a tight rope upon the challenge of a rope-walker, or to cross an arm of the sea upon the defiance of a professor of swimming? And even though the chances were equal between us, when one concludes a treaty he must hope to gain something thereby; now, if I kill you, what shall I gain? And if I am killed by you, then what shall I gain? You see, in either case I should make a dupe's bargain. You repeat that every man challenged to a duel must fight. What! if a murderer of the highway should stop me at the corner of a wood, I should feel no scruple in escaping from him with the aid of my good legs, but, when a murderer of the drawing-room places a challenge under my nose, I must feel myself obliged to throw myself upon the point of his sword?

"According to you, when an individual whom you know only from accidentally having stepped on his toe, writes to you: 'Monsieur, be present at such an hour, at such a spot, in order that I may have the satisfaction of killing you, in reparation of the insult which you have offered me,' one must submit to the orders of this person, and furthermore take good care not to keep him waiting. Strange thing! there are men who would not risk a thousand francs to save their friend's honor or their father's life, and who risk their own life in a duel on account of an equivocal word or a squinting glance. But then, what is life? It is, then, no longer a blessing without which all others are of little consequence? It is, then, a rag to be thrown to the passing rag-picker, or a piece of worn-out money to be abandoned to the first blind man that sings beneath your window? They require that I shall stake my life against that of M. de Pont-Cassé in a game of swords, whereas, if I should play a game of cards for a hundred francs, I should be a man ruined in reputation, and the poorest cobbler among them all would not have me for a son-in-law. According to them, I should be more prodigal of my life than of my money. And must I, who pride myself on being a philosopher, regulate my conduct by the opinions of such casuists?

"In fact, what is this public which assumes to judge our actions? Grocers who sell with false weights, clothiers who give false measure, tailors who dress their brats at the expense of their customers, men of property who live on usury, mothers of families who have lovers, and, in short, a heap of crickets and grasshoppers who know not what they sing, ninnies who say yes and no without knowing why, an areopagus of imbeciles incapable of giving reasons for their conclusions. I should be in pretty business, I, a doctor, if I should decide, because these boobies believe that Saint Hubert cures of the rabies, to send a patient suffering with hydrophobia to Ardennes to kneel at the shrine of that great saint. Choose those among them who pride themselves on being sages, and you will see how consistent they are with themselves. Their philosophers utter loud cries when one speaks to them of those poor women of Malabar who throw themselves, alive and decked in all their finery, on the funeral-pile of their husband; and when two men cut each other's throats for a straw, they award them a crown for intrepidity.

"You say that I am a coward when I have the good sense to decline a challenge; but what is cowardice, then, in your opinion? If cowardice consists in recoiling from useless danger, where will you find a courageous man? Who of you, when his roof is cracking and flaming above his head, remains calmly dreaming in his bed? Who, when he is seriously sick, does not call the doctor to his aid? Who, finally, when he falls into a river, does not clutch at the bushes on the banks? Once more, what is this public? A coward that preaches temerity. Suppose that M. de Pont-Cassé were to challenge, not me, Benjamin Rathery, but the public to fight a duel, how many out of the whole crowd would dare to accept this defiance?

"And besides, has a philosopher any other public to consider than the men who think and reason? Now, in the eyes of such people is not the duel the most absurd as well as the most barbarous of prejudices? What is proved by the logic that is learned in an armory? A well-delivered sword thrust is a magnificent argument, is it not? Parry tierce, parry quarte, you can now demonstrate anything you like. It is a great pity, indeed, that, when the pope excommunicated as heretical the revolution of the earth around the sun, Galileo did not think of summoning His Holiness to a duel to prove that this revolution was a fact.

"In the Middle Ages the duel had at least a reason; it was the consequence of a religious idea. Our grandparents thought God too just to allow an innocent man to fall under the blows of a guilty man, and the issue of the combat was regarded as a decree from on high. But with us, who are, thank Heaven, well recovered from those mad ideas, and who believe in the temporal justice of God only to such extent as we like, how can the duel be justified and of what use is it?

"You fear that they will accuse you of lacking in
courage if you decline a challenge ; but those wretches
who make murder a profession and defy you because
they feel sure of killing you, what, then, do you think
of their courage ? What do you think of the courage
of the butcher who kills a sheep with its feet bound, or
that of the huntsman who fires pitilessly at a hare in
its form or at a bird singing on its branch. I have
known several of these people who had not pluck
enough to have a tooth pulled ; and among the number
how many are there who would dare to obey their conscience against the will of the man upon whom they
are dependent? I can understand that the cannibals
dwelling in the islands of the new world should kill
men of their own color in order to roast them, and,
after they have been well cooked, to eat them ; but
with what sauce will you, a duelist, eat the body of
the man you challenge, after you have killed him?
You are more guilty than the assassin whom justice
condemns to die upon the scaffold ; he at least was
pushed to murder by poverty,—a praiseworthy sentiment perhaps in its origin, however deplorable in its
results. But what is it that puts the sword in your
hand? Is it vanity, or an appetite for blood, or curiosity to see how a man writhes in the convulsions of
the death-agony? Do you picture to yourself a wife
throwing herself, half-crazed with grief, across the
body of her husband, children filling the widowed
house, draped with black, with their lamentations, a
mother praying God to receive her in the place of
her son in his coffin? And it is you who, moved by
a tiger's self-love, have caused all these miseries! You

wish to kill us if we do not give you the title of a man
of honor! But you are not worthy of the name of
man : you are only a brute thirsting for blood, only a
viper that bites for the pleasure of killing without
profiting by the evil that it does; and even the viper
respects itself in its fellows. When your adversary
has fallen, you kneel in the mud mixed with his blood,
you try to stanch the wounds you have made, you aid
him as if you were his best friend; but then, why did
you kill him, wretch? A great deal society cares for
your remorse! Will your tears replace the blood that
you have shed? You, fashionable assassin, you, respectable murderer, you find men to take your hand,
mothers of families to invite you to their parties;
those women who faint at the sight of the executioner
dare to press their lips against yours, and suffer you to
rest your head upon their bosom. But these men and
women judge things only by their names : they are
horrified at the murder that is called assassination, and
they applaud the murder that is called a duel. And
after all, how much time have you in which to enjoy
this applause which they shower upon you? On high,
beside your name is written homicide. You have on
your brow a stain of clotted blood which the kisses
of your mistresses will not wipe out. You have found
no judge on earth, but in heaven a judge awaits you who
will not be taken in by your tall talk about honor. As
for me, I am a doctor, not to kill, but to cure, do you
hear, M. de Pont-Cassé? If you have too much blood
in your veins, only with the point of my lancet can I
let it out for you."

Thus reasoned my uncle to himself. We shall soon
see how he put his doctrine in practice.

Night does not always bring good counsel. My uncle rose the next day, determined not to cower before the provocation of M. de Pont-Cassé, and, in order to end the adventure as soon as possible, he started that very day for Corvol. Whether he had not breakfasted, or did not perspire freely, or suffered from an unfinished digestion of the day before, he felt an unusual melancholy creeping over him in spite of himself. In a very pensive mood, like Racine's Hippolyte, he followed the successive slopes of the mountain of Beaumont; his noble sword, which generally fell with rigorous perpendicularity along his thigh-bone and threatened the earth with its point, affecting now the trivial attitude of a *broche*, seemed to conform to his sad thought; and his three-cornered hat, which usually stood proud and straight upon his head with a slight inclination toward the left ear, now sat sheepishly upon his neck, and seemed itself preoccupied with sinister ideas; his stony eye had softened. He contemplated with a sort of emotion the valley of Beuvron which stretched away stiff and shivering at his feet; those large walnut trees in mourning, which, with their dark branches, resembled a vast polyp; those long poplars that had but a few red leaves left on them, and on the tops of which thick clusters of ravens sometimes balanced themselves; that wild copse browned by the frost; the dark river that flowed between its banks of snow toward the mill-wheels; the dungeon of La Postaillerie, gloomy and vaporous like a column of clouds; the old feudal castle of Pressure, crouching among the brown reeds of its moats and seeming to have a fever; and the village chimneys throwing out together their light thin smoke, like the breath of a man who blows between his fingers. The tic-tac of the mill, that friend with which he had conversed so often on his way back from Corvol in the fine moonlight nights of autumn, was full of sinister notes; it seemed to say in its spasmodic language:

> Porteur de rapière,
> Tu vas au cimetière.

To which my uncle replied:

> Tic-tac indiscret,
> Je vais où il me plaît;
> Si c'est au trépas,
> Ca n'te r'garde pas.

The weather was gloomy and sickly: huge white clouds, pushed by the north wind, dragged heavily across the sky, like a wounded swan; the snow, deprived of its glitter by a grayish day, was dull and dim, and the horizon was closed in every direction by a girdle of fogs that dragged along the mountains. It seemed to my uncle that he would never again see, lighted by the joyous sun of spring and adorned with its festoons of verdure, this landscape over which winter now had spread so thick a veil of sadness.

M. Minxit was absent when my uncle arrived at Corvol; he entered the drawing-room. M. de Pont-Cassé was installed upon a sofa, by the side of Arabelle. Benjamin, without paying any attention to the pout of his *fiancée* and the provoking airs of the musketeer, threw himself into an arm-chair, crossed his legs, and laid his hat on a chair, like a man in no hurry to go. When they had talked for some time about M. Minxit's health, the probabilities of a thaw, and the grippe, Arabelle became silent, and my uncle could get nothing more out of her beyond a few sharp and shrill monosyllables, like the notes which an apprentice musician elicits with great difficulty and at rare intervals from his clarinette. M. de Pont-Cassé walked up and down the drawing-room, twirling his moustache and sounding his big spurs on the floor; he seemed to be studying to himself the best way of picking a quarrel with my uncle.

Benjamin had divined his intentions, but he had the air of paying no attention to him, and took up a book that was lying on a sofa. At first he contented himself with turning over the leaves, watching M. de Pont-Cassé out of the corner of his eye; but, as it was a medical work, he soon became absorbed in its interesting contents and forgot the musketeer. The latter decided to bring things to a crisis: he halted before my uncle, and, surveying him from head to foot, said to him:

"Do you know, Monsieur, that your visits here are very long?"

"It seems to me," answered my uncle, "that you were here when I came."

"And also very frequent," added the musketeer.

"I assure you, Monsieur," replied my uncle, "that they would be much less frequent if I expected always to find you here."

"If you come here on Mlle. Minxit's account," continued the musketeer, "she begs you by my lips to rid her of your long person."

"If Mlle. Minxit, who is not a musketeer, had any orders to give me, she would give them more politely; at any rate, Monsieur, you will allow me to wait before retiring until she has explained herself on this subject and until I have interviewed M. Minxit."

And my uncle went on with his chapter.

The officer went up and down the drawing-room a few times more, and then, again placing himself opposite my uncle, he said to him :

"I pray you, Monsieur, to interrupt your reading for a moment, as I have a word to say to you."

"Since it is but a word," said my uncle, turning down the leaf that he was reading, "I can easily waste a moment in listening to you."

M. de Pont-Cassé was exasperated at Benjamin's *sang-froid*.

" I declare to you, Monsieur Rathery," said he, "that, if you do not go out on the instant through the door, I will throw you through the window."

" Really ! " said my uncle. " Well, I, Monsieur, will be more polite than you; I shall throw you through the door."

And taking the officer by the middle of the body, he carried him to the head of the steps and locked the door behind him.

As Mlle. Minxit was trembling, my uncle said to her :

" Do not be too much afraid of me ; the act of violence which I have permitted myself toward this man was superabundantly justified by a long series of insults. And besides," he added, bitterly, "I shall not embarrass you long with my long person ; I am not one of those dowry-marryers who take a woman from the arm of the man she loves and fasten her brutally to the foot of their bed. Every young girl has received from heaven her treasure of love : it is just that she should choose the man with whom it pleases her to share it; no one has the right to pour the white pearls of her youth into the street and trample them under foot. God forbid that a base greed for money should lead me to commit a bad action! So far I have lived poor; I know the joys of poverty, and I am ignorant of the miseries of wealth; in exchanging my mad and laughing indigence for a cross and snarling opulence, perhaps I should make a bad bargain; at any rate, I should not like this opulence to come to me with a woman who detested me. I beg you, then, to tell me, in all the sincerity of your soul, whether you love M. de Pont-Cassé; I need your reply in order to determine my conduct toward you and your father."

Mlle. Minxit, affected by Benjamin's frankness, answered:

"If I had known you before M. de Pont-Cassé, perhaps you would now be the object of my love."

"Mademoiselle," interrupted my uncle, "it is not politeness, but sincerity that I ask of you; tell me frankly whether you think that you would be happier with M. de Pont-Cassé than with me."

"What shall I say, Monsieur Rathery?" answered Arabelle; "a woman is not always happy with the man she loves, but she is always unhappy with the man she does not love."

"I thank you, Mademoiselle; now I know what I have to do. Will you kindly order some breakfast for me? The stomach is an egoist which has little sympathy with the tribulations of the heart."

My uncle breakfasted as Alexander or Cæsar prob-

ably breakfasted on the eve of battle.   He did not want
to await M. Minxit's return ; he did not feel the courage
to face his grieved expression when he should learn
that he, Benjamin, whom he treated almost as a son,
had abandoned the design of becoming his son-in-law.
He preferred to inform him by letter of his heroic de-
termination.

At some distance from the town he saw the friend of
M. de Pont-Cassé walking majestically up and down
the road.   The musketeer advanced to meet him, and
said to him :

"Monsieur, you keep those who have a reparation to
ask of you waiting a very long time."

"I was eating breakfast," answered my uncle.

"I have to hand you, in behalf of M. de Pont-Cassé,
a letter to which he has charged me to bring back a
reply."

"Let us see, then, what this estimable nobleman has
to say to me: 'Monsieur, in view of the enormity of
the outrage which you have inflicted upon me' . . . —
What outrage ? I have carried him from a drawing-room
to the steps ; I wish some one would thus outrage me by
carrying me to Clamecy. . . . — 'I consent to cross swords
with you.' — The grand soul ! . . . What ! he condescends to grant me the favor of being crippled by him !
If that is not generosity, then I am mistaken ! — 'I hope
that you will show yourself worthy of the honor which
I do you, by accepting it.' — Why, of course ! it would
be base ingratitude on my part to refuse.   You may say
to your friend that, if he kills me like the brave Desrivières, the intrepid Bellerive, etc., etc., I wish them to
write upon my tombstone in golden letters: 'Here

lies Benjamin Rathery, killed in a duel by a nobleman.'
— 'Postscript.'— What! your friend's note has a postscript?—'I will await you to-morrow at ten o'clock in
the morning at the place known as Chaume-des-Fertiaux.' — At the place known as Chaume-des-Fertiaux!
Upon my honor, a process-server could not have drawn
it up better. But Chaume-des-Fertiaux is a good league
from Clamecy; I, who have no burnt sorrel horse, have
not time to go so far to fight. If your friend will con-
descend to go to the place known as Croix-des-Michelins, I shall have the honor to await him there."

"And where is this Croix-des-Michelins?"

"On the Corvol road, at the height of the faubourg
of Beuvron. Your friend must be very pessimistic if
he does not like that spot; from there one may enjoy a
panorama worthy of a king; before him he will see the
hills of Sembert with their terraces loaded with vines,
and their big bald craniums with the forest of Frace on
their necks. At another season of the year the view
would be still finer, but I cannot revive the springtime
with a breath. At their feet the town, with its thousand wavy plumes of smoke, presses between its two
rivers and climbs the arid slopes of Crot-Pinçon like
a man pursued. If your friend has any talent for draw-
ing, he will be able to enrich his album from this point
of view. Between its great gables, which, covered with
dark moss, resemble pieces of crimson velvet, rises the
tower of Saint Martin, invested with its turrets and
decorated with its jewels of stone. This tower in itself
alone is worth a cathedral; by its side extends the old
basilica, which throws to the right and to the left, with
admirable boldness, its great arch-shaped counter-forts.

Your friend cannot help comparing it to a gigantic spider resting on its long claws. Toward the south run, like a succession of sombre clouds, the bluish mountains of Morvan; then " . . .

"Oh, enough of banter, if you please! I did not come here for you to show me the magic lantern. To-morrow then, at Croix-des-Michelins."

"To-morrow? One moment, the affair is not so pressing that it cannot be postponed. To-morrow I am going to Dornecy to taste a cask of old wine which Page proposes to buy; he relies on my judgment as to quality and price, and you must see that I cannot, for the sake of your friend's fine eyes, fail in the duties that friendship imposes on me; day after to-morrow I breakfast in town; I cannot, in decency, give the preference to a duel over a breakfast; Thursday I am to tap a patient of mine, who has the dropsy; as your friend wishes to cripple me, it would be impossible for me to perform the operation afterward, and Doctor Arnout would not do it well; for Friday . . . yes, that's a fast day; I believe I have no engagement for that day, and I see nothing to prevent me from playing your friend's game."

"We are obliged to comply with your desires; at least, you will do me the favor to bring a second with you, in order to save me from playing the tiresome *rôle* of spectator."

"Why not? I know that you are a pair of friends, you and M. de Pont-Cassé: I should be sorry to separate you. I will bring my barber, if he has time, and if that suits you."

"Insolent fellow!" said the musketeer.

"This barber," answered my uncle, "is not a man to be despised: he has a rapier long enough to spit four musketeers upon, and moreover, if you prefer me to him, I will willingly take his place."

"I take note of your words," said the musketeer.

My uncle, as soon as he had risen, went in search of Machecourt's inkstand. He began to compose in his finest style and his clearest penmanship a magnificent epistle to M. Minxit, in which he explained to him why he could not become his son-in-law. My grandfather, who was given an opportunity of reading it, has told me that it would make a jailer weep. If the exclamation point had not then existed, my uncle certainly would have invented it. The letter had been in the post-office scarcely a quarter of an hour, when M. Minxit in person arrived at my grandmother's, accompanied by the sergeant, who was himself accompanied by two masks, two foils, and his respectable poodle.

Benjamin was just then breakfasting with Machecourt off a herring and the patrimonial white wine of Choulot.

"Welcome, Monsieur Minxit!" cried Benjamin; "wouldn't you like a bit of this fish?"

"Fie! do you take me for a thrasher?"

"And you, sergeant?"

"I have given up this sort of thing since I had the honor to join the band."

"But your dog, what would he think of this head?"

"I thank you for him, but I believe he has little taste for sea-fish."

"It is true that a herring is not as good as a pike cooked in court-bouillon" . . .

"And how about a carp stewed in Burgundy wine?" interrupted M. Minxit.

"To be sure, to be sure," said Benjamin; "you might even say a jugged hare prepared by your own hand; but at any rate herring is excellent when you haven't anything else. By the way, I mailed a letter to you a quarter of an hour ago; you probably have not received it yet, Monsieur Minxit?

"No," said M. Minxit, "but I come to bring you the answer. You pretend that Arabelle does not love you, and because of that you will not marry her."

"M. Rathery is right," said the sergeant. "I had a bed-fellow who did not like me, and whose dislike I cordially returned; our household was a regular police-station. When one wanted turnips in the soup, the other put in carrots; at the canteen, if I asked for currant wine, I e sent for gin. We quarrelled to see which should have the best place for his gun. If he had a kick to give, he bestowed it on my poodle, and when he was bitten by a flea, he would have it that it came from this poor Azor. Would you believe it, we once fought in the moonlight because he wanted to sleep on the right side of the bed, and I insisted that he should take the left. To get rid of him I was obliged to send him to the hospital."

"You did quite right, sergeant," said my uncle: "when people do not know how to live in this world, we sentence them to the other forever."

"There is some truth in what the sergeant says," said M. Minxit. "To be loved is more than to be rich, for it is to be happy; consequently, I do not disapprove your scruples, my dear Benjamin. All that I ask of

you is that you continue, as in the past, to come to
Corvol. That you do not wish to be my son-in-law is
not a reason why you should cease to be my friend.
You will no longer be obliged to play the languishing
lover to Arabelle, to go after water to sprinkle her
flowers, or to go into ecstasies over the ruffles which
she embroiders for me and over the superiority of her
cream-cheeses. We will breakfast, we will dine, we
will philosophize, we will laugh, that is as good a
pastime as any other. You are fond of truffles, I will
perfume my whole pantry with them; you have a predilection for *volnay*,—a predilection which I do not
share,—but I shall always have some in my wine-cellar;
if you take a notion to hunt, I will buy you a double-
barrelled gun and a pair of hounds. I give Arabelle
less than three months to get sick of her nobleman and
to love you madly. Do you accept or not? Answer
me, yes or no. You are aware that I am not fond of
fine phrases."

"Well, yes, Monsieur Minxit," said my uncle.

"Very well, I expected nothing less from your friendship. And now you are going to fight a duel?"

"Who the devil told you that?" cried my uncle.
"I know that urines hide nothing from you; can you
have consulted my urine without my knowledge?"

"You are to fight with M. de Pont-Cassé, you rogue;
you are to meet him three days hence at Croix-des-
Michelins, and, in case you rid yourself of M. de Pont-
Cassé, the other musketeer will take his place: you see
that I am well informed."

"What, Benjamin!" cried Machecourt, turning paler
than his plate.

"What, wretch!" added my grandmother, "you are to fight a duel?"

"Listen to me, you, Machecourt, you, my dear sister, and you too. Monsieur Minxit: it is true that I am to fight with M. de Pont-Cassé. My mind is made up; so save yourself the representations which would weary me without causing me to abandon my design."

"I do not come," answered M. Minxit, "to place obstacles in the way of your duel; I come, on the contrary, to furnish you a means of coming out of it victoriously, and furthermore of making your name famous throughout the country. The sergeant knows a superb thrust, with which he could disarm in an hour the entire corporation of fencing-masters. As soon as he has drunk a·glass of white wine, he shall give you your first lesson; I leave him with you until Friday, and shall remain here myself to watch you, lest you may waste your time in the taverns."

"But," said my uncle, "I have only to make your thrust, and moreover, if your thrust is infallible, what glory should I win in triumphing by this means over our vicomte? Homer, in rendering Achilles invulnerable, deprived him of all the merit of his valor. I have reflected; my intention is not to fight with the sword."

"What! you want to fight with the pistol, imbecile! Now, if it were with M. Arthus, who is as big as a wardrobe, that would be all very well."

"I fight neither with the pistol nor with the sword; I wish to serve these bullies with a duel of my own making; I reserve for you the pleasure of the surprise; you shall see, Monsieur Minxit."

"Very well," answered the latter; "but learn my thrust all the same: it is a weapon that will not embarrass you, and one never knows what one may need."

My uncle's room was in the second story, over that occupied by Machecourt. So after breakfast. he shut himself up in his room with the sergeant and M. Minxit to begin his fencing-lessons. But the lesson was not of long duration: at Benjamin's first appeal Machecourt's worm-eaten floor gave way under his feet, and he went through up to his arm-pits.

The sergeant, amazed at the sudden disappearance of his pupil, remained standing with his left arm gently curved on a level with his ear and his right arm extended in the attitude of a man who is about to make a thrust. As for M. Minxit, he was seized with such a desire to laugh that he came near suffocating.

"Where is Rathery?" he cried. "What has become of Rathery? Sergeant, what have you done with Rathery?"

"I see M. Rathery's head well enough," answered the sergeant, "but devil take me if I know where his legs are."

Gaspard just then was alone in his father's room; at first he was a little astonished at the abrupt arrival of his uncle's legs, which certainly he did not expect, but soon his surprise changed into mad shouts of laughter, which mingled with those of M. Minxit.

"Hello, there, Gaspard," cried Benjamin, who heard him.

"Hello, there, my dear uncle," answered Gaspard.

"Place your father's leather arm-chair under my feet, I beg of you, Gaspard."

"I have not the right," replied the scamp; "my mother has forbidden anybody to stand on it."

"Will you bring me that arm-chair, accursed cross-bearer?"

"Take off your shoes, and I will bring it to you."

"And how do you expect me to take off my shoes? My feet are in the first story, and my hands are in the second."

"Well, give me a franc to pay me for my trouble."

"I will give you a franc and a half, my good Gaspard, but the arm-chair at once, I beg of you; my arms will soon separate from my shoulders."

"Credit is dead," said Gaspard : "give me the franc and a half at once; otherwise, no arm-chair."

Fortunately Machecourt came in at this moment; he gave Gaspard a kick, and put an end to the suspension of his brother-in-law. Benjamin went to finish his fencing-lesson at Page's, and he proved so apt a pupil that in two hours' time he was as skilful as his teacher.

THE dawn, a dull and grimacing dawn of February, had scarcely thrown its leaden tints upon the walls of his room, when my uncle was up. He dressed himself gropingly, and softly descended the stairs, being especially desirous of not waking his sister. But, as he was crossing the stair-landing, he felt a woman's hand on his shoulder.

"What, dear sister!" he cried, in a sort of fright, "you are already awake?"

"Say rather that I am not yet asleep, Benjamin. Before you go, I wanted to say farewell to you, perhaps a last farewell, Benjamin. Do you imagine how I suffer when I think that you leave this house full of life, youth, and hope, and that perhaps you will re-enter it borne on the arms of your friends, and your body pierced with a sword? Is your mind firmly made up? Before coming to a decision, did you think of the grief with which your death would fill this sad house? For you, when your last drop of blood has gone, all will be over; but many months and years will pass before our grief is exhausted, and the tear-grass over your grave will have been long withered before our tears cease to flow."

My uncle went away without answering, and perhaps he was weeping; but my grandmother caught him by the skirt of his coat.

"Run, then, to your murderous rendezvous, ferocious

beast," she cried; "do not keep M. de Pont-Cassé waiting.   Perhaps honor requires you to start without kiss-
ing your sister; but at least take this relic which cousin
Guillaumot has lent me; perhaps it will preserve you
from the dangers into which you are about to throw
yourself so heedlessly."

My uncle thrust the relic into his pocket and slipped
away.

He ran to awaken M. Minxit at his tavern.   They
took Page and Arthus in passing, and all went to breakfast together in a wine-shop at the extremity of Beuvron.
My uncle, if he was to fall, did not wish to depart this
life with an empty stomach.   He said that a soul which
reaches the tribunal of God between two glasses of wine
has more courage and pleads his cause better than a
poor soul full of nothing but sweetened water.   The
sergeant was present at the breakfast; when they were
at dessert, my uncle asked him to go to Croix-des-Michelins to carry a table, a box, and two chairs, which he
needed for his duel, and to build a big fire there with
vine-poles from the neighboring vineyard; then he called
for coffee.

M. de Pont-Cassé and his friend were not slow in
arriving.

The sergeant did the honors of the bivouac to the
best of his ability.

"Gentlemen," said he, "be good enough to sit down
and warm yourselves.   M. Rathery begs you to excuse
him if he keeps you waiting a little, but he is at breakfast with his seconds, and in a few minutes he will be
at your disposition."

Benjamin arrived, in fact, a quarter of an hour later

holding Arthus and M. Minxit by the arm, and singing with bare throat:

> " Ma foi, c'est un triste soldat
> Que celui qui ne sait pas boire ! "

My uncle saluted his two adversaries graciously.

" Monsieur," said M. de Pont-Cassé, haughtily, " we have been waiting for you twenty minutes."

" The sergeant must have explained to you the cause of our delay, and I hope that you will find it legitimate."

" Your excuse is that you are a plebeian, and this is probably the first time that you have had a duel with a nobleman."

" What do you expect? We plebeians are ·accustomed to take coffee after each of our meals, and because you call yourself Vicomte de Pont-Cassé, that is no reason why we should violate this custom. Coffee, you see, is beneficent, it is a tonic, it agreeably stimulates the brain, it gives movement to the thought. If you have not taken coffee this morning, the weapons are not equal, and I do not know whether I can conscientiously measure myself against you."

" Laugh, Monsieur, laugh while you can; but I warn you that he laughs best who laughs last."

" Monsieur," rejoined Benjamin, " I do not laugh when I say that coffee is a tonic: that is the opinion of several celebrated doctors, and I myself give it as a stimulant in certain diseases."

" Monsieur ! "

" And your burnt sorrel horse? I am greatly astonished not to see him here; is it possible that he is indisposed ? "

"Monsieur," said the second musketeer, "enough of your wit; you undoubtedly have not forgotten why you have come here?"

"Oh, ho! it is you, number two? Delighted to renew my acquaintance with you; indeed I have not forgotten why I come here, and the proof," he added, pointing to the table on which the box was placed, "is that I have made preparations to receive you."

"And what need have we of this juggler's apparatus in order to fight with the sword?"

"But," said my uncle, "I do not fight with the sword."

"Monsieur," said M. de Pont-Cassé, "I am the insulted party; I have the choice of weapons; I choose the sword."

"It is I, Monsieur, who was first insulted; I will not yield my privilege; and I choose chess."

At the same time he opened the box which the sergeant had brought, and, having taken out a chess-board, he invited the nobleman to take his place at the table.

M. de Pont-Cassé turned pale with anger.

"Are you trying to make sport of me?" he cried.

"Not at all," said my uncle; "every duel is a game in which two men stake their lives: why should not this game be played as well with chess as with the sword? However, if you doubt your strength at chess, I am ready to play you a game of *écarté* or of *triomphe*. In five points, if you like, without a return game or a rubber; in that way it will be soon over."

"I have come here," said M. de Pont-Cassé, scarcely able to contain himself, "not to stake my life like a bottle of beer, but to defend it with my sword."

"I understand," said my uncle; "you are of superior

skill with the sword, and you hope to have an advantage over me, who never hold mine except to put it at my side. Is that a nobleman's fairness? If a mower should propose to fight you with the scythe, or a thrasher with a flail, would you accept, I ask you?"

"You will fight with the sword," cried M. de Pont-Cassé, beside himself; "otherwise," he added, lifting his riding-whip . . .

"Otherwise what?" said my uncle.

"Otherwise I will cut you across the face with my riding-whip."

"You know how I answer your threats," retorted Benjamin. "No, Monsieur, this duel shall not be accomplished as you hope. If you persist in your unfair obstinacy, I shall believe and declare that you have speculated on your bravo's skill, that you have set a trap for me, that you have come here, not to risk your life against mine, but to cripple me, do you understand, M. de Pont-Cassé? And I shall hold you for a coward, yes, for a coward, my nobleman, for a coward, yes, for a coward."

And my uncle's words vibrated between his lips like a rattling window-pane.

The nobleman could endure it no longer; he drew his sword and rushed upon Benjamin. It would have been all up with the latter, if the poodle, by throwing himself upon M. de Pont-Cassé, had not changed the direction of his sword. The sergeant having called off his dog, my uncle cried:

"Gentlemen, I call you to witness that, if I accept the combat, it is to save this man from committing a murder."

And, flashing his sword in the air in turn, he sustained
the impetuous attack of his adversary without retiring
a step.   The sergeant, seeing no sign of his thrust,
stamped on the grass like a war-horse tied to a tree,
and twisted his wrist till he nearly threw it out of joint,
to indicate to Benjamin the motion that he ought to
make in order to disarm his man.   M. de Pont-Cassé,
exasperated at the unexpected resistance which he met,
had lost his *sang-froid* and with it his murderous skill.
He no longer tried to parry the thrusts which his adversary might make at him, but sought only to pierce him
with his sword.

"Monsieur de Pont-Cassé," said my uncle, "you
would have done better to play chess : you never parry;
I could kill you at any moment."

"Kill, Monsieur," said the musketeer; "that is what
you are here for."

"I prefer to disarm you," said my uncle, and, quickly
passing his sword under that of his adversary, he sent it
into the middle of the hedge.

"Well done! bravo!" cried the sergeant; "I could
not have sent it so far myself.   If you could only take
lessons of me for six months, you would be the best
swordsman in France."

M. de Pont-Cassé desired to begin the combat again.
The seconds, however, were opposed to this.   But my
uncle said :

"No, gentlemen, the first time does not count, and
there is no game without a return game.   The reparation to which Monsieur is entitled must be complete."

The two adversaries put themselves on guard again;
but at the first thrust M. de Pont-Cassé's sword went

flying into the road. As he ran to pick it up, Benjamin said to him, in his sardónic voice:

"I ask your pardon, Monsieur Comte, for the trouble that I give you; but it is your own fault: if you had been willing to play chess, you would not have had to disturb yourself so often."

A third time the musketeer returned to the charge.

"Enough!" cried the seconds; "you abuse M. Rathery's generosity."

"Not at all," said my uncle; "Monsieur undoubtedly wishes to learn the thrust: permit me to give him another lesson."

In fact, the lesson was not long in coming, and M. de Pont-Cassé's sword escaped from his hand for the third time.

"At least," said my uncle, "you would have done well to bring a servant with you to run after your sword."

"You are the demon in person," said the vicomte; "I would rather have been killed by you than treated so ignominiously."

"And you, my nobleman," said Benjamin, turning to the other musketeer, "you see that my barber is not here. Do you wish me to fulfil the promise that I made to you?"

"By no means," said the musketeer; "to you the honors of the day: there is no cowardice in retiring before you, since you do not lift your sword against the conquered. Although you are not a nobleman, I hold you as the best swordsman and the most honorable man that I know; for your adversary wanted to kill you, but you, who had his life in your hands, respected it.

If I were king, you should be at least a duke and
peer. And now, if you attach any value to my friendship, I offer it to you with all my heart, and ask yours
in exchange."

He extended his hand to my uncle, who grasped it
cordially in his own. M. de Pont-Cassé stood before
the fire, gloomy and sullen, his brow charged with a
stormy cloud. He took his friend's arm, saluted my
uncle freezingly, and went away.

My uncle hastened to return to his sister; but the
report of his victory had spread rapidly through the
faubourg. At every step he was intercepted by a self-
styled friend who came to congratulate him on his fine
feat of arms and to shake his arm clear to the shoulder
under pretext of grasping his hand. The urchins, that
population which each fresh event gathers in the street,
swarmed about him and deafened him with their hur-
rahs. In a few moments he became the centre of a
horribly tumultuous crowd, who tagged at his heels,
spattered his silk stockings, and tumbled his three-
cornered hat into the mud. He was still able to exchange a few words with M. Minxit, but, under pretext
of completing his triumph, Cicero, the drummer whom
you already know, placed himself at the head of the
crowd with his drum, and began to beat the charge
vigorously enough to shatter the bridge of Beuvron;
Benjamin even had to give him thirty sous for his din.
The only thing lacking to complete his misfortune was
an harangue. That is how my uncle was rewarded for
having risked his life in a duel.

"If, on the height of Croix-des-Michelins," he said to
himself, "I had given a few louis to a wretch dying

of hunger, all these loungers now shouting about me
would let me pass quietly enough. My God! what,
then, is glory, and to whom does it appeal? This noise
that they make around a name, is it a blessing so·rare
and so precious that, to obtain it, one should sacrifice
rest, happiness, sweet affection, the finest years of one's
life, and sometimes the peace of the world? The lifted
finger that points you out to the public, upon whom,
then, has it not been fixed? The child whom they take
to church to the sound of pealing bells, the ox that they
lead through the city, decorated with flowers and ribbons, the six-footed calf, the stuffed boa-constrictor, the
monster pumpkin, the acrobat who walks a wire, the
aëronaut who makes an ascension, the juggler who swallows balls, the prince who passes, the bishop who
blesses, the general who returns from a far-off victory,—
have not all these had their moment of glory? You
think yourself celebrated, you who have sown your
ideas in the arid furrows of a book, who have made men
out of marble and passions out of ivory-black and white-
lead; but you would be much more famous if you had
a nose six inches long. As for that glory which survives us, it does not belong to everybody, I admit; but
the difficulty is to enjoy it. Find me a banker who dis-
counts immortality, and from to-morrow I will toil to
make myself immortal."

My uncle wanted to have a family dinner at his sister's with M. Minxit; but the worthy man, although
his dear Benjamin stood before him, safe, sound, and
victorious, was sad and preoccupied. What my uncle
had said in the morning to M. de Pont-Cassé came back
continually to his mind. He said that a voice rang in

his ears summoning him to Corvol. He was seized
with a nervous agitation like that felt by persons who
have drunk a strong cup of coffee when not accustomed
to it. He was frequently obliged to leave the table
and take a turn about the room. This undue excite-
ment frightened Benjamin, and he himself urged him
to depart.

CHAPTER XX

MY uncle, however, escorted M. Minxit as far as Croix-des-Michelins, and then returned to go to bed. He was in that profound annihilation produced by the first hours of sleep when he was awakened by a violent knock at the outside door. This knock gave my uncle a painful shock. He opened his window; the street was as dark as a deep ditch; nevertheless he recognized M. Minxit, and thought he perceived in his attitude indications of distress. He ran to open the door; scarcely had he drawn the bolt, when the worthy man threw himself into his arms and burst into tears.

"Well, what is it, Monsieur Minxit? Come, speak out; tears do not end in anything; certainly no misfortune has happened to you?"

"Gone! gone!" cried M. Minxit, choking with sobs, "gone with him, Benjamin!"

"What! Arabelle has gone with M. de Pont-Cassé?" said my uncle, divining at once what he meant.

"You were quite right to warn me to distrust him; why did you not kill him?"

"There is still time," said Benjamin; "but first we must start in pursuit."

"And you will accompany me, Benjamin; for in you lies all my strength, all my courage."

"Accompany you! Of course I will; and directly.

And, by the way, did it occur to you to supply yourself with money?"

"I haven't a bit of cash, my friend; the poor girl carried off all the money that there was in my secretary."

"So much the better," said my uncle; "you can at least be sure that she will want for nothing until we catch her."

"As soon as it is light, I will go to my banker to get some funds."

"Yes," said my uncle, "do you think that they will amuse themselves in making love on the greensward by the roadside? When it is light, they will be far from here. You must go at once to awaken your banker, and knock at his door until he has counted out a thousand francs for you. You will have to pay twenty per cent. instead of fifteen, that is all."

"But what road have they taken? We must wait for daylight in order to make inquiries."

"Not at all," said my uncle; "they have taken the Paris road: M. de Pont-Cassé can go only to Paris; I have it on good authority that his leave of absence expires in a few days. I am going at once to get a carriage and two good horses; you will join me at the Golden Lion."

As my uncle started to go out, M. Minxit said to him:

"But you have nothing on but your shirt."

"True, you are right," said Benjamin, "I had forgotten that; it was so dark that I did not notice it; but in five minutes I shall be dressed, and in twenty minutes I shall be at the Golden Lion; I will say good-bye to my dear sister when I return from our journey."

An hour later my uncle and M. Minxit, in a rickety vehicle drawn by two jades, were driving along the execrable cross-road that then led from Clamecy to Auxerre. By daylight winter is tolerable, but at night it is horrible. With the utmost diligence they could employ, it was ten o'clock in the morning when they arrived at Courson. Under the porch of La Levrette, the only tavern in the neighborhood, a coffin was exposed, and a whole swarm of old women, hideous and in rags, were croaking around it.

"I have it from Gobi, the sexton," said one, "that the young lady has promised to give three thousand francs to be distributed among the poor of the parish."

"We shall get some of that, Mother Simonne."

"If the young lady dies, as they say she will, the proprietor of La Levrette will take everything," answered a third; "we should do well to go and see the bailiff, that he may look after our inheritance."

My uncle called one of these old women, and asked her to explain to him what this meant. The latter, proud at having been singled out by a stranger who had a two-horse carriage, gave her companions a look of triumph, and said:

"You have done well to ask me, my good Monsieur, for I know all the details of this matter better than they do. He who is now in this coffin was this morning in that green carriage that you see yonder in the coach-house. He was a grand lord, worth millions, who was going with a young lady to Paris, to court perhaps, and he stopped here, and he will remain in that poor ceme-

tery to rot with the peasants whom he so despised. He
was young and handsome, and I, old Manette, who am
all worn out and good for nothing, shall go to sprinkle
holy water on his grave, and in ten years, if I live so
long, his rottenness will have to make room for my old
bones. For in vain are all these grand gentlemen rich,
sooner or later they have to go where we go ; in vain do ,
they dress themselves in velvets and taffetas, their last
coat is always made of the planks of their coffin; in
vain do they care for and perfume their skin, the worms
of the earth are made for them as well as for us. To
think that I, the old washerwoman, shall be able to go,
when I like, to squat on a nobleman's grave. Oh, my
good Monsieur, this thought does us good; it consoles
us for being poor, and avenges us for not being nobles.
For the rest, it is really his fault that he is dead. He
wanted to take possession of a traveller's room because
it was the finest in the tavern. A quarrel ensued between them ; they went to fight in the garden of La
Levrette, and the traveller put a ball through his head.
The young lady, it seems, was with child, poor woman.
When she learned that her husband was dead, she was
taken in labor, and is scarcely better off just now than
her noble husband. Doctor Débrit left her room just
now ; as I do his washing, I inquired of him regarding
the young woman, and he answered: 'Ah! Mother
Manette, I would rather be in your old wrinkled skin
than in hers.'"

"And this grand lord?" said my uncle, "had he not
a red coat, a light wig, and three plumes in his hat?"

"He had all those, my good Monsieur; perhaps you
knew him?"

"No," said my uncle, "but I may have seen him somewhere."

"And the young lady?" said M. Minxit, "is she not tall, and has she not red spots on her face?"

"She is a good five feet three inches in height," answered the old woman, "and has a skin like the shell of a turkey's egg."

M. Minxit fainted.

Benjamin carried M. Minxit to his bed, and cared for him; then he asked to be taken to Arabelle; for the beautiful lady·who was dying in the pains of child-birth was M. Minxit's daughter. She occupied the room that her lover had obtained at the cost of his life. A gloomy room, truly, the possession of which was scarcely worthy quarrelling about.

There Arabelle lay in a bed of green serge. My uncle opened the curtains and looked at her for sometime in silence. A moist and dull pallor, like that of a white marble statue, had spread over her face; her half-open eyes were faded and expressionless; her breath escaped in sobs. Benjamin lifted her arm that lay motionless along the bed; having felt her pulse, he sadly shook his head, and ordered the nurse to go for Dr. Débrit. Arabelle, on hearing his voice, trembled like a corpse under the influence of a galvanic current.

"Where am I?" said she, throwing a wild look about her; "have I, then, been the plaything of a sinister dream? Is it you, Monsieur Rathery, whom I hear, and am I still at Corvol in my father's house?"

"You are not in your father's house," said my uncle; "but your father is here. He is ready to forgive you;

he asks of you but one thing,—that you will allow yourself to live that he may live also."

Arabelle's eyes chanced to fix themselves upon M. de Pont-Cassé's uniform, which was hanging on the wall, still soaked in blood. She tried to sit up in bed, but her limbs twisted in a horrible convulsion, and she fell back heavily, as a corpse falls back that has been raised in its coffin. Benjamin placed his hand upon her heart; it was no longer beating. He held a mirror at her lips; the glass remained clear and brilliant. Misery and happiness, all were over for the poor Arabelle. Benjamin stood erect at her bedside, holding her hand in his, and plunged in an abyss of bitter reflections.

Just then a heavy and uncertain step was heard on the stairs. Benjamin hastened to turn the key in the lock. It was M. Minxit, who knocked at the door, and cried:

"It is I, Benjamin; open the door; I wish to see my daughter; I must see her! She cannot die until I have seen her."

It is a cruel thing to suppose a dead person to be alive, and to attribute acts to her as if she were still in existence. My uncle, however, did not shrink from this necessity.

"Go away, Monsieur Minxit, I beg of you. Arabelle is better; she is resting: your sudden presence might provoke a crisis that would kill her."

"I tell you, wretch, that I wish to see my daughter," cried M. Minxit; and he made such a violent effort against the door that the staple of the lock fell on the floor.

"Well," said Benjamin, hoping still to deceive him,

"you see your daughter is quietly sleeping. Are you satisfied now, and will you go away?"

The unhappy old man threw a glance at his daughter.

"You are lying," he cried, in a voice that made Benjamin tremble; "she is not asleep, she is dead!"

He threw himself upon her body and pressed her convulsively to his breast.

"Arabelle!" he cried; "Arabelle! Arabelle! Oh! was it thus, then, that I was to find you again? She, my daughter, my only child! God leaves the brow of the murderer to cover itself with white hairs, and he takes from a father his only child. How can they tell us that God is good and just?" Then, his grief changing into anger against my uncle, he continued: "It is you, miserable Rathery, who caused me to refuse her to M. de Pont-Cassé; but for you she would be married and full of life."

"Are you joking?" said my uncle. "Is it my fault if she has become smitten with a musketeer?"

All passions are nothing but blood rushing to the brain. M. Minxit's reason had doubtless given way under this terrible grief; but in the paroxysm of his delirium his scarcely-closed vein (it will be remembered that my uncle had just bled him) reopened. Benjamin allowed the blood to flow, and soon a salutary swoon succeeded this superabundance of life, and saved the poor old man. Benjamin gave orders and money to the proprietor of La Levrette, in order that Arabelle and her lover might receive an honorable burial. Then he came back to station himself at M. Minxit's bedside, and watched over him like a mother over her sick child.

M. Minxit remained three days between life and the grave; but, thanks to the skilful and affectionate care of my uncle, the fever which was devouring him gradually disappeared, and soon he was in a condition to be carried to Corvol.

CHAPTER XXI.

A FINAL FESTIVAL.

MONSIEUR MINXIT had one of those antediluvian constitutions that seem made of more solid material than our own. It was one of those deep-rooted plants that still preserve a vigorous vegetation when winter has withered the others. Wrinkles had been unable to ruffle this granite brow; years had accumulated upon his head without leaving any trace of decline. He had remained young till past his sixtieth year, and his winter, like that of the tropics, was still full of sap and flowers; but time and misfortune forget nobody.

The death of his daughter, coming after her flight and after the revelation of her pregnancy, had dealt this powerful organization a mortal blow; a slow fever was silently undermining him. He had renounced those noisy inclinations that had made his life one long festivity. He had put aside medicine as a useless embarrassment. The companions of his long youth respected his sorrow, and, without ceasing to love him, they had ceased to see him. His house was silent and sealed, like a tomb; and scarcely could its occupants get a few stealthy glimpses of the village through the blinds occasionally half-opened. The yard no longer rang with the noise of people going and coming; the early weeds of the spring had taken possession of the avenue, and high domestic plants grew along the walls, forming a circle of verdure.

This poor soul in mourning needed nothing now but
obscurity and silence. He had done as the wild beast
that retires, when it wishes to die, into the gloomiest
depths of its forest. My uncle's gayety had proved
powerless to overcome this incurable melancholy.
M. Minxit answered his joyousness only by a sad and
gloomy smile, as much as to say that he had understood and thanked him for his good intentions.

My uncle had counted on the spring to bring him back
to life. But the spring, which dresses the dry earth anew
in flowers and verdure, cannot revive a grief-stricken
soul, and, while all else was being born again, the poor
man was slowly dying.

It was an evening in the month of May. He was
walking in his field, resting on Benjamin's arm. The
sky was clear, the earth was green and fragrant, the
nightingales were singing in the poplars, the dragon-
flies were hovering among the reeds of the brook with
a harmonious rustling of their wings, and the water, all
covered with hawthorn blossoms, was murmuring under
the roots of the willows.

"This is a fine evening," said Benjamin, trying to
rouse M. Minxit from the gloomy reverie which en-
wrapped his mind like a shroud.

"Yes," answered the latter, "a fine evening for a
poor peasant who goes between two flowering hedges,
with his pick on his shoulder, toward his smoking hut,
where his children await him; but, for the father in
mourning for his daughter, there are no more fine
evenings."

"And at what fireside," said my uncle, "is there not
some vacant chair? Who has not in the field of rest

some grassy hillock, where every year, on All Saints' day, he comes to shed pious tears? And in the streets of the city what throng, however pink and gilded, is not stained with black? When sons grow old, they are condemned to put their old parents in the grave; when they die in their prime, they leave a desolate mother on her knees beside their coffin. Believe me, man's eyes were made much less for seeing than for weeping, and every soul has its wound, as every flower has its insect nibbling at it. But also, in the path of life, God has put forgetfulness, which follows death with slow steps, effacing the epitaphs which death has traced and repairing the ruins which death has made. Are you willing, my dear Monsieur Minxit, to follow a piece of good advice? Believe me then, go eat carp on the shores of Lake Geneva, macaroni at Naples, drink Xérès wine at Cadiz, and taste ices at Constantinople; in a year you will come back as fat and round as you used to be."

M. Minxit allowed my uncle to harangue as long as he liked, and, when he had finished, he said to him:

"How many days have I still to live, Benjamin?"

"Why?" said my uncle, amazed at the question and thinking he had misunderstood him; "what do you mean, Monsieur Minxit?"

"I ask you," repeated M. Minxit, "how many days I have still to live."

"The devil!" said my uncle, "that is a very embarrassing question: on the one hand, I should not like to disoblige you; but, on the other, I know not whether prudence permits me to satisfy your desire. They announce to the condemned man the news of his execu-

tion only a few hours before his journey to the scaffold,
and you " . . .

" It is a service," interrupted M. Minxit, " which I
impose upon your friendship, because you alone can
render it.   The traveller must know at what hour he is
to start, in order that he may pack his *porte-manteau*."

" Do you wish me, then, to speak frankly and sincerely,
Monsieur Minxit?   Will you, on your honor, not be
frightened at the sentence that I shall utter?"

" I give you my word of honor," said M. Minxit.

" Well, then," said my uncle, " I will speak as if it
were myself."

He examined the old man's dried-up face; he inter-
rogated his dim, dull eye, which still reflected but a few
gleams of light; he consulted his pulse, as if listening
to its beating with his fingers; and for some time was
silent; then he said:

" To-day is Thursday; well, on Monday there will
be one house more in mourning in Corvol."

" A very good diagnosis," said M. Minxit; " what
you have just said, I thought myself; if you ever find
an opportunity to introduce yourself, I predict that
you will make one of our medical celebrities; but does
Sunday belong to me entirely?"

" It belongs to you from beginning to end, provided
you do nothing to hurry the end of your days."

" I have nothing more to do," said M. Minxit; " do
me now the service of inviting our friends for Sunday
to a solemn dinner; I do not wish to go away on bad
terms with life, and it is with glass in hand that I desire
to make my farewell.   You will insist on their accept-
ance of my invitation, making it, if necessary, a duty
on their part."

"I will go myself to invite them," said my uncle, "and I guarantee that none of them shall fail you."

"Now, let us pass to another order of ideas. I do not wish to be buried in the churchyard; it lies in a valley, it is cold and damp, and the shadow of the church stretches over its surface like crape. I should be uncomfortable in that spot, and you know that I like my ease. I desire you to bury me in my field, at the edge of this brook of whose harmónious song I am so fond." He tore up a handful of grass, and said: "See, here is the spot where I wish you to dig my last resting-place. You will plant here a bower of vines and honeysuckles, in order that the verdure may be mingled with flowers, and you will come here sometimes to dream of your old friend. In order that you may come oftener, and also in order that they may not disturb my sleep, I leave you this domain and all my other property. But this is on two conditions: first, that you shall live in the house that I am about to leave empty; and, second, that you shall continue to attend my patients as I have attended them for thirty years."

"I accept with gratitude this double inheritance," said my uncle, "but I warn you that I will not go to the fairs."

"Granted," answered M. Minxit.

"As for your patients," added Benjamin, "I will treat them conscientiously and according to the system of Tissot, which seems to me founded on experience and reason. The first one of them to leave this world shall bring you news of me."

"I feel the cold of evening creeping over me; it is time to say farewell to this sky, to these old trees which

will never see me more, to these little birds that sing,
for we shall not come back here till Monday morning."

The next day he shut himself up with his friend, the
tabellion. The day after that he grew weaker and
weaker and kept his bed; but, when Sunday came, he
rose, had himself powdered, and put on his best coat.
Benjamin, as he had promised, had been to Clamecy to
extend the invitations; not one of his friends had failed
to respond to this funeral call, and at four o'clock they
found themselves all gathered in the drawing-room.

M. Minxit was not slow in making his appearance,
tottering and resting on my uncle's arm. He shook
hands with all of them, and thanked them affectionately
for having conformed to his last desire, which was, he
said, the caprice of a dying man.

This man whom they had seen sometime before, so
gay, so happy, and so full of life, grief had broken; old
age had come upon him at one stroke. At sight of
him, all shed tears, and Arthus himself suddenly felt
his appetite leave him.

A servant announced that dinner was ready. M.
Minxit placed himself as usual at the head of the table.

"Gentlemen," said he to his guests, "this dinner is
to me a final dinner; I wish my last looks to be fixed
only on full glasses and merry faces; if you wish to
please me, you will give free course to your accustomed
gayety."

He poured out a few drops of Burgundy, and extended his glass to his guests. They all said together:

"To M. Minxit's health!"

"No," said M. Minxit, "not to my health; of what
use is a wish that cannot be gratified? But to your

health, to you all, to your prosperity, to your happiness, and may God keep those of you who have children from losing them!"

"M. Minxit," said Guillerand, "has taken things too much to heart; I should not have thought him capable of dying of sorrow. I too have lost a daughter, a daughter whom I placed at school with the Sisters. It pained me for a time, but now I am none the worse for it, and sometimes, I confess, the thought occurs to me that I have no longer to pay her board."

"A bottle broken in your wine-cellar," said Arthus, "or a scholar taken from your school would have caused you more sorrow."

"It well becomes you," said Millot, "to talk thus, you, Arthus, who fear no misfortune except the loss of appetite."

"I have more bowels than you, song-maker," answered Arthus.

"Yes, for digestive purposes," said the poet.

"Well, it is of some value to be able to digest well," replied Arthus; "at least, when you go in a cart, your friends are not obliged to fasten you to the cart-stakes, for fear of losing you on the way."

"Arthus," said Millot, "no personalities, I pray you."

"I know," answered Arthus, "that you bear me ill-will because I fell on you on the way from Corvol. But sing me your 'Grand-Noël,' and we shall be quits."

"And I maintain that my song is a fine bit of poesy; do you wish me to show you a letter from Monseigneur the bishop, who compliments me upon it?"

"Yes, put your song on the gridiron, and you will find out what it is worth."

" I recognize you there, Arthus; you value nothing that isn't roasted or boiled."

" What would you ?   My sensitiveness resides in my palate ; and I like as well to have it there as anywhere else.   Is a solidly-organized digestive apparatus worth less, for purposes of happiness, than a largely-developed brain ?   That is the question."

" If we should leave it to a duck or a pig, I do not doubt that they would decide it in your favor; but I take Benjamin for judge."

" Your song suits me very well," said my uncle :

" ' A genoux, chrétiens, à genoux ' :

That is superb.   What Christian could refuse to kneel when you invite him to do so twice in a line of eight syllables ?   But I am of the opinion of Arthus ; I prefer a cutlet in papers."

" A joke is not a reply," said Millot.

" Well, do you think that there is any moral sorrow that causes as much suffering as a tooth-ache or an ear-ache ?   If the body suffers more keenly than the soul, it must likewise enjoy more energetically ; that is logic ; pain and pleasure result from the same faculty."

" The fact is," said M. Minxit, " that, if I had my choice between the stomach of M. Arthus and the over-oxygenated brain of J. J. Rousseau, I should take the stomach of M. Arthus.   Sensitiveness is the faculty of suffering ; to be sensitive is to walk barefooted over the sharp pebbles of life, to pass through the crowd that rubs against and jostles you, with an open wound in your side.   Man's unhappiness consists of unsatisfied desires.   Now, every soul that feels too keenly is a bal-

loon that would like to mount to heaven but cannot go
beyond the limits of the atmosphere. Give a man good
health and a good appetite, and plunge his soul into
perpetual somnolence, and he will be the happiest of all
beings. To develop his intelligence is to sow thorns in
his life. The peasant who plays at skittles is happier
than the man of wit who reads a fine book."

All the guests became silent after these words.

"Parlanta," said M. Minxit, "what is the status of
my suit against Malthus?"

"We have a warrant for his arrest," said the sheriff's
officer.

"Well, you will throw all the documents into the
fire, and Benjamin will reimburse you for the costs.
And you, Rapin, how does my trouble with the clergy
in relation to my music come on?"

"The case is postponed for a week," said Rapin.

"Then they will sentence me by default," answered
M. Minxit.

"But," said Rapin, "perhaps there will be a heavy
fine. The sexton has testified that the sergeant insulted the vicar when the latter summoned him to evac-
uate the square in front of the church with his band."

"That is not true," said the sergeant; "I only
ordered the band to play the air: 'Where are you
going, Monsieur Abbé?'"

"In that case," said M. Minxit, "Benjamin will flog
the sexton at the first opportunity; I want the scamp to
remember me."

They had reached the dessert. M. Minxit made a
punch, and poured into his glass a few drops of the
flaming liquor.

"That will hurt you, Monsieur Minxit," said Machecourt.

"And what can hurt me now, my good Machecourt?
I must make my farewell to all that has been dear to
me in life."

Meanwhile his strength rapidly grew less, and he
could express himself only in a weak voice.

"You know, gentlemen," said he, "that it is to my
funeral that I have invited you; I have had beds prepared for all of you, in order that you may be in readi-
ness to-morrow morning to escort me to my last resting-
place. I wish no one to weep over my death: instead
of crape, you will wear roses in your coats, and, after
wetting the leaves in a glass of champagne, you will
strew them over my grave. It is the cure of a sick
man, the deliverance of a captive, that you celebrate.
And by the way," he added, "which of you will undertake my funeral oration?"

"It shall be Page," said some.

"No," answered M. Minxit, "Page is a lawyer, and
at the grave the truth must be told. I prefer that it
should be Benjamin."

"I!" said my uncle; "you know very well that I am
no orator."

"You are enough of an orator for me," answered M.
Minxit. "Come, speak to me as if I were lying in my
coffin; I should be much pleased to hear while living
what posterity will say of me."

"Indeed," said Benjamin, "I really don't know what
to say."

"What you like, but make haste, for I feel myself
sinking."

" Well," said my uncle, " 'he whom we lay under this foliage leaves behind him unanimous regrets.' "

" 'Unanimous regrets' is not good," said M. Minxit; " no man leaves behind him unanimous regrets; that is a lie that can be retailed only from a pulpit."

" Do you prefer ' friends who will weep over him for a long time ' ? "

" That is less ambitious, but it is no more exact. For one friend who loves us loyally and without reserve, we have twenty enemies hidden in the shadow, who await in silence, like a hunter in ambush, an opportunity to injure us; I am sure that there are in this village many people who will be happy at my death."

" Well, ' he leaves behind him inconsolable friends,' " said my uncle.

" 'Inconsolable' is another falsehood," answered M. Minxit. " We doctors do not know what part of our organization sorrow affects, or how it makes us suffer; but it is a disease that is cured without treatment and very quickly. Most sorrows are to the heart of man only slight scabs that fall almost as soon as they are formed; none are inconsolable except fathers and mothers who have children in the grave."

" 'Who will long preserve your memory'; does that suit you better? "

" That will do," said M. Minxit; " and that this memory may be more lasting, I provide a permanent fund for a dinner to be eaten at each anniversary of my death, at which you will all be present as long as you remain in this · part of the country; Benjamin is charged with the execution of my will."

" That is better than a service," said my uncle; and

he continued in these terms: "'I will not speak to you of his virtues.'"

"Say 'qualities,'" said M. Minxit; "that savors less of exaggeration."

"'Nor of his talents: you have all been in a position to appreciate them.'"

"Especially Arthus, from whom I have won during the past year forty-five bottles of beer at billiards."

"'I will not tell you that he was a good father; you all know that he is dead from having loved his daughter too well.'"

"Alas! would to Heaven that that were true!" answered M. Minxit, "but it is a deplorable truth, which I can no longer conceal, that my daughter is dead because I did not love her enough. My conduct toward her has been that of an execrable egoist: she loved a nobleman, and I did not wish her to marry him because I detested noblemen; she did not love Benjamin, and I wished him to become my son-in-law because I loved him. But I hope that God will pardon me. We did not make our passions, and our passions always govern our reason. We must obey the instincts that he has given us, as the duck obeys the imperative instinct that takes it toward the river."

"'He was a good son,'" continued my uncle.

"What do you know about it?" answered M. Minxit. "That is the way in which epitaphs and funeral orations are made. Those paths that run through our cemeteries lined with graves and cypresses are like the columns of a newspaper,—full of lies and falsehood. The fact is that I never knew either my father or my mother, and it is not clearly demonstrated that I was born of the union of a man and a woman; but I have never complained of the abandonment in which I was left; it did not prevent me from making my way, and, if I had had a family, perhaps I should not have gone so far: a family embarrasses and thwarts you in a thousand ways; you must obey its ideas, and not yours; you are not free to follow your vocation, and, in the path in which it often throws you, from the first step you find yourself in the mire."

"'He was a good husband,'" said my uncle.

"Indeed, I am not too sure of that," said M. Minxit; "I married my wife without loving her, and I have never loved her much; but with me she always had her own way: when she wanted a dress, she bought one; when a servant displeased her, she discharged him. If that is what makes a good husband, so much the better! But I shall soon know what God thinks about it."

"'He has been a good citizen,'" said my uncle: "'you have been witnesses of the zeal with which he has labored to spread among the people ideas of reform and liberty.'"

"You can say that now without compromising me."

"'I will not say to you that he was a good friend.'"

"But then what will you say?" said M. Minxit.

"A little patience," said Benjamin. "'His intelligence has enabled him to win the favor of fortune.'"

"Not precisely my intelligence," said M. Minxit, "although mine is as good as another's; I have profited by the credulity of men; that takes audacity rather than intelligence."

"'And his wealth has always been at the service of the unfortunate.'"

M. Minxit gave a sign of assent.

"'He has lived as a philosopher, enjoying life and causing those around him to enjoy it, and he has died as a philosopher also, surrounded by his friends, after a grand feast. Passers-by, drop a flower upon his grave.'"

"That is pretty nearly right," said M. Minxit. "Now, gentlemen, let us drink the stirrup-cup, and wish me a pleasant journey."

He ordered the sergeant to carry him to his bed. My uncle wanted to follow him, but he was opposed to it, and insisted that they should remain at table until the following day.

An hour later he sent for Benjamin. The latter hurried to his bedside; M. Minxit had only time to take his hand, and then expired.

The next morning Monsieur Minxit's coffin, surrounded by his friends and followed by a long procession of peasants, was about to leave the house.

The priest presented himself at the door, and ordered the bearers to take the body to the churchyard.

"But," said my uncle, "it is not to the churchyard that M. Minxit intends to go; he is going to his field, and no one has a right to prevent it."

The priest objected that the remains of a Christian could rest only in consecrated ground.

"Is the ground to which we carry M. Minxit less consecrated than yours? Do not the flowers and the grass grow there as well as in the churchyard?"

"Then," said the priest, "you wish your friend to be damned?"

"Allow me," said my uncle: "M. Minxit has been in the presence of God since yesterday, and, unless his case has been postponed a week, he is now judged. In case he has been damned, it will not be your funeral ceremony that will revoke his sentence, and, in case he has been saved, of what use will the ceremony be?"

The priest cried that Benjamin was an impious man, and ordered the peasants to leave. All obeyed, and the bearers themselves were disposed to follow their example; but my uncle drew his sword and said:

" The bearers have been paid to carry the body to its last resting-place, and they must earn their money. If they perform their task well, each shall have his pay: if, on the contrary, one of them refuses to go, I will beat him with the flat of my sword till he falls to the ground."

The bearers, even more frightened by Benjamin's threats than by the priest's, made up their mind to march, and M. Minxit was laid in his grave with all the formalities that Benjamin had indicated.

On his return from the funeral, my uncle had an income of ten thousand francs. Perhaps we shall see later what use he made of his fortune.

THE END.

APPENDIX.

CLAUDE TILLIER.[*]

AT the beginning of the fifties, while I was saunter-
ing through Paris one day and standing before one of
those itinerant news stalls that exhibit their wares on the
ramparts of the quais and under the archways of the
houses, my eyes caught sight of a stitched volume, of
damaged appearance. No cover, no title-page, no preface, neither author nor printer,—nothing but a dirty
title pasted on with the three words: *Mon Oncle Benjamin.* I do not know what attraction these three
words had for me, but they seemed to look at me in a
friendly way, as if to say: "Only turn the leaves, you
will not regret it." I was not long to be entreated, and,
indeed, scarcely had I hurried through a few pages
when both style and contents began to fascinate me in
such a degree that I bought the book for a few sous and
put it in my pocket. Then I went to the Luxembourg
garden, took a seat beneath a chestnut tree, and did not
rise again until I had read the book to the end.

For a long time no book had yielded me such deep
satisfaction; but by whom was it? The simple, con-
cise, and direct style seemed to be that of the eighteenth
century; the narrative, so natural and without reserve
and circumlocution, recalled Voltaire, Diderot, and Le

*This sketch of Claude Tillier's life and works is translated from the
German of Ludwig Pfau by George Schumm.

Sage; the genuine feeling for nature and mankind maybe also conveyed a suggestion of the sentimentalism of Rousseau. But the whole manner of expression was more spontaneous, popular, and richer in color; and even if the author had not introduced himself as a grand-child of that generation, the spirit of liberty and equality that permeates his book betrayed too much of modern thought not to have lain at the breasts of the Revolution. Moreover, in spite of all that family resemblance, the character of the author was so independent, his humor so peculiar, as to permit of explanation only by the individuality of the man.

Greatly as I was delighted, therefore, by the beauty of the book, greater almost was my astonishment to find its author so entirely forgotten. How came it that a man of such talent was not in everybody's mouth? How could a writer who so easily wins the sympathies of the reader remain wholly in concealment? For a long time I made vain inquiry among *littérateurs* and the trade, until I finally succeeded in discovering the traces of my Great Unknown, who in the meantime, to be sure, has acquired a certain popularity. I secured the four volumes of his writings that were published at Nevers in 1846, and learned now that his name was Claude Tillier, that he had lived in the province, died in the province, and was therefore being ignored by Paris.

Claude Tillier is probably the only highly-gifted French writer of this century who could decide to play his modest part in the obscurity of a small town. A child of the Revolution, he was born on the 21st of Germinal in the year IX. of the republic, or on the 10th of April, 1801, in Clamecy, a small town in the department of

Nièvre. His father was a locksmith. Already as a boy he was wont to take the part of the weaker in the fights of his comrades and oppose the stronger. In consequence of this pernicious inclination he came home one day with a broken arm. But his talents kept equal pace with his courage, and he so distinguished himself while at school as to win the town scholarship of Clamecy in 1813 among numerous competitors. With this assistance he completed his studies at the lyceum of Bourges.

During the first Restoration, Claude, the child of the Revolution, who, as he himself says, drank his mother's milk out of the field-flasks of the daughters of the regiment, rebelled against the new order of things. Placing himself at the head of a riot at school, he met the shout: *Vive le roi!* with the exclamation: *Vive l'empereur!* He tore up the white cockade and wrote his mother an enthusiastic letter, which later fell into hostile hands and shut him out from the career of a public instructor during the second Restoration.

Completing his studies in 1819, Tillier left the college of Bourges. He now became an assistant teacher, first at the college of Saissons, and later at a boarding school in Paris. In 1821 he was drawn into military service and obliged to take part in the campaign of 1823 as subaltern of the artillery. The son of liberty, he must march in favor of the Holy Alliance against the Spaniards! After passing six years, full of disgust and weariness, in military service (where, moreover, he laid the seeds of the lung trouble that was to prove fatal), he returned home in November, 1828. He became teacher of the communal school and got married.

Now Tillier begins to attract attention as a writer; he becomes a zealous contributor to a small opposition paper that was founded in Clamecy in 1831 under the title, "L'Indépendant." Not satisfied with teaching the young, he wishes also to instruct the old. But people unwilling to learn prove unfriendly towards those who give them lessons, and they revenged themselves on the writer at the expense of the schoolmaster. His opponents moved, in public meeting, to appoint a second principal, and to divide the salary between the two. Tillier defended himself with his "hard and pointed weapons," as he himself calls them. He submitted a remonstrance to the common council, in which he brought out the incongruity of the proposition in a humorous way, by comparing the union of two teachers to a double team consisting of a horse and a donkey. But, tired of the squabble, he finally consented to the discharge of the horse, and left the vehicle to the other companion. The police court, however, took the part of the donkey, and the unharnessed schoolmaster had to atone for the directness of his speech with eight days' imprisonment.

Tillier now founded a private school, which was originally well attended. But the antagonisms that led to the catastrophe of 1848, the dissensions between a rotten *bourgeoisie* that had shared the spoils of 1830 with royalism and the outraged people who had gained nothing, were at that time coming to a head. True to himself, Tillier took the part of the oppressed, and soon the whole camp of corruption — official robe, cowl, and money-bag — had entered into a conspiracy against him. These natural enemies of every free and noble character strove to cut the poor schoolmaster off from the economic means of life. Political hatred and religious persecution placed themselves in ambush to draw away his pupils. Fatted *bourgeois* and fanatical confessors belabored the fathers and terrified the mothers until the private school more and more melted away.

But as it ever happens that the evil principle incurs its own defeat by its victory, so also Tillier was urged on to his literary calling by these persecutions, and his mighty pen dealt the reactionaries far severer and more effective blows than his teacher's rod could ever have done. In 1840 he published his first pamphlet under the title: "A Raftsman, to the Common Council of Clamecy." This was followed by the "Letters on Electoral Reform," which appeared in the "National." In 1841 there was already such a good ring to his name that he received a call to Nevers to assume the editorial chair of the journal, "L'Association." Here he wrote for the *feuilleton* two stories: his "Oncle Benjamin" and "Belleplante and Cornelius." The first, a charming sketch of the Nivernese manners and customs of the eighteenth century, combines the spiritual freshness of Gallic presentation with that German humor that laughs through tears, and is in this respect unique in French literature. As if in play and by a few strokes, the masterful description endows a character with flesh and blood, and places him, as by magic, in full life before the eyes of the reader. Experienced rather than invented, sprung from the fulness of artistic observation, the "Oncle Benjamin" belongs to those favored spiritual children of which the most fortunate father produces but one; to those rare books which by the delicate —

because unconscious — blending of the ideal and the real become the common property of all times and places and pass from generation to generation in eternal youth. The other story treats of the joys and sufferings of the inventor in battle with the commonplace; it is more of a fantastic nature, but rich in beautiful passages.

The "Association" finally succumbed to a systematic persecution; but Tillier, although ill, did not lay down the pen. He now wrote a first series of twenty-four pamphlets, then a second one of twelve. The wealth of satirical fire, philosophical humor, and poetical power that he spent in these pamphlets is something amazing. The elector, the tax-collector, the prefect, the bishop, the priest, the professor, the mayor, the miracle-performing saint, and the severe beadle, all the half-gods of the district, the giants of the country town, must take the floor and play their part. But his favorite antagonist, his hereditary foe, is the late M. Dupin, president of the chamber of the republic and deputy of the July revolution and subsequent attorney-general and senator of the second empire. Nor can one imagine two more complete opposites than these two men; the modest, unselfish pamphleteer, full of tenderness and fidelity of thought, and the greedy, venal political parasite, shameless and without principle. When this type of corruption appears on the scene in his great galoches, the style of Tillier also puts on clouted shoes, the better to step on the feet of his adversary. The "Pamphlets" constitute a history of the liberal aspirations of the province under Louis Philippe; they furnish a comprehensive picture of the struggles and battles which the democratic opposition fought in all departments with the July government. Tillier did not live to see the appearance of the second series. His lung trouble passed into consumption, and so he faded away, pen in hand, like a sentinel who in his fall still exclaims: "Comrades, here is the enemy!" He died at Nevers, October 12, 1844, aged forty-three years.

Such is, in few words, the life — so brief and so full, so modest and so meritorious — of a man of genius. As child,— a broken arm; as boy,— a rebellion; as youth, — a soldier's fate; as man,— a school-room, then prison, persecution, struggle, misery, and finally death! He died poor as he had lived, but, notwithstanding his poverty, he frequently made himself responsible for his friends and found means, when necessary, to pay for them. The abstemiousness of the philosopher and the carelessness of the artist constituted the features of his character. In all questions we find him on the side of truth, liberty, and justice. Whether he attacks the superstition and intolerance of an ambitious clergy or the selfishness and corruption of a wealthy *bourgeoisie;* whether he champions the right of suffrage and the liberty of the press, or writes against the dotation of the Duke of Nemaurs and in derision of the thighbone of Sainte Flavia, all these little masterpieces of polemics reveal the same warm feeling of justice, the same healthy common sense, and the same relentless logic that will never let go of what it has once seized, and which a miracle-performing saint will no more escape than a royal prince.

A master of form and abounding in matter, thinker and artist, politician and poet, bright and clear, graceful and pointed, Claude Tillier is the genuine expression of French literature. Born in the centre of ancient Gaul, near the Loire, in the true home of the Gallic spirit, on the boundary line between Troubadour and Trouvère, he has, like the wine its bouquet, the peculiar taste of the soil whose product he is. This happy zone has brought forth many a writer of precious humor, keen intellect, and biting satire; but notably Tillier's spiritual kinsman, Paul Louis Courier, and the father of the pamphlet and of satire, the master of Montaigne, Molière, and Voltaire, the jolly Rabelais. Tillier is the legitimate son of this family, and his polemical writings, which are still read with undiminished pleasure, take their place beside the pamphlets of Paul Louis Courier. The two countrymen are equals in respect to fire and dash, charming nature and artistic skill, wealth of sentiment and power of irony; and, if Tillier is sometimes left in the rear by his predecessor in the matter of elegance of language and delicacy of description, he excels him in point of novelty and spontaneity, he has the unexpected turn and the surprising metaphor. Tillier has the frank expression, the scent of the country, the spicy strength of the people from whom he sprang; his style overflows with sap and force, like the wild tree in the free country. "What do I care," he remarks somewhere, "that you call a simile trivial, if it is only correct and picturesque, if it only embodies the idea and makes it tangible to eye and ear? A fine reason, that, to refrain from the use of a word because thirty millions of others use it."

II.

Better, however, than any biography do Tillier's
writings tell us who and what he was. For as a poet
of lyrical feeling and plastic power he weaves his life
into his writings, and gives us, as none else, himself in
every line. Nothing, for instance, could furnish a
more realistic picture of the sufferings and struggles
of his youth than the following description of his life
as an assistant teacher:

" I who jest and laugh with you have passed through
life's severest trials. I was pupil, assistant teacher, soldier, and schoolmaster. With these employments I always combined that of the poet. The corporal, the
school-director, the ill-bred children, the tender mothers,
and the rhyme were my five inexorable enemies that pursued me incessantly. . . . Now I am a pamphleteer, a
pamphleteer with somewhat pointed tooth and nail by
whom a number of people carry scars, but I shall never
say anything so bad of society as it has done to me.

" Before I got to be a soldier, I was an assistant
teacher. But of all serving men the most unfortunate
is without doubt the assistant of a boarding school.
With terror I recall the miserable state of mind I was
in when, my certificate in' my pocket, I offered my services to those Latin hucksters of the capital who trade
in the languages of Homer and Virgil. . . . I was
nineteen years old; suffering early marked me out for
her own, and I could not without great difficulty earn
the piece of bread that easily falls to the lot of every
beggar. During four weeks I wandered through the
streets of Paris with my grandmother; we had searched

the farthest suburbs, we had knocked at the doors of
all institutions known to the guide-board; but the good
old woman might say as often as she would: 'Claude
has passed through all the grades, and in philosophy he
even stood second best'—in vain! My unfortunate
nineteen years were to blame that I was everywhere
left on the hands of my grandmother. From door to
door we were turned away with thunder tones: 'We
need nobody.' A joking principal of a boarding school
even pretended to consider me as a pupil who was
being brought him. Finally my grandmother succeeded in finding a corner for me in an institute, Avenue de Lamothe-Piquet. The excellent institute was
situated between the House of Invalids and the Military Academy, just opposite a school for trained dogs
that were taught to fetch and carry things and give the
paw."

.The neighborhood gave rise to a mistake that Claude
relates drolly enough. A lady who was looking for the
dog school for her little quadruped was mistaken by the
master of the institute for a mother who wanted to
place her child there.

"In this house," Tillier continues, "I had my washing, board, and lodging in the dormitory of the pupils;
in view of my great youth, I was to receive no salary at
the beginning. I conducted the studies and recitations,
I watched over the recreation hours, and accompanied
the pupils on their walks. That was a dearly bought
morsel of bread.

"The proprietor of the institute had nothing to prove
himself a teacher except his sign. He did not understand Latin, not even thieves' Latin. In order to con-

ceal his ignorance, he sought to gain fame as a *savant*; to that end he published "The Beauties of French History," and was now engaged on the historical beauties of other nations. This sort of books were the fashion at that time; every nation was presented with the beauties of its history in a duodecimo volume, neither a page more nor less.

"There are persons who will make a fine book out of one good page; there are others who cannot get up even a page with the aid of a whole book. Monsieur R. belonged to the latter. He was one of those spiritual journeymen who mutilate rather than abbreviate, who take a folio, dissect it, throw away the meat, and keep the bones; one of those scullions of literature who, when they pare an apple, leave nothing but the core. His beauties of French history gave him the right to assume the title of a writer, a title that served that of teacher as no mean armament. He passed his days in the public libraries in the preparation of extracts, and his evenings in the *salons* of the Faubourg Saint-Germain, where he was admitted in consequence of the purity of his royalism. During his absence, the crown descended to the female line. The female line ruled in the person of Madame R., a red-haired, pale-faced Englishwoman, who had a skin like the shell of a turkey's egg, or like white satin that has for some time been exposed to the indignities of flies. The pupils liked her very much, because she always maintained that they were right; the assistant teachers despised her just as much, because she always said they were wrong.

"There were from twenty to twenty-five Englishmen in the institute of Monsieur R., whom his wife had brought as her dowry, and about as many Frenchmen who represented his share. This mixture of two nationalities constituted the educational system. The Englishmen of the wife were to initiate the Frenchmen of the master into the language of Byron at the ball and other games; and these were at the same time to teach the former the language of Racine. In consequence of this unfortunate exchange, the substantives had lost their articles, the adjectives their genders, and the verbs their conjugations. There arose such a hodgepodge of the two languages, such gibberish that, as at the tower of Babel, no one any longer understood his neighbor. . . .

"During the first days that I passed in this house I felt terribly unhappy. The loss of liberty was intolerable torture to me. I envied secretly the boot-black who went by the windows singing and whistling. How gladly would I have exchanged all my treasures of wisdom for his dirty stool and his black hands! Sometimes I was almost choked by tears, but I dared not cry; I had to await the night to permit myself this luxury. Often I said to myself: Why did not my father teach me his trade? Then I should have all I need: bread and liberty; more I have never asked for, and here I have neither bread nor liberty. The good man had imagined that I must make my way as so many others with the help of the education that he had given me; but instead of gold pieces he put counters in my purse. I am too simple, too awkward, too ingenuous to make my fortune in pedagogy. Fortune is like the tall trees, only the insect that creeps or the bird that flies can build its nest on them.

"However, I was only at the beginning of my troubles. After two or three days my charges had lost all respect for my person. The two nations that had daily made war upon each other made a truce, and combined themselves against me. My gray dress coat — a gray dress coat which the best tailor of my town had made and which my grandmother had said was splendid — was the target of their jests, and often even of their missiles. It was useless to punish them for it, large and small laughed at my punishments; to be kept after school was recreation to them, for I had to preside. Again and again I was tempted to take instant and summary revenge on these impudent and, in their practical jokes, so cruel fellows. But if I were sent away, what should I do? How should I meet my parents, who believed me to be on the road to success? And even if I had wished to come to this decision, how should I pay my seat on the stage coach? I was literally without a penny. My family granted me a monthly allowance of five francs, which came to me through my grandmother; but these five francs I had long ago spent in rolls and bretzels that I ate on my walks, for I was always hungry."

But at last poor Tillier lost his patience anyway, and, after he had one day deservedly whipped an insolent young Englishman, he was obliged to leave the institute in the fall of 1820.

"I had settled with Monsieur R.," he continues. "There were still coming to me twenty-two francs and ten centimes which he gave me. They leaped into my pocket. My traps were soon together. My whole trunk consisted of an old neckerchief tied together by the four corners, and contained more scribbled paper than linen. An old stump of a cigar that was hidden in my pocket came accidentally into my hands. It seemed to me becoming to depart with the cigar in my mouth. I lit it in the kitchen and marched proudly over the yard, like a garrison that leaves the fortress all covered with military glory. At the large gate stood a boy who seemed to be waiting for some one. This young pupil had been my neighbor at the table in the workroom, and I had often helped him in his tasks. As soon as he saw me coming, he came running up to me and extended some square-looking object wrapped in paper to me.

"'I beg you, Monsieur Claude, take this; it is vanilla chocolate. I know you have not earned much at Monsieur R.'s. That will make a few breakfasts. Do not fear you are robbing me; Christmas is at hand, mamma will give me some more chocolate, and perhaps nobody will give anything to you.'

"This unexpected manifestation of tender affection embarrassed me. I am possessed of a very foolish excitability, and my emotions, once aroused, lack all self-control. Instead of expressing my thanks to this lovable boy, I began to cry like a donkey. In the meantime he attempted to force the package into my coat-pocket, and I — blinded by tears, choked by sobs, unable to speak — tried to stay his hands, but in vain. As soon as the chocolate was in my pocket, the dear little rogue took his flight like a bird that is chased from one bush into another. A short distance from me he stopped:

"'Monsieur Claude,' he cried, 'if you will promise

me to keep the chocolate, I will come to you again; I have something more to say to you.'

" ' O dear little fellow, I promise you, I will always keep it in memory of our friendship.'

" He came back and took both my hands.

" ' Now you must promise me further that you will let me know what institute you will enter. I don't like Monsieur R., because he is a royalist, nor Madame R., because she is an Englishwoman; but you I loved from the first hour, I don't know why, and I will entreat mamma so long to take me to you until she consents.'

" ' Well, my child, I will promise you also that.'

" And as I took my hands out of his, I fled to the street, for I felt that I was again to be overcome by crying. At some distance I saw my friend standing on the terrace. He was looking after me with eyes that were surely filled with tears.

" Afterward I forgot this child. I was unfeeling enough to eat his chocolate without notifying him of the institute I had entered. I have forgotten him, as the wanderer forgets the tree under which he rested for a moment on his journey through the desert. This poor, deceased love, here it lies in a corner of my heart under some rose-colored crape; for it is the fate of man to forget. At the bottom of every human heart lies, ah! a little heap of ashes and dross. Our soul is a church-yard full of graves and inscriptions, a bed where young blossoms strike their roots in dead flowers. Oblivion is a blessing of God, for if man, while round about him all is changing and passing away, had not the faculty of oblivion, he would be the unhappiest of all creatures, his life would be one perpetual pain, and his eye an inexhaustible well of tears."

The sorrows of the assistant are followed by the tortures of the schoolmaster. The vivid description of them furnishes at the same time an intimation of the struggles Tillier had to wage with the clergy. He writes:

"Which of us earns the more honest bread, you bishops or we schoolmasters? In the midst of a troop of children from morn till night who yelp like a pack of hounds, we wrack ourselves to set in motion the cumbersome, rusty machine called the school, and spend our energy, like the wood-chopper who drives a wedge into a block of wood, by forcing letters and syllables into the hard heads of children, and ruin our health by repeating tiresome explanations a hundred times. The poor road-mender can put aside his shovel for a moment in order to press the hand of an old acquaintance who is passing along; the brick-layer on the scaffolding turns his head in the direction of the street and looks a long time after a girl whom he has given a friendly nod; the locksmith, while pulling up and down his bellows, dreams of his home and of the day of his return; the tailor, sewing his coat, discovers in a fold of the cloth a merry song that he hums again and again, as the peasant jingles a gold piece that he wishes to test. But we, we must stand guard over our head like a sentinel over his post; we must inexorably turn away from us every dream, every memory, every wish; we must see and speak at the same time, restrain this one, spur on that one, preserve order here, call out the spirit of industry there; in short, we must do the

work of three.   Some of us are magnificently gifted,
but if their spirit wishes to soar into higher regions,
they must nail their pinions to the desk; they have a
golden tool and must break stones with it.   And you,
you bishops, what are you doing meanwhile?   You
preach from your pulpit, you promenade like little gods
under a canopy, you let Levites flatter you, or you even
banish some old priest out of his congenial parish.
For this arduous labor the government pays you ten
thousand francs a year, but you are not of the kind to
content yourself with anything so small.   You make a
journey every year, and when you have travelled a
hundred miles or so, you return, weary and exhausted,
into your palace to rest yourself, and for this toilsome
trouble you ask no less than two thousand francs'
'travelling fees,'   Ah! how many of us would count
themselves overhappy if they received for the hard
labor of a year only one-half of what you earn in eight
days by breakfasting, dining, and triumphal proces-
sions.

   " Do you perhaps claim that your abilities merit such
grand rewards?   But who tells you that a bishop
requires more brains than a schoolmaster?   A good
teacher must know everything, even a little theology;
but a bishop, what does he need to know except a
little theology?   Honestly, don't you think something ·
more is needed for a good arithmetician or a good
grammarian than for the manufacture of holy oils?
I will wager that the person of Monsieur Dupin con-
tains enough material for ten bishops; but I deny that ,
a single schoolmaster could be made out of him.   Or
do you even claim that the size of your salary is deter-

mined by the utility of your works? This would be a second self-delusion; in this respect also ve have the advantage. For four months the diocese was without a bishop, and nobody noticed it. The bells tolled, masses were read, women went to confession now as before; there was only a priest less in the city, and since the return of His Eminence there is one more, that is all. But if the diocese should be four months without a schoolmaster, do you think that would be immaterial, too? Do not, therefore, reproach us again by saying that we give instruction to earn money, for, you see, we are capable of answering you."

III.

In the following picture of Dupin, Tillier furnishes splendid proof of the power of his pen and the penetration of his thought. When he sketched it in the beginning of the forties, this professional renegade stood in the zenith of his glory and was the idol of the department. To-day nobody any longer doubts the likeness of the picture:

"Verily, I say to you, Monsieur Dupin, there is a certain species of egotism that would even make a great man ridiculous: namely, that shameless and garrulous egotism that forever and ever prates of itself, that would monopolize the attention of the entire world, and write its name upon every wall. You, Monsieur Dupin, are the most perfect type of this sort of egotism. You love money, you love it with a measureless passion, you love it as well as the law permits it to be loved, and yet there is one thing that you love still more, and the more so the more it is denied you, and that thing is popularity. As the people fail you, you have made yourself a people out of the *bourgeoisie.* You need people who are well-dressed, well-shaven, well-brushed, well-polished, and who continually run up and down stairs. You need newspapers that are forever on the alert and exclaim every moment: ' O, the great man!' To live obscurely would mean to you not to live. If one should discover some luminous article that could shed its radiance over a circumference of from two to three miles, you would have to get a piece of it for a wide dress-coat, and if every yard should cost a lawsuit.

" You have an insatiable craving to shine. Wherever there are compliments to reap, you rush in instantly. There can be no festivity in Clamecy but what you appear, clad in your wide dress-coat, majestically escorted by firemen. Should the king of Monaco attend one of these ostentatious festivities, he could but exclaim: ' Upon my honor, if I were not king of Monaco, I would be Monsieur Dupin!'

" Certain simple folks imagine that you harbor an implacable hatred against me who committed the blasphemy of defaming your great name, that hatred which never vanishes, but, like the dagger of the savage, eternally preserves its poison. These people do not know you. Your mortal enemy, Monsieur Dupin, is he who appears not to notice your importance and who basely curtails you of the required attention. You would much rather hear it said: ' This is Monsieur Dupin, the lickspittle, the counsel of all abuses, the defender of all wrongs; Monsieur Dupin, the turncoat, who deserted the camp of the people under a **great**

flourish of trumpets ' — than, ' Who is this old gentleman ?'

" You have that voracious appetite for flattery which,
without nicety of choice, devours everything that is
thrown at it: you think more of quantity than quality.
It would require large bells to execute the serenade
that would truly delight you. There is a shoemaker in
Clamecy, a ridiculous poetaster whom everybody de-
rides. Nine out of every ten lines of the doggerel
which the lame muse of this Apollo of the last welds
together are addressed to the great Dupin, ' the king of
orators.' While awaiting your return, he has always a
poem on his last and a wreath in his tub. And you,
the academician, who are accustomed, moreover, to the
gilded flatteries of the court, you pride yourself with
this crown as if it were of roses and laurels. The fetid
incense that he wafts towards you is sweet perfume to
you ; you wear the disgraceful mark of his praises on
your forehead as if it were the most precious jewel of
popularity. And to complete the bargain you send him
your addresses for his pathos ! . . .

" I will tell you what you are, Monsieur Dupin:
above all you are a Dupinian. You belong to no party,
you resemble those marshes between two rivers that
are neither land nor water, but treacherous quicksand.
You may now throw aside your honest man's mask ;
your hypocritical sturdiness no longer deceives any one.
You are not the peasant of the Morvan, you are the
fawner upon ministers at court. You take off your
iron-bound laced shoes in order to walk on the polished
floors of the *salons*. You are a lion that offers his
paw.

"You were a liberal when you were young, if you really ever were young. But liberty was only a poor grisette, who lavished all the wealth of her love on you while you were plotting a marriage for money with a lady of high degree, royalty. Had the Restoration lasted longer, you would have turned to her. Half *bourgeois*, half nobleman, half prelate, half minister, we should have seen you figure in a ministry of reconciliation. The Restoration was awaiting you. . . .

"You have in turn attacked and defended the same people. You danced now on the right foot, now on the left. You placed yourself as a hyphen between progress and the reaction. You expected people would regard your instability of principle as a sign of independence of character, and say: 'Monsieur Dupin recognizes no master save his own conscience; he extols the good and rebukes evil wherever he meets it, regardless of party.' But the art of your dissimulation wore too clumsy galoches to sneak in unawares, and people simply said: 'Monsieur Dupin wishes to enjoy at one and the same time the rewards of servility and the honors of independence.' From time to time you antagonized the ministers, but your opposition was so gentle that it reminded me of the tactics of your old schoolmaster, who used to punish his favorite pupils with a goose-quill. It reminded me of the valorous deeds of those bears which, trained to sham-fighting, seize the dogs of their masters between their paws as if they would crush them, and suffer them to run away after pulling out a few hairs.

"No, if I were the electorate, I should not have anything to do with a delegate who occupies two seats. I should say to you : 'Monsieur Dupin, are you the friend, the foe, or the accomplice of the government? You do not wish to submit your creed in order not to limit your independence? Well, then, Monsieur Dupin, you remain mayor of Gacogne!'

"You have exerted a lamentable influence on the district of Clamecy, Monsieur Dupin. Your protection has killed every noble aspiration in its shadow. Our young people got to be calculating old men in their twentieth year. We came to be accustomed not to engage in any political work without first asking ourselves what you, the public conscience of the district, would say of it. The fear of incurring your ill-will and the hope of winning your applause have been our sole guide for ten years. You have raised among us the most pernicious spirit of selfishness and intrigue. Out of our honest fat ciphers you have made State parasites and office seekers. Blockheads were sent to high schools because in the mist of the future people discerned your hand, ready to guide and to provide. People married the daughters of your servants, in order to gain your protection as dowry, and you paid the dowry. Your recommendation took the place of acquired rights and replaced virtue and capacity. Integrity that appeared without your marginal notes was basely turned away from the door. The talent that your fingers did not plant on a candlestick was suffered to miserably perish under the bushel. You were looked upon as the providence of the town. Favors, official positions, advantages, everything came to us out of your hands. Presently we should have entreated you for rain and sunshine; and if you had wanted an altar in the church of Clamecy, the common council would have built two for you.

"But what use have you made of your influence, Monsieur Dupin? How have you distributed your favors among the crowd of petitioners who daily made a show of their pretended misery before your door, and whom I used to call the poor of Monsieur Dupin? It is just as if you had intentionally selected the very worst. Let us look at some of your favorites at random. There is, for instance,—but, no! You would make me run the gauntlet of your laws, which in certain cases punish truth for libel. . . .

"This revolution—that was taking place by your side, without you, and perhaps in spite of you—you have despoiled of the better part of the booty, washed it clean of blood, and distributed it among your creatures. O, Monsieur Dupin, will we be burdened much longer by the public calamity of your influence? I think not. Since your last address, you have terribly fallen off. You are no longer anything but a smoking wick. There is already a certain odor of the peerage about you. On the day when the miserable cry: 'Monsieur Dupin will be a peer, Monsieur Dupin is a peer'' echoes through the district like a thunderclap, there will be an end of you. You are not the man who can make a weapon out of his quill when the platform is taken from you. Your speech is good at one time and bad at another; but if your tongue should be cut out, what would remain of your person? A demonetized gold coin still retains the greater part of its value, but a depreciated *assignat*, what is that worth, Monsieur Dupin? In ten years, when our young people will ask about the Monsieur Dupin who made such a noise in the district, they will find nothing but an old pettifogger."

IV.

What could better reveal the magnanimity of the poet and the integrity of the poor man that Tillier possessed in so eminent a degree than the following passage:

"There is unfortunately no law against corruption; undisputed we must suffer this public calamity to scatter down on our cities the infectious miasma out of its wide pinions. . . . If a soldier should deliver into the hands of the Prussians the poorest hamlet on your boundary, he would be sentenced to a shameful death; but the scoundrels who, to gratify their greed, sell our liberties, violate our contracts, and hold the nation by the throat while it is being placed in fetters are rewarded with positions of honor and wealth untold. According to what rule do you judge of human actions? If treason, instead of a gorget, wears a stand-up collar, and a pen behind the ear instead of a sword by the side, does it then cease to be treason? Does crime, by merely changing coats, become a virtue? A few moss-grown boundary stones — are they of greater value in your sight than the law of the land?

"But however base we esteem venality in general, the basest is that of the writer. Those who have a voice strong enough to make themselves heard by the masses are the natural champions of the noble cause. God has loosened their tongue and commanded them to preach the service of liberty. If they prove false to their sacred calling, if they, like wicked shepherds, lead their flocks to the shambles, they deserve all the contempt of which a human soul is capable. That is just as if the light-house were to desert the coast that it ought to point out to the storm-tossed ship and station itself on a cliff. I am one of the least of those who write for the people; I wield only a wren's quill; but God forbid that I should ever sell it to our oppressors! O, no! and if hunger with his iron fingers should tug at my vitals, I would not so degrade myself. If I must beg my bread, it shall at least not be in the ante-chambers of the ministers. Rather would I recite my pamphlets from door to door and hold out my hand to those who have a heart for liberty and the people. And surely calmer dreams would visit me on my straw than many another on his silken couch.

" Between the icy steppes of poverty and the wearisome Eden of wealth where heaven eternally reflects the same blue and the earth the same green lies a temperate zone where want and superfluity alike are unknown. Here the soil yields nothing to the weakling who will not till it; but whoever digs a furrow is sure of a rich harvest. Under these changeful skies there are indeed gloomy and rainy days, but often also the sun smiles mildly and gloriously through the rifts of the clouds. Here I have pitched my modest tent between two blooming bushes. I am perfectly contented on this spot, and have no desire to leave it. My wants are few and my stomach is small. Since a little rib is sufficient to fill it, why should I mortgage myself to a butcher in order to have a leg? . . . Great ladies I do not frequent, my dress costs me very little consequently, and theirs costs me nothing at all. I hold that a garment in the closet does not serve as clothing, and so my entire wardrobe consists of a great coat of agreeable thickness for winter and of a thin coat for the mild days of the pleasant season. I try to make these garments last as long as possible ; and it concerns me very little if fashion looks at me askance when I meet her. My respect does not suffer thereby among those who know me, and the rest may think what they like about it. When I am saluted, I can at least feel assured that the salute is not meant for my coat. . . .

"Should you appeal to my fatherly feelings, I will answer you that I love my children with all my heart, but that I cannot sell my conscience in order to enrich them. Besides, I have not placed them in the world that they should grow rich ; it would vex me if they should. Their cradle was made of willows, and it is not necessary that their death-bed should be carved of mahogany. We Tilliers, we are made of the hard, knotty wood of which the poor people are made. My two grandfathers were poor, my father was poor, I am poor ; my children shall not depart from their kind. If my son should take a notion to accumulate wealth, my enraged shade would rise up before him and throw his money-bags out of the window. And do not imagine I am exaggerating ; for I tell you : the lame old cobbler who mends shoes in yonder street corner and whom you despise earns his bread more honestly than the loftiest plumed crest among our great lords or the weightiest money-bag among our skilful financiers.

"And, moreover, why should I trouble myself about

the lot of my children? When **my last** coughing fit has come, when my quill together with my soul has returned to God, will the sun darken then and the earth cease growing green? The All-Father who supplies the young of the birds with food, will he deny it to the little ones of the pamphleteer? My parents gave me nothing, and I am grateful to them for it; had they given me much, I should perhaps not dare to sign their name to my pamphlets. When I left the paternal roof, I had not even a calling. I fell into this world like a leaf that the storm shakes from the tree and rolls along the highway. But I did not lose courage: I always hoped that out of the wings of some bird sweeping the skies a quill would fall down, fitted to my fingers, and I have not been disappointed. The rich man is a plant that springs from the earth full-grown in leaf and flower. I was a poor grain cast among thorns; with bleeding head I raised the hard shells that were oppressing me and forced my way towards the sun. Why should not the modest blades that I leave on my root-stalk grow as I grew? Instead of selling myself to the powerful, I made war upon those who sold themselves to them, and I do not regret it. That is, after all, the best road to an honorable grave. Of that I am convinced; and if this my pamphleteer's quill should grow out of my grave, and my son had the cunning to use it, I should urge him to grasp it, even if he should meet a prison in the middle of his course. When one can say to himself: the oppressor fears you and the oppressor puts his trust in you — that is the noblest riches, riches for which I would willingly give all else.

"And of what avail if I, like those gentlemen, were one of the most important philistines in my small town? A fine honor to be the thickest stalk of asparagus in a bunch or the largest radish in a basket-full! I cannot walk on stilts, and in order to rise above the heads of the rest, I will not get on a muck-heap. Whoever desires to be proud must at least know why; but these philistines who with their thick paunches put on such great airs, what are they proud of? They do not know it themselves, and those who take off their hats so slavishly before them do not know it either. These gentlemen despise the people and consider themselves therefore as half noblemen; but they are only butterflies that despise caterpillars. . . .

"And, moreover, man is not born alone to live, but also to die. Who of us would not cast a glance behind the dark curtain that brings our existence to a close? All that dies leaves a trace of its life: when the wind is dispersed in space, the leaves still tremble which it has kissed; when the wild thyme is crushed between the great jaws of the ox, it still leaves its fragrance in the meadow for a time; when the string of a violin snaps asunder under the rude strokes of the bow, its vibrating ends still emit a sibilant sound. But all the people who bartered away their conscience — when the last sound of the bells that toll them to the grave has died away; when the silver-paper tears that have been shed over them are laid away in their bier; when the smoke of the thundering guns that offer the last salute to what is mortal in them has cleared away, — what remains of them? A disgraceful memory and a dishonored name, something like the stench that survives an extinguished candle. After their flatterers will come the people whom they have betrayed, and spit on their tomb. But I, if I have neither a marble slab nor gilded letters on my coffin, I wish at least that the modest hillock that shall cover it may spread a sweet perfume; and, haply, when a pious duty shall lead the friend of liberty into the garden of the dead, he will go a few graves farther and salute my shade." . . .

And again:

"The name pamphleteer that you hurl at me as something opprobrious, I take it up and wear it as a badge of honor. To tell people the truth is, notwithstanding all your talk, a noble calling. What does it concern me if a couple of old crickets and two or three barnbeetles that have lost their teeth angrily buzz at me in their little rage? I am conscious of having put to good use what small portion of reason God gave me. I am rather at peace with myself than with others, and my self-respect is of greater value to me than that of a whole troop of jackanapes who neither know nor understand me.

"With what can they reproach me as a writer? I have always taken the part of the weak against the strong; I have always lived beneath the tattered tents of the conquered and slept by their hard bivouac. It is true, I have cancelled a number of too pompous adjectives which certain names had appropriated to themselves; and now and then I have also pricked the bubble of some bloated self-conceit. But the persons whom I have treated so were on the side of the enemy, and I had a right to explode their airs. I did not

violate the law of war against them; and if they complain about me, it is just as if an old soldier of the
empire should complain because he was wounded at
Austerlitz by a Frenchman. Call it personalities —
what of it? Every one has his own way of making
war: the others shoot into the masses at half the height
of a man; but I select my man and take a good aim.
But if a plumed crest happens to pass by my door, I
always give him the preference.

"My name is lost among the many which the great
city daily rolls in its wide mouth; but nevertheless I
flatter myself that my pen is not useless. The hedge is
low, and its branches hang into the grass; but with its
thorns it pricks the wrong-doer who would trespass
upon strange premises; its wild flowers it gives to the
shepherdess who passes by the way, and the little birds
build their nest with security in its branches. I would
rather be a law-protecting hedge than a tall useless tree.
A shameful employment, that of the penny-a-liner who
sells to the powers that be an old duster of a quill with
which no scrub woman would sweep away the ashes in
the stove, and who for a handful of money lives a life
of falsehood and lies. I should indeed not like to be in
his place.

"I am, then, a writer of pamphlets; but am I indeed
so godless as the black-coated gentry would like to
have their pious souls believe? According to their
religion, may be; but not according to the religion of
God. Would the supreme judge, if I were to appear
before his tribunal to-morrow, have so very much to
hold up against me? I did not fill my hands with
gold; I did not sell my thoughts. I gave them to the

people, whole and unalloyed, as the tree gives them its fruits. I took my daily bread out of God's hand, without ever asking for more. If this bread is black, I do not complain; if it is white, I eat it with a good appetite; but black or white, I never let anything remain over for the coming day. I go straight ahead, without looking backwards or forwards; only the stone before my feet I seek to avoid, and in this, too, I do not always succeed. If I see some weed on my way, I pull it up by the roots; if I find a good grain, I dig a hole in the earth and plant it there; if it does not come forth for me, it will yet grow for some one else. I do as the butterfly that enjoys itself during the summer without thinking of the winter, and that does not dream of building itself a nest for the few days it will remain on earth. I advise my children to do as I do. I will them my example: that is, after all, the best riches, for which they will at least not have to pay any inheritance tax. I do not pray, for the reason that God knows better than I what he must do; because I might ask things of him that would not be good for me; and because without our asking he lets the sun rise every morning and the earth bring forth fruit and herbs every year, for, if he has created us, he is also bound to care for our maintenance. He cannot be like those wretched fathers who place their children before the doors of foundling hospitals. Nor do I adore him, because he does not need adoration, and the worship that the masses offer him is nothing but the flattery of selfish creatures who want to enter paradise. But if I have a penny to spare, I give it to the poor.

"I have said what *I* am; may those now who call me

godless tell us just as sincerely what *they* are, and we shall soon see that they are less religious than I."

V.

Nothing can give us a better idea of the fortitude and strength of soul of the poor sufferer than the following passage, full of mockery and resignation, with which Tillier laughed death in the face. The Monsieur Gaume mentioned here is an abbé, who had brought the thigh-bone of Sainte Flavia from Rome to Nevers for his bishop, Monsieur Dufêtre, and who thereby challenged the scorn and ridicule of the pamphleteer:

"In the congregation of Monsieur Gaume," writes Tillier, "a schism has broken out on my account; for a portion of the virgins declare that, struck by the avenging thigh-bone of Sainte Flavia, I am about to die; but another, more impatient portion claim that I have already died, that I am as dead as a rat, and even buried. Very well, then, I am about to die; that is possible. It is indeed long since the years of youth, these beautiful birds of passage whom winter drives away, have flown from me. I have travelled over half of my course. I am on the other slope of life, where the valleys stretch before us in sombre twilight, where the trees have retained hardly a few leaves, and where the gray sky is thick with snow-flakes. When one has once reached the downward course, the descent is more like rolling than walking. But that I am dead I deny. Besides, my death is a ready-made miracle for Sainte Flavia; I may die to-day, or to-morrow, or in ten years — nothing will prevent the superannuated virgins of Monsieur Gaume from claiming that their saint killed me.

"I confess I was frightened by this threatening announcement of my impending doom; but Claudius, my venerable patron saint, appeared before me one night recently:

"'Do not fear, my dear Claude,' he said to me, 'the Lord Christ has read your pamphlets, and he liked them very much, and if he does not become a subscriber to them, it is only because he would not like to offend M. Dufêtre. You are the defender of religion, and its enemies are those Jesuits who shape and utilize it to their own advantage as if it were their property. You are coughing, I know, I hear up yonder how you cough, and, without meaning to flatter you, I can say that you cough pretty well. But don't take any of that medicine, that's poor stuff; go early to bed, rise late, and drink the wholesome country air; I do not claim that this diet will cure you. I am not one of those empirical saints who pursue the art of healing as if they had to live by it. But if this Flavia touches your chest, she shall learn to know a Claude: with a single stroke of my crosier I will break that thigh-bone of hers into a thousand pieces.'

"'Dear patron,' I answered him, 'is your crosier perhaps loaded with lead? But in any case, you cannot mean to wield it against a woman?'

"'A woman,' he answered me, 'a woman! Is malice invulnerable, then, as soon as it is coupled with weakness? And you yourself, Claude, although you are a whole-souled Claude, do you hesitate to kill the fly that has stung you for the simple reason that you are stronger than it?'"

The warmth of his feeling, the tenderness of his
heart, how powerfully they burst forth once more in
these last lines which he wrote on his death-bed :

"My mother stands beside my invalid's chair ; she is
deaf, poor woman, and my voice is weak ; we can
hardly make ourselves understood. But she is here,
she envelopes me in her glances, she seeks to read in
my eyes what I want, she can divine by the smallest
fold on my forehead what I dislike. She has left the
other half of her family, the half that can spare her ;
she wishes to have her part of my death-struggle. The
same care that once watched over my childhood she
now bestows on my early old age. One son she has
already seen dying, and now she comes to lend me also
the support of her arm and to lead me gently down the
slope of life. . . .

"Poor mother ! with what heavy hand did God
measure out the tears that he stored beneath your
lids ? Or is God unjust to the mothers ? A son can
only once bury his mother ; but a mother, how many
sons may she mourn ! Am I at least the last child she
must bury ? Will a last one remain to close her eyes
and lay her dear body beside our bones ? Or must
it be her lot to take the key of our poor house with
her ? . . .

"Ah ! how much less am I to be commiserated than
she ! . . . I die a few days before my schoolmates, but I
die at that age when youth is nearing its end and life
is but a long decay. Unimpaired I return to God the
gifts with which he intrusted me ; free my thought
still soars through space, time could not bleach the
feathers of his wings. . . . I am like the tree that is cut

down and still bears fruit on the old trunk amidst the young shoots that come after. Pale, beautiful autumn! this year thou hast not seen me on thy paths that are fringed with fading flowers; thy mild sun, thy spicy air have refreshed me only through my window; but we depart together! With the last leaf of the poplar, with the last flower of the meadow, with the last song of the birds I wish to die, aye, with all that is beautiful in the space of the year; may the first breath of frost call me away! Happy he who dies young and need not grow old!"

This farewell requires no rhymes to be a poem; poetry has not created anything more touching and more genuine. Rarely do we find a combination of so much lyrical charm and so much polemical power and logical rigor as in the writings of Tillier. But his works reflect his character. He was one of those beautiful natures of native nobility, who rise out of the depth of society, and who, in spite of temptation and misery, pass unsullied through the filth of life. Wholly of the third estate and of the people, he loved liberty passionately and battled for her heroically on the remote outpost that accident had intrusted to him. Regardless of personal matters, he lived for his idea and found his reward in himself. Unselfishness was his virtue and human dignity his religion.

After I had learned to know this knightly figure by his writings, I determined to revive his memory among my countrymen. I visited his sunken grave, held out my hand to his pensive shade, and spoke to him: "Here you rest now, quietly and forsaken, under your modest sod, brave champion! And six feet of earth is

all that death gave you after life denied you so much.
I, too, am an exiled disciple of liberty, travelling along
your paths and come for devotion to your grave.
Slumber on in your ungrateful earth, disinherited one!
I, the refugee, will erect a monument to you in my
home. I will translate your 'Benjamin,' who resembles
you in noble pride and true love of man, into a language that appeals to forty millions of hearts; and
your portrait, you faithful counsellor of the oppressed,
I will exhibit it among my countrymen, for you are the
true man of the people whom all nations recognize as
their own.— Look you, our enemies consider us as poor
in wealth and as weak in power; but we are rich in
the spirit and strong of will, and we are their masters
by the might of wisdom. The fools! They do not
know that above them an eternal law holds sway and
that its mighty spirit is leading the world gently, but
irresistibly, towards *our* goal: the liberation of the
human race, the reign of justice. They do not see the
foot-prints of his progress, they do not hear the verdicts
of his tribunal; but to us, his messengers, he appears in
all his glory, saying: 'Do not complain! I am with
you; and instead of the things of time I promise you
the things of eternity. See these poor, they pride
themselves on their spoils and — nothing is their inheritance; for their deed is without seed and their
bequest without heirs, they are in the service of decay.
But you are the workers of the resurrection, your work
grows from generation to generation and has eternal
life.'— Sleep on, then, with your honors, your poor
grave will outlive their marble vaults. Let them glis-
ten and glitter, let them mock and deride, the unjust:

their soul will vanish without a trace, like the stalk
that bears no fruit; but you, chosen one, you will live
among the living. Your brain sleeps and rests, but
your thought is awake and working. You have dug
your furrow in the field of time; many a harvest will
come and go, and none will erase it. Thousands of
spirits will receive you, thousands of hearts will bless
you!"

What's To Be Done?

A NIHILISTIC ROMANCE.

By N. G. TCHERNYCHEWSKY.

WITH A PORTRAIT OF THE AUTHOR.

WRITTEN IN PRISON.

SUPPRESSED BY THE CZAR.

THE AUTHOR OVER TWENTY YEARS AN EXILE IN SIBERIA.

PRESS COMMENTS.

Boston Advertiser.—"To call the book the 'Uncle Tom's Cabin' of Nihilism is scarcely extravagance."

Boston Courier.—"It is perhaps the book which has most powerfully influenced the youth of Russia in their growth into Nihilism."

Providence Star.—"As a revelation of folk life it is invaluable: we have no other Russian pictures that compare with it."

329 LARGE PAGES.

Price: In cloth, $1.00; in paper, 35 cents.

Sent, postpaid, on receipt of price, by the Publisher,

BENJ. R. TUCKER, - - Box 3366,
BOSTON, MASS.